Diondray's Journey

(Book 2 of The Diondray Chronicles)

Marion Hill

Part 1:
Santa Teresa

Chapter 1

Sunlight filtered through the high arched windows of the kahall, and outside, I could see birds rapidly flying by without concern for what was happening inside. I returned my attention to the morrim, who was pacing behind the pulpit, wearing his custom white shawl with red trim as if it were unusually heavy today.

"I want to thank everyone for coming to today's kahall service," the morrim of the kahall of Santa Teresa began after pacing for several moments. "There is something I must discuss with the congregation. Something placed on my mind and heart by the Eternal Comforter."

I saw a concerned look on the morrim's face. The lines on his forehead dug deep into his skin, and his mouth worked like a fish. I wondered what was so troubling the morrim that he had to speak about it here and now.

"As you know, our city is dealing with a serious issue about marriage," the morrim continued. "Our custom and tradition is for women to be married when they reach the age of twenty-one. But it seems in the last few years that a lot of women who reach that age do not want to get married. They are trying to become resas or moving away to the other cities north of the Great Forest. Some women are considering a move to the cities south of the great forest. I've been told they feel trapped by this custom and believe it's not an accurate representation of what is written in the Book of Kammbi."

I glanced to the right at Diakono Copperwith and saw a thin smile as he held Annalisa's hand. She reciprocated the gesture. Their affection seemed in direct contradiction to the morrim's opening statement. I noticed the gray strands in their hair; my traveling companions had to be twice my age. They had probably been married as long as I had been alive.

"I'm tired of these unmarried women deciding to go against the Book of Kammbi!" a voice said to the left of me.

I turned to find out where that outburst was coming from. I looked past Maisa, who was sitting next to me, and saw a man wearing a sky-blue jumpsuit standing up from his seat.

I had never heard someone give an outburst in a kahall service during my short time in these cities north of the great forest. I hadn't thought that a morrim could be challenged by a parishioner in this manner. I had seen the reverence Diakono Copperwith and other diakonos gave to the morrim of the kahall in Santa Sophia just two days ago at the morrim's feast before the Festival of Sinquinta. I shifted for a better view, intrigued to see how the outburst would play out in front of the rest of the congregation.

"These women believe because Teresa never married that it gives them the right to follow in her footsteps. But they have not read the entire chapter where she said she was not against marriage. It was not for her. They need to learn how to read the Book of Kammbi," the man continued bitterly.

"Parishioner, I can appreciate your anger about this issue. But my message was going to address what you just mentioned about Teresa."

"Was it really, Morrim Pomodore? Why do I doubt that?"

By this time, several second esperahs had reached this man. He gave a quick glance at the uniformed kahall servants as they came to remove him from the service, then turned his eyes back on the unfortunate morrim.

"Morrim Pomodore, aren't you single? What made you change your mind all of a sudden? Are you sure it was from the Eternal Comforter?"

"Enough!" the morrim snapped. "I will not have another parishioner disrespect a kahall service. Get him out of here."

"I've touched a nerve," the man said as three second esperahs surrounded him.

I turned away from the man being removed and looked up at Diakono Copperwith, who stood up stiff as a board and began to approach the troublemaker with menacing steps. I believe he would have removed him if the guards hadn't reached him first. I had never seen him so angry before.

"What kind of believer and follower of Kammbi are you that would disrespect a morrim like that?" Diakono Copperwith asked the man.

He gave the diakono a contemptuous look. "Who are you, Diakono? Are you single just like the morrim you serve under? Men of the cloth should support my position and make these women get married!"

"I've heard enough from you," one of the second esperahs said. He began moving the man down the aisle.

"Parishioner, I'm Diakono Copperwith from the kahall of Santa Sophia, and I do not serve under this morrim, to answer your first question. And I'm married to my lovely wife, Annalisa, who is sitting amongst the congregation, to answer your second. However, you have not given a good reason why you would disrespect a morrim while he's teaching a kahall service."

"Because the morrims of this city have only been talking about the problem of women not getting married instead of forcing them to do the right thing, like our custom and tradition has been for years. I'm tired of morrims talking about it instead of doing something."

"Being disrespectful to the one who has been chosen to speak for Kammbi will never get you the results you want. As a believer and follower of Kammbi, you are to trust in him that he will do what needs to be done according to the Book of Kammbi."

"You are just like the morrims here in this city, even though you are from Santa Sophia. At least you have a wife."

The second esperahs lifted the man up the aisle and toward the exit of the congregation hall. He continued to yell out as he was leaving.

Diakono Copperwith returned to his seat. I could feel the anger from his body as he walked in front of me.

"Thank you, Diakono Copperwith," Morrim Pomodore said. "Morrim Martinez must be honored to have someone like you serving under him."

Diakono Copperwith bowed to the morrim before sitting. "My pleasure, Morrim Pomodore."

"I would like to speak with you after the service," Morrim Pomodore asked.

The diakono nodded as the morrim continued with the kahall service.

#

The kahall service ended, and the second esperahs motioned for us to remain seated. Diakono Copperwith whispered to me that Morrim Pomodore would come back out to the congregation hall and talk to us.

The diakono was still angry from the parishioner's outburst.

Diakono Copperwith had always come across as calm and measured since I met him. Now I knew what could draw out his anger.

I was still trying to grasp everything that had happened since I arrived in Santa Sophia on the first day in the fourth month of Lir. I realized that fifty-two days had already passed since my arrival in the north. It seemed like I had just been on the plane from my home in Charlesville a few days ago, yet my life had changed for good.

The Festival of Sinquinta was still on my mind, and how the people of Santa Sophia had acknowledged me after the festival was surprising. I'd thought Reuel the Leopard would be coming with us on this second expedition, and I kept looking for that cat during the entire drive from Santa Sophia. But Reuel had disappeared just as quickly as he appeared at the festival. I knew his coming was a sign that I was truly the prophesied successor to Oscar Ortega, a prophet of Kammbi and my ancestor. But beyond that, I wasn't sure I understood much of what was happening to me. I wasn't even sure how fully I believed in Kammbi, never mind being his prophet!

Diakono Copperwith placed his left hand on my shoulder, and I rose from my seat in anticipation of Morrim Pomodore's arrival. Maisa rose as well. She gave me a quick smile, and I returned the gesture. I could have stared into her piercing eyes and perfectly oval-shaped face for the rest of the day. Of all the companions who had come with me from Santa Sophia, I was particularly glad she had decided to come along.

Morrim Pomodore arrived, escorted by two men. The morrim had taken off his customary shawl for a beige v-neck jumpsuit with a light green shirt underneath. The other two men wore brown jumpsuits that contrasted with the morrim's outfit.

Diakono Copperwith bowed, and the morrim touched his shoulders. I assumed the diakono was submitting himself to the morrim's authority while we were at the kahall of Santa Teresa.

"First Esperahs Rondoe and Feller, please bring something to drink for our guests," the morrim said. I had learned from Diakono Copperwith that first esperahs were servants for the morrim, while second esperahs served the diakonos and everyone else who worked at the kahall. The first esperahs nodded and left.

"I wanted to thank you again, Diakono Copperwith, for your action during the service," the morrim continued. "That was the third time a parishioner has interrupted the kahall service in the last thirty days. I was beginning to lose my patience."

"My pleasure, Morrim Pomodore." Diakono Copperwith replied. "But why are parishioners disrespecting kahall services?"

The morrim gave a thin smile. "Disrespect is a strong word, Diakono Copperwith. However, I do believe it's quite appropriate. That parishioner was actually right in one aspect of his outburst: the morrims of Santa Teresa have only *talked* about this issue of our women not getting married by the age of twenty-one. It's creating problems in the city. We do need to address it with action, not words alone."

The first esperahs returned and handed each of us a glass of cherry juice. I drank my juice immediately even though it was tart.

"Why do you have a custom for women getting married at age twenty-one?" I asked.

The morrim faced me. "Young man, you are?"

"Diondray Azur from Charlesville."

"If I had seen those shorts you are wearing during the service, I would have mentioned that we had a visitor from south of the Great Forest."

"Do you get visitors from south of the Great Forest often?" I asked.

"Not often," the morrim replied. "But enough to recognize dark brown skin like yours, contrasting against us lighter-skinned people of the congregation. Not to mention your rather different sense of style."

The morrim gave a warm smile after that comment. It disarmed me, and I knew I was not to take offense to what he said.

"Shorts," the morrim continued. "I guess the young people are always wearing the latest style of clothing."

"Latest style indeed," a voice said behind me.

"Mr. Cortes, I thought I had the second esperahs dismiss everyone after service," Morrim Pomodore said. He didn't look pleased to see the parishioner who had suddenly appeared. Cortes stood next to the morrim. He towered over everybody. Mr. Cortes had to be about seven feet tall or so. His presence filled the area, and I sensed he had quite an influence with Morrim Pomodore. Also, my eyes were drawn to the thick silver necklace that dangled over his sun-yellow jumpsuit.

"My apologies, Morrim Pomodore. I wanted to meet our visitors. Hello, I'm Frederic Cortes, owner of Cortes Holdings. And young man, you have on a piece of clothing that no man in this city is wearing."

The morrin still looked annoyed. "Mr. Cortes, I will have time for you later this evening."

"Okay, Morrim Pomodore," Mr. Cortes said while staring at me. "Nice to meet you . . ."

"Diondray Azur."

"Welcome to Santa Teresa." Mr. Cortes nodded slightly and started to leave.

I watched him being escorted out of the congregation hall by those first esperahs, and they looked like little children next to him. Mr. Cortes's stare bothered me for some reason. It did not feel right. I hoped I did not run into him anymore.

"It seems my day is full of interruptions," Morrim Pomodore said. "Welcome, Diondray Azur. How do you know Diakono Copperwith?"

"Morrim Pomodore, he is the one who is going fulfill Oscar's prophecy," Maisa interjected.

The morrim's face changed from a thin smile to shock.

Diakono Copperwith spoke up next. "Maisa is correct, Morrim Pomodore. Diondray Azur came to Santa Sophia in the month of Lir, and he had Oscar Ortega's copy of the Book of Kammbi—the very one he left in Charlesville after trying to reconcile with his son. I have spent the last fifty-two days with Diondray in our city, and everything that has happened since his arrival tells me Oscar's prophecy will be fulfilled by him. He will unite the two lands and lead all our peoples in the worship of Kammbi."

The morrin looked pale. "Oh, my," he whispered. "In prayer this morning I heard the Eternal Comforter tell me that someone special was coming to our service and that everything would change."

"I heard the same thing in prayer after Diondray arrived in Santa Sophia, Morrim Pomodore," Diakono Copperwith said.

The morrim nodded suddenly, as though he had made up his mind about something. "First Esperahs Rondoe and Feller, please prepare the visitor rooms for Diakono Copperwith and his guests. We have a lot to discuss while they are here in Santa Teresa."

Chapter 2

When I first (of three times over the years) arrived here in the lower valley of these hills from the northwest, I was immediately taken by the presence of this woman. She was tall and slender, with sharp eyes, and she stood like a queen amongst her tribe. The woman was not beautiful like my Sophia or Adrianna. She seemed to be all angles, suggesting masculinity. However, when she spoke to me for the first time, I knew she was deeply feminine.

I spent fifty days with Teresa and her tribe. I taught Kammbi's teachings and told them how the Eternal Comforter could come into their lives once they believed and followed Kammbi. Teresa took to my teaching the fastest, and she told me she knew this was the path her people needed to take.

The elders of the tribe came along more slowly than Teresa. They still had their suspicions, and I got a sense that they thought Teresa was taken with me.

We spent a lot of time together repeatedly going over Kammbi's teachings. Teresa told me she wanted to understand every bit of Kammbi's teachings before I left her and the tribe. There was nothing romantic or sexual about our private times together. I had already committed an act of passha with Adrianna. I had learned my lesson. Besides, I never wanted to hurt Sophia again like I had when she found out about my relationship with Adrianna.

I knew Teresa had suitors amongst the leadership of the tribe. I noticed that when I first arrived. A short, stocky man named Leopolde was the most prominent of these. His gaze at Teresa when she asked questions during our teaching sessions revealed his love for her.

The day before I left the tribe, Teresa told me that Leopolde had asked to marry her. She wanted advice from me on how to ask the Eternal Comforter about rejecting his proposal. Teresa felt marriage would compromise her growing belief in Kammbi, and she wanted to devote all her time and energy to becoming a totally committed follower and believer. She also spoke about how the young women of the tribe were getting married as soon as their first menstrual cycle came. Teresa thought that was not the right path for them. They should be able to choose marriage when they found the man they truly loved, not be forced into it by the elders of the tribe. She felt the Eternal Comforter had told her to choose this path but had not told her how to reject Leopolde's proposal. She wanted to do the right thing in her newfound beliefs and wanted my help before I traveled east and north to find more followers and believers in Kammbi.

I read the opening part of chapter 4 from the Baramesa in the Book of Kammbi after I arrived in my room. We were staying in the visitors' area at the kahall of Santa Teresa. The room resembled the one I'd stayed in at the kahall of Santa Sophia. It had a floor-to-ceiling window on the left side and a huge bed next to it. Above the bed, a wall-sized picture of Kammbi floating in the air with the words "He's always with us" underneath reminded me of my first night in Santa Sophia.

On the right side of the room were a desk, a bookcase, and a second wall-sized picture, this one of a tall, angular woman wearing a brown shawl. I knew this had to be Teresa, founder of this city and a member of that tribe Oscar Ortega had met on his journey.

I returned my attention to the pages I was reading in the Book of Kammbi. This was the second time I had read this chapter since arriving north of the Great Forest. I reread this chapter in order to see how, when the book clearly stated that Teresa chose not to get married and opposed forced marriage in the tribe, a tradition could have arisen like the one I was encountering now. How could someone start and continue a tradition that directly contradicts what has been written in their sacred book?

I did not grow up with a sacred book that wrote out our spiritual beliefs. In my culture, the lifechart we received at birth, validated by the *oraki,* our version of a morrim, determined one's path in life. There was no way possible for misinterpretation or contradiction by those who received their lifechart.

I needed a break from reading, and I got up from the chair at the desk. I paced the room in order to clear my head and absorb what I had read.

Today was the twenty-fourth day in the fifth month of Aym, and we had arrived in Santa Teresa yesterday. So this second expedition in the service of Kammbi had started two days before Oscar Ortega's expedition two hundred fifty years ago.

The timing was not by coincidence. This time frame had been chosen for a reason. It only made me even more convinced of my role in fulfilling Oscar's prophecy.

I had to start writing a themily about this turn of events.

Is anything really a coincidence? Or is everything connected? Does history repeat itself from one generation to the next? Does something that's old become new again but is really old the whole time?

I have been north of the Great Forest for nearly two months as a stranger and am now starting to feel more connected to this area, like I was back home in Charlesville.

Maybe we are not the strangers to others as we make ourselves out to be. History, traditions, and beliefs are supposed to differentiate one group of people from another group of people. But perhaps they are just barriers put up by people to make them feel connected to those who are closest to them and keep out the stranger. Those barriers can be removed when you are a part of something that's bigger than any person or group of people.

I guess there is no such thing as coincidences when we realize that we are truly connected to each other.

I heard a knock on the door right after I wrote the last sentence. I got up and looked across the room, glancing briefly out the window. The sun had risen and was lightening the horizon. In the distance, I could see the Ortega Hills. I appreciated seeing those hills and began to understand why Oscar Ortega wrote about them so eloquently in his section of the Book of Kammbi. I hoped to have some inspiration of my own for a themily about those hills while I was here.

I had been up all night, and I could feel the pull of sleep calling me to the bed even as I walked to the door. I opened the door and smiled at the tiny woman wearing her customary second esperah green shawl. She wore eyeglasses that looked too big for her face, and her cute, plump cheeks made her appear a few years younger than myself.

"Hello, Diondray Azur. I'm Second Esperah Annika Dorrado, here to serve your needs while you are staying in the visitors' area at the kahall of Santa Teresa."

She faced me and gave the customary bow after entering the room. I remembered how formal second esperahs could be from my interaction with Second Esperah Leo Carranza at the kahall of Santa Sophia. Second esperahs served under the diakonos and did all menial work for the kahall.

"I thought I would get a first esperah after meeting with Morrim Pomodore," I replied.

"Morrim Pomodore chose me to serve you," she said. "I'm grateful that he picked me instead of a first esperah for this duty."

The savory smell from the *changa* on the plate diverted my attention from Second Esperah Dorrado's youthfulness. A changa was a combination of sliced cherries, corn, and strips of meat on a hard-crusted white piece of circular bread. I'd had my first changa on the second day I arrived in Santa Sophia, and it was delicious. She placed the changa and a glass of cherry juice on the desk. My stomach rumbled, knowing that food had entered the room.

"Are you a writer?" she asked, her back to me as she glanced at the paper on the desk.

"I write themilys."

"What is a themily?" she asked while looking at the paper on the desk.

"Words written on a single sheet of paper that are meant to inspire, encourage, or admonish an audience."

"You read this themily to an audience?"

"I did back in my hometown of Charlesville."

Second Esperah Dorrado faced me and smiled. "You are the first person I've ever met from south of the Great Forest."

I chuckled. Even if everyone else insisted on seeing me as a stranger, I was glad I was ceasing to feel like one. "I've gotten that a lot since I've been here, and in Santa Sophia."

"Could you read this themily to me? I'd like to hear it."

I searched her face and was drawn in by her cheeks. She had an innocence that attracted me. "I will read it to you."

She handed me the paper, and I read the themily.

"Those are beautiful words," she said. "I've never heard anyone talk about coincidences and being connected like that before."

"Thank you."

"I have been feeling like an outcast recently," she said and looked away.

Her comment surprised me. Why would she feel like an outcast? Second Esperah Dorrado did not come across as someone who would be shunned by others. "What do you mean?"

She kept her eyes downcast. "I'm supposed to get married on the first day in the seventh month of Yul. I'm supposed to look forward to it. But I don't."

"You do not want to get married." As those words came out of my mouth, I thought about that parishioner at the kahall service. I could imagine that if he had a daughter like Second Esperah Dorrado, he would make life difficult for her.

"Yes. But I turned twenty-one yesterday, and it is our custom for women to get married at this age."

"Yes, I heard that from the previous kahall service."

"I have told my family that I don't feel anything about the man they have arranged to be my husband. I don't want to marry him."

Tears welled up in her eyes, and sadness showed on her face. I embraced her.

"What are you doing, Second Esperah Dorrado?" a male voice said from behind me. I turned around and saw another second esperah and Maisa standing at the doorway to the room.

"I must go, Diondray," Second Esperah Dorrado said. She pulled away from my embrace. I saw a wan smile on her face and knew she appreciated my comfort. "I will return in a little while to clean up your breakfast." She left the room, following the other second esperah.

I watched her go, troubled by the exchange. How could a city have a custom like this—one that forced young women to marry men they did not love? Was this one of the costs paid by a young woman who did not want to follow tradition? I felt sympathetic toward her plight and began thinking about ways to help. Had Teresa addressed in the Book of Kammbi how the tribe accepted her decision not to marry? Again, I found myself wondering why Teresa's clear choice had been ignored by the people of this city. There was something missing, and I wanted to find out what it was.

Maisa was still standing at the doorway, and her blank expression caught my attention. Our eyes connected, and I saw disappointment in her face. She lowered her eyes and left the doorway.

I knew I had done something wrong.

Chapter 3

"You have learned about Second Esperah Annika Dorrado's dilemma?" Morrim Pomodore said.

I had requested a meeting with Morrim Pomodore after hearing about Second Esperah Dorrado's upcoming marriage. I met with Diakono Copperwith later that evening, and he had set it up. It took three days for the meeting, and she had kept her interaction with me formal since her confession.

Now, facing the morrim, I realized he wasn't surprised that I was here. In fact, I had the sudden sense that he had planned this. "Is that why you let Second Esperah Dorrado attend to me? Instead of a first esperah?" I asked.

Seated behind his desk, Morrim Pomodore stared hard at me for a moment. "Diakono Copperwith was right about you. You are perceptive. If you are the one to fulfill Oscar's prophecy, then I want to see how you handle a situation like this one."

I looked over at Diakono Copperwith and Annalisa. They were sitting in chairs opposite the morrim on the left side of the desk. The Copperwiths looked solemn, but I could not read how they were reacting to the morrim's comments.

"I have read Teresa's section in the Book of Kammbi, and she did not dissuade anyone from getting married," I continued. "Yet, neither does she require that anyone do so. I don't understand why there is a custom of having women marry at twenty-one. It appears that the people of this city have created a belief outside of their sacred book."

"We have, Diondray," the morrim answered. Because of Teresa's position in the Book of Kammbi and her status in our city, the leaders since her death to the current day have wanted to make sure the women of the city did not want to become just like her and see marriage as a burden, or as something that might divide them between belief in Kammbi and having a relationship with a husband."

"So the leaders of this city have believed throughout the years that most of the women here would pursue the route of Teresa instead of getting married if they were given a choice," I shot back.

The morrim grimaced and replied, "We need future generations of our people to keep Santa Teresa in existence."

I looked away from the morrim and started to pace the room. I did not like where this discussion was going. It seemed the women of this city were forced into marriage and motherhood without their consent. But their sacred book contradicted this custom and featured women prominently throughout its pages. I was reminded of my family, especially Uncle Xavier and Mother, in their total belief in the lifechart determining my life's path. I had hated those conversations, and it was one of the reasons I had to leave my family home. Did believers or followers of any spiritual persuasion have a choice to determine one's own life? Or did following a spiritual persuasion demand coercion?

"Are you all right, Diondray?" the morrim asked.

"Yes, he is," Diakono Copperwith answered.

I stopped pacing and glanced at Diakono Copperwith. His expression calmed me down. It seemed like he knew what I was going to say next. I shook my head. "With all due respect, Morrim Pomodore, this custom seems quite unfair to me."

"I can see that you believe in fairness. That's quite noble of you, Diondray. You do come from a family of wealth and privilege?" Morrim Pomodore asked.

"I do." I thought back to my youth and to the abuses I'd seen against those who were powerless. My voice grew more heated as I continued, "I've seen how members of my family used their wealth and power to determine the fate of those beneath them. This situation is similar. Something is wrong with that, and I'm surprised a morrim would continue to let it happen."

"Diondray Azur, please speak to the morrim in a respectful tongue." Diakono Copperwith interjected. He glared at me, but I wasn't going to back down.

"It's okay, Diakono Copperwith," the morrim replied. "I like that he has fire. He will need that as you all continue on this second expedition."

"How can I stop Second Esperah Dorrado from getting married?"

"You cannot break custom, Diondray," Annalisa said.

I glanced at Annalisa and noted the pained look on her face. I knew she had married Diakono Copperwith around the same age as Second Esperah Dorrado. The women of Santa Sophia weren't under the control of a custom, but they were pressured to get married at a young age nevertheless. Even so, Annalisa was happy with her husband: I had no doubt she believed that she had made the right choice by marrying Diakono Copperwith, and Second Esperah Dorrado would do the same.

"Her family is arranging a marriage with a man she does not love. Does love not get to have a choice?"

"You can grow to love someone. Passion of the flesh can lead to deception of the heart, Diondray." Annalisa shot back.

I shook my head in frustration. "I guess this is where our beliefs from Charlesville differ with yours in the north. You should not marry someone you do not love."

"I would agree with Mrs. Copperwith," Morrim Pomodore said. "Passion of the flesh is often disguised as love. It takes more than that for a marriage."

I felt anger flaring up in me again. Of course it took more than passion to make a marriage—but did they really think a custom could create that "more"? That forcing a woman into marriage was the ideal answer? This discussion wasn't helping me. "Well, Morrim Pomodore, I would like to thank you for your time. But I do not believe that Second Esperah Dorrado should marry a man she does not love. I have made up my mind to help her get out of it. I do not know if you will help me. But I'm going to help her anyway."

To my surprise, Morrim Pomodore smiled. "Diondray Azur, I will help you. I'm beginning to believe you are the one to fulfill Oscar's prophecy. If you can help change a custom that has been going strong for over two hundred years, then I will know by the Eternal Comforter you are the one."

#

I came back from my meeting with Morrim Pomodore a few hours later. I didn't know how I was going to help Second Esperah Dorrado. I had to find a way to show the people of this city the contradiction between their custom and the Book of Kammbi. Weren't the people of Santa Teresa faithful believers and followers in Kammbi, just like the people of Santa Sophia? If so, why would they create a custom outside of the Book? It should have not taken a stranger from south of the Great Forest to point it out.

The smell of dinner coming from the desk diverted my attention from Second Esperah Dorrado's problem. She must have brought dinner a short time before I returned to the room. Steam rose from the bluefish and vegetables on the plate. I took a sip of the cherry juice and swished the tartness around my mouth before eating. The aroma from the bluefish reminded of what I ate back home. Diakono Copperwith must have told the first esperahs what kind of food I liked.

I had eaten a couple of bites of the bluefish when I heard a knock on the door. I took another sip of cherry juice and got up from the desk. It was Maisa. Her eyes were watery like she had been crying.

"Are you fond of her?" she asked and entered the room. Leave it to Maisa not to beat around the bush.

I was caught off guard by the question. Had she misunderstood our embrace the other day? "Second Esperah Dorrado?"

She nodded.

"I want to help her. She is being forced into marrying a man she does not love. I don't believe that is right."

Maisa faced me, and the tears streamed over her cheeks. I didn't know why she was questioning me about Second Esperah Dorrado.

"I saw the way she looked at you. I want to know if you felt the same way about her."

Even though Second Esperah Dorrado was only two years younger than myself, she appeared to me like a younger sister. I wasn't sure what Maisa saw in that embrace, but it hadn't been romantic from my perspective. "I read a themily, and she told me about her upcoming marriage. I don't understanding why you are questioning me like this."

"You don't get it, Diondray. I have watched how you look at me," Maisa said with her piercing eyes staring right through me. I sensed that she could read all my thoughts at that moment. She wore an ocean-blue jumpsuit that hugged her perfectly. I found it difficult not to stare. She'd worn that outfit for my benefit and knew it would affect me like this.

"And I know how you feel about me even though you have not spoken it. I understand you wanting to keep your distance because we are on this second expedition. But I thought there would be a time for us to have that discussion. I've been waiting for it."

What discussion? I was not sure that I wanted to talk about my feelings with her. She'd known of my attraction to her since we first met in Santa Sophia. I had not felt this way about any woman since Mara. But why would I want to go through that kind of pain again? I walked up to Maisa and embraced her. Maisa sobbed into my chest as I consoled her. I did not have anything to say after that.

"Maisa Merez!"

I released Maisa from my embrace as Annalisa Copperwith entered the room. Did the woman never knock?

Annalisa did not look happy. "You know the rule the diakono put in place. At night, an unmarried man and woman should not be in the same room together."

Maisa had a disgusted look. "I know, Annalisa. But I had to talk to him about something important."

"What was so important that you needed to be in his arms?"

"I was crying! Can't Diondray even comfort me?" Tears welled in Maisa's eyes again.

This was my fault, I thought. "Annalisa, I did not know about this rule. I did not hear about this in Santa Sophia."

"Diondray, I have seen how you've looked at her since the Festival of Sinquinta. I'm a woman, and I know that kind of look from a man. I'm married. I do not want you to be led in the wrong direction. I know you are the one to fulfill Oscar's prophecy, and you must not have anything to distract you from that calling."

"You think I would distract Diondray from fulfilling Oscar's prophecy?" Maisa snapped. "Annalisa, you do not know me at all. That's disrespectful."

"Disrespectful!" Annalisa said. "Being in an unmarried man's arms is disrespectful. Modesty should be a woman's virtue at all times."

Maisa sobbed and ran for the door. She paused and looked back at me just before she exited. "Diondray, I want you to know that I would never be the one to distract you from fulfilling Oscar's prophecy. I'm on this expedition because I believe in you and want to see the prophecy fulfilled. Despite what the diakono's wife thinks of my intentions."

I watched Maisa leave the room. Her hips and backside swayed in a seductive fashion even though she was upset.

"That look on your face is why you must keep your distance," Annalisa said when Maisa was gone.

#

Four days passed before I saw Maisa again. I was unhappy about that. I had to admit our embrace had been warm and inviting. I could have held her for the rest of that evening. I did not know if Annalisa had told her to stay away because of our interaction. Or was Maisa avoiding me of her own volition?

The Copperwiths had spent the last few days with Morrim Pomodore and helped around the kahall. They wanted to meet Maisa and me before today's duties. I was not ready to talk about my feelings for Maisa with them. But I knew this had to be addressed before we could continue any further on this expedition.

We met in the kahall's cafeteria. It was a small, square-shaped room with only a few tables and chairs. The room's lighting was dim and unappealing. I could not imagine that the morrim, the diakonos, or any of the first or second esperahs ate in here. I assumed the Copperwiths wanted to meet with us here because we would have complete privacy.

The Copperwiths and Maisa were already seated when I arrived.

I glanced at Annalisa and could still see the anguished look on her face from the other night. I cut my eyes to Maisa, who looked like she did not want to be here. And Diakono Copperwith had a solemn look on his face, adding to the mood of the room.

I sat across from Maisa as my new second esperah placed a plate of changas and cherry juice in front of me. Even the aroma of those delicious changas could not stir up my appetite.

"Diondray, you know why we are here," Diakono Copperwith started.

I nodded, still looking down at my plate, not meeting his gaze.

"My wife saw both of you together in a compromising position a few nights ago. I heard Maisa's side of the story about it. I want to hear yours."

I looked up but still avoided the diakono's eyes. "I really have nothing to discuss. Maisa was emotional, and I embraced her. I do not believe I did anything wrong."

"You are both unmarried," Annalisa interjected. "And I saw how you have looked at her."

I glanced at Annalisa and saw the disappointment in her eyes. It was like she knew something about Maisa that I did not. "Yes, I'm fond of Maisa. I cannot deny that. But there was nothing happening when you saw us."

I didn't see any need to go into detail about Maisa's questioning about Second Esperah Dorrado. I felt it was out of place for the Copperwiths to know that conversation.

Maisa smiled at me after my comment. I was confirming what she already knew. I could only look at her briefly, because I did not want those piercing, sharp eyes exposing all my feelings for her.

"Annalisa believes that I will distract you from the reason you are on this expedition," Maisa said bitterly. "I have no intention of doing that, Diondray. I have heard the Eternal Conforter in my prayers, and I believe you are the one."

"Then you should know what happened to Oscar," Annalisa shot back. "Do you want the same thing to happen to Diondray?"

I looked at both women. Their interaction reminded me of a mother-daughter conflict. Maisa and I were the Copperwiths' children for this journey. Apparently my childhood had not ended, even though I had left my family's home in Charlesville three years ago.

"I have my own reasons for being here," Maisa countered. "My family will not be forgotten."

Diakono Copperwith stiffened after that comment and replied, "No one has forgotten the contributions of your family. They were instrumental in helping create Santa Sophia."

Maisa glared at the diakono. "Then why are they not mentioned in the Book of Kammbi? Oscar recognized the Carranza and Ortega families in his writings. My family married into the Ortega family generations ago and are not even mentioned in the Book of Kammbi. And you tell me they are not forgotten!"

Her outburst caught me totally by surprise. The Carranza and Ortega families were indeed written about in Oscar Ortega's section in the Book of Kammbi; I had read about them there. I did not know that another family belonged in those pages as well. I was beginning to realize that Maisa might not be here just because of me.

"The konseho of Kammbi decided what writings of Oscar went into the Book of Kammbi. That will have to be addressed with them," Diakono Copperwith said.

Her eyes flashed. "Oh, it will be, Diakono Copperwith."

"Konseho of Kammbi," I said. "You mentioned that briefly when we were in Santa Sophia."

My eyes finally met the diakono's. "You are correct, Diondray," he said. "We did have a brief discussion about it. The konseho of Kammbi is the governing council for all the cities north of the great forest. They put together the Book of Kammbi after Oscar's death in the Year 58 A.O.A. Oscar had a lot of writings compiled over his expedition, and the konseho of Kammbi wanted to create a book for all believers and followers of Kammbi to live their lives by."

I nodded at his explanation. 'The konseho of Kammbi is in the city of Issabella?"

"Correct," Diakono Copperwith answered.

"Are we going to the city of Issabella?"

"Yes, we are," Maisa interjected.

I looked at her as she stood from the table. "Where are you going?" I asked.

"I have a meeting with Frederic Cortes. And I was going to ask if you could join me."

"What for?" I replied.

"You will see," she answered and stared down at me with those piercing eyes.

"Diondray is not going with you. That's what we were here to discuss in the first place," Annalisa said.

"The Eternal Conforter has spoken to me these past several nights. And we are going to need help with the konseho of Kammbi. I have cultivated a relationship with Frederic Cortes since our arrival in this city," Maisa said.

"I can't believe you, Maisa Merez—" Annalisa said.

"Diondray, please join me?"

I looked over at the Copperwiths. The diakono nodded, while Annalisa stared at Maisa in disbelief.

"I will go with you, Maisa."

Maisa grinned at her victory over Annalisa. I got up from the table and followed her out of the cafeteria.

#

A driver for Frederic Cortes was waiting in front of the kahall's main entrance. I was relieved to leave the cafeteria. The tension between the Copperwiths and Maisa and I was as thick as several days' of uncut grass. Plus, I did not like the fact that I was the one who had caused the tension. I'd grown fond of the Copperwiths, and it felt like I was disappointing them. Annalisa's anguished look reminded me of my mother when I decided to leave the family home and move to the westside of Charlesville. She had been disappointed in me for that decision, and looking at Annalisa brought those memories back again.

Maisa had arranged the meeting with Mr. Cortes at his office on the other side of the city. Even though I had just agreed to go with Maisa, I was starting to feel some uneasiness coming from my stomach. Maybe it was due to not getting a chance to eat those delicious changas for breakfast. I hoped that was the only reason.

I followed Maisa onto the autobus. She was wearing a mid-thigh cloud-white midi dress with an orange flower pattern that flowed as she walked to the first seat opposite of the driver. I sat down next to her, thinking about how Annalisa would not like it.

"I'm glad you wore shorts today," Maisa said. "Mr. Cortes has been looking forward to talking with you, Diondray."

"About my shorts?"

"Yes," she replied. "Mr. Cortes owns the largest fashion company in all the cities north of the Great Forest. When he saw you at the kahall service with those shorts, it gave him an idea for a new clothing line."

I looked at my light gray shorts and wondered what this meeting with Mr. Cortes had to do with Second Esperah Dorrado's dilemma. What was Maisa thinking?

Maisa placed her hand on my right thigh and added, "He wants to help with Second Esperah Dorrado."

I glared at Maisa. "Did you tell him about our conversation?"

She nodded. "Yes. I'm sorry for the way I acted. When I left your room I had to think about what you said. Also, I prayed, and the Eternal Comforter revealed to me that what you said was true. So I told Mr. Cortes about her forthcoming marriage and how you wanted to stop it."

I looked away from Maisa as the driver left the Kahall. The uneasiness in my stomach continued, and I knew it was not just because I was hungry.

Chapter 4

Fifteen minutes later, we arrived at Cortes Holdings. I had stared out the seat's window for the entire drive. The long and sandy-colored rectangular buildings were similar to what I had seen in Santa Sophia. Santa Teresa's scenery was unremarkable and serene at the same time. It had a calming effect on me as I thought about Maisa. She said she had prayed to the Eternal Comforter and that changed her mind about Second Esperah Dorrado. How could the Eternal Comforter do that? I was still unclear on this particular aspect of belief in Kammbi. The entire Baramesa section of the Book of Kammbi explained through Oscar's writings how the Eternal Comforter was received as a gift once you became a believer and follower in Kammbi. But how did you receive that gift? Oscar and Teresa had made declarations for their gift, while Alicia and Issabella were immersed in the river for it. Which was correct, and why the difference amongst the four main people written about in the second half of the Book of Kammbi?

My thoughts about the Eternal Comforter subsided as the Cortes Holdings building came into view. It was the tallest building in the Kammbi district of the city and towered over everything else in the area. Maisa explained that the city of Santa Teresa was divided into three districts: Kammbi, Teresa, and Ortega. The Kammbi district housed most of the city's commerce and government facilities, and Mr. Cortes made sure his building stood out.

A tall, well-dressed woman wearing a red mid-thigh dress with a sun-like pattern over the stomach area greeted Maisa and me. My eyes lowered to the pattern as she approached us. I assumed that dress was one of Mr. Cortes's newest fashions.

"Welcome, Diondray Azur. I'm Felicia Hargrove, Mr. Cortes's executive administrator here at Cortes Holdings. We are pleased that you accepted Mr. Cortes's invitation to visit us here at headquarters. I will make sure your visit here today is hospitable and welcoming."

I shook Ms. Hargrove's hand, and she smiled. Her greeting felt genuine even though I still had misgivings about her boss. Then Felicia turned to Maisa, and her tone changed dramatically. "Hello, Maisa Merez," Felicia said. She had a contemptuous look on her face. I was taken aback by Felicia's look after her warm greeting to me. Was there some history between the two women? Maisa had told me on the way to Santa Teresa that she came to visit the city quite often.

"Hello, Felicia," Maisa replied. "You can be hospitable to all visitors."

Felicia's thin smile was not friendly. I could feel the tension between the two women as Felicia led us into the building. I noticed her long, blonde hair that stopped in the middle of her back and wondered how long it took her to grow it.

"This is our main lobby area, Diondray. We will take the elevator to Mr. Cortes's office, which is on the thirty-sixth floor."

I surveyed the lobby area as Felicia led us to the elevator. People were staring as we walked by. Their eyes lowered to look at my shorts. Some people smiled. Some gaped. Others laughed. I hadn't realized wearing shorts would cause this type of reaction.

"I'm used to everyone staring at me," Maisa laughed. "Your shorts have captured everybody's attention."

"Thirty-sixth floor," Felicia said to the tall, olive-skinned man who was standing inside the elevator. I glanced at Felicia, and still she had a look of contempt on her face toward Maisa. I did like not how she looked at Maisa, and I suddenly felt protective toward my companion.

The man pushed a button on the elevator panel, and we were heading to Mr. Cortes's office. The uneasiness in my stomach returned. I wanted to get this meeting over with as quickly as possible.

"Welcome to Cortes Holdings," Frederic Cortes said as we entered his office. He sat at a large conference table in the back of his office. Even seated, his height made me feel like I was a child again. "Diondray and Maisa, the travelers from Santa Sophia. My favorite city outside of Santa Teresa."

Felicia led us to the table, past artwork on the walls and oval-shaped lights that hung from the ceiling. The lighting made it darker than I'd expected for a businessman's office.

"Can you bring us drinks and starter food?" Mr. Cortes asked Felicia as we were seated across from him.

"Yes, Mr. Cortes." She quickly walked out of the office.

"Maisa. Please stand up and let me see how beautiful you are."

Maisa giggled and readily obeyed Mr. Cortes's request. She walked over to the other side of the table and extended her hand to him as she approached.

"Love the color combination, Maisa. At least someone in Santa Sophia knows how to dress." He twirled Maisa with a smile.

"Thanks, Mr. Cortes. At least someone knows how to appreciate a beautiful woman."

Both of them looked at me after that comment. I cut my eyes away from their stares and saw a large painting of a man wearing a white shawl that floated in the air.

"Is that Kammbi?" I asked.

Mr. Cortes smiled. "It is. I can see you have read the Book of Kammbi. I'm impressed that someone from south of the Great Forest has read our sacred book."

I nodded. "There's a statue at the marperia in Santa Sophia that reminded me of him."

"You have good recollection as well. Maybe you are the one to fulfill Oscar's prophecy?"

I felt the churning in my stomach while he talked get even worse with that last statement. I did not know why I felt this way around Mr. Cortes. Something about him did not sit well with me.

"Did Morrim Pomodore tell you about Diondray?" Maisa said after she returned to her seat next to me.

"Of course. Morrim Pomodore keeps me informed on everything that happens at the kahall of Santa Teresa. And it's not every day we get a visitor from south of the Great Forest claiming he's the one."

Felicia returned to the office and brought a pitcher of cherry juice and a plate full of changas. They smelled delicious, and maybe eating a few them would help my stomach. She placed them in the middle of table and turned to leave the room.

"Help yourself to the changas. A staple of Santa Teresa cuisine," Mr. Cortes said and grabbed one.

Felicia returned to the table with plates and glasses. She served Maisa and I before sitting down next to Mr. Cortes.

"I didn't claim to be the one who would fulfill Oscar's prophecy. That was placed upon me," I replied after eating a changa. They helped the uneasiness immediately. My stomach stopped rumbling. Were the changas imbued with the Eternal Comforter somehow?

"I know about how you arrived in Santa Sophia," Mr. Cortes said. "However, that's not the only reason I invited you and Maisa to my office."

How did he know about my arrival in Santa Sophia? Did he know the morrim at the kahall of Santa Sophia as well? "I know you wanted to see my shorts."

"Yes, we wanted to see you in those shorts so we could start to design our own version," Mr. Cortes said. "Felicia has gotten everything I needed in terms of that. We will have our own version of shorts for sale by the first day in the seventh month of Yul. I have to thank you for that."

How did Ms. Hargrove get what she needed about these shorts? Were pictures of me being taken as I entered the building? My uneasiness came back. This meeting needed to end soon. I wasn't sure how much longer I could stand being here.

Felicia held up a folder and slid it across to me. Inside were pictures of myself as I arrived and walked through the lobby area. The pictures caught every angle of my shorts and confirmed my suspicion.

"Do you need something to drink that's stronger than cherry juice?" Felicia asked.

"You work fast," I replied, ignoring her offer. My hands were trembling. "I did not know there would be pictures taken of me in this manner."

"That's why Cortes Holdings is the top business in all the cities north of the Great Forest," Felicia said as I slid the folder back to her.

"Diondray Azur, I invited you to my office because I have an offer to make."

"An offer?" Maisa asked.

I glanced at Maisa and saw a surprised look. She did not know about this. I had no idea what Mr. Cortes could possibly have to offer me, but I waited for him to continue.

"I understand that you want to help Second Esperah Annika Dorrado escape her fate. You do not believe in our custom of forcing women to marry at twenty-one. I agree with you, and I want to offer my assistance in that endeavor."

"How would you do that?" I said.

"I'm a powerful man in this city, and I have my eyes and ears into everything that goes on. Felicia is not married because of my influence and power. And I believe I can help Second Esperah Dorrado in the same way."

"What's your angle?" Maisa said.

Mr. Cortes gave a thin smile while staring at me. My stomach was doing flips, and I thought I was going to vomit. I grabbed the glass of cherry juice and gulped it.

"I would like to be part of your expedition. I know my influence can help you fulfill Oscar's prophecy."

Maisa's jaw dropped into her chest. It was all I could do to keep mine steady.

"I do not know how to respond to your offer," I said.

"I will give my assistance with Second Esperah Dorrado's marriage issue, and you can make your decision before you leave Santa Teresa."

I got up from my chair and began to leave the room. I couldn't take this a moment longer.

"Where are you going, Diondray?" Maisa called out to me.

"You have forty-six days to make a decision. I'm usually not that patient. But I am convinced that you are the one. I will offer my assistance and wait for your decision. I believe you will make the right choice before you leave the city."

#

I got up early the next morning after our meeting with Mr. Cortes. It was the twenty-ninth day in the fifth month of Aym, and I had forty-five days left in Santa Teresa. I had the same time frame to make a decision about the businessman. Should I allow Mr. Cortes to come with us on the expedition? If I said no, what would that mean for the rest of our journey? Would he use his wealth and influence to make it difficult for us in the cities of Issabella and Alicia? How would Diakono Copperwith and Annalisa react if I allowed him to join us?

I opened the Book of Kammbi, hoping to find some guidance from Oscar Ortega on making a big decision. I flipped through the pages, but nothing caught my attention in regard to what I needed to do.

I closed the book and picked up my pencil. I wrote the word *decision* on a blank sheet of paper. Before I could ponder what words would come next, someone knocked on the door.

I got up to open the door. Second Esperah Dorrado entered the room with the breakfast but did not make eye contact with me. I was surprised to see her.

"I thought they assigned me another second esperah?" I asked as she placed the food on the desk.

She kept her back turned to me. "Morrim Podomore allowed me to continue my duty. But I cannot get in trouble again by overstepping my position."

I grabbed her shoulders and turned her to face me. "I understand. I did not want to get you in trouble. But I'm here to help you. You do not have to get married to a man you don't love."

"Diondray, I do not want to talk about this. I have to maintain my role with you." She pulled away and turned her attention back to the food on the desk. I felt more determined than ever to change things for her.

"I'm still going to help you. You will not be getting married on the seventh day in the seventh month of Yul."

"Is that a Book of Kammbi?" she asked.

"Yes."

"I have never seen one that worn looking before." She glided her fingers over the book.

"I brought it with me from Charlesville. It is the copy Oscar

Ortega had when he came south of the Great Forest to reconcile with his son. My family hid it in my hometown for years until it was shown to me recently."

She gave me a surprised look. "Are you telling the truth?"

I nodded.

"May I pick it up?"

"Go ahead.

She opened the Book of Kammbi like someone who had just received a precious gift. "Amazing. When I was a child, my mother would read to me every night from the story about Oscar going south of the Great Forest to reconcile with his son from that woman."

My body stiffened after that comment. I assumed the people of Santa Teresa thought of Mother Adrianna the same way the people of Santa Sophia did. She could not even say her name. Was that one of the consequences for committing an act of passha? "That woman is Mother Adrianna. I'm a fourth-generation member of her family."

She looked at me again, even more surprised now. "I'm sorry, Diondray. I did not mean to be hurtful in my comments. But I only knew about Mother Adrianna, as you call her, as the woman who caused Oscar Ortega to commit an act of passha."

I watched as Second Esperah Dorrado slowly turned the pages of the Book of Kammbi. She seemed entranced by it. However, I was still angered by her comments about Mother Adrianna. My ancestor had risked everything when she was forced to leave her tribe because of her illicit relationship with Oscar Ortega. And I could tell from Oscar's writings in the Book of Kammbi that he loved Mother Adrianna even though he was married. I believed that people of these cities north of the Great Forest should treat Mother Adrianna more respectfully despite the act of passha committed.

"That has to be the oldest copy of the Book of Kammbi still in existence," Second Esperah Dorrado continued. "You may be the one who will fulfill Oscar's prophecy."

"So do you want me to help you?"

She closed the Book of Kammbi and looked up at me. "Yes, I do, Diondray Azur. I do not love Turner Perez. And you said earlier that I should not marry a man I do not love. If you are the one to fulfill Oscar's prophecy, then I know your help would receive honor from the Eternal Comforter."

Second Esperah Dorrado smiled and caressed the Book of Kammbi. I knew what I had to do.

But first, there was a certain businessman to answer.

#

I spent the next three days writing themilys and going through the Book of Kammbi looking for anything that would help me make the decision about Mr. Cortes. Diakono Copperwith and Annalisa were doing duties for Morrim Pomodore and the kahall of Santa Teresa. I had not seen them since our meeting in the cafeteria and had not told them about the offer from the businessman.

I did not know how they would react to Cortes's offer. Would they accept him? Would they not accept him? How would he fit with us? It seemed like the Copperwiths had become Maisa and my honorary parents. Would Mr. Cortes become like another sibling? I could already guess the businessman would not respond favorably to being treated in such a fashion. His wealth and influence demanded that people follow his lead, not the other way around. Even so, I hoped that whatever decision I made would receive their endorsement. Especially Diakono Copperwith's. His presence in my life had meant a lot since I arrived in the north.

Second Esperah Dorrado brought breakfast, lunch, and dinner every day, and her formal demeanor returned. We did not talk any more about her upcoming marriage to Turner Perez.

On the third day, she left a piece of paper next to my breakfast plate. I opened it after eating. It read,

Diondray, I would like you to come to my home for dinner this evening. I have told my mother everything, and she would like to meet you. I told her about the Book of Kammbi you have and asked if you could bring it with you to dinner. She wants to see if it's actually real. My work shift ends at 6:00 this evening, and I will come for you one hour later. See you then, Annika.

I folded the paper and held it in my left hand. Did she always sign letters with her first name, or did it mean something? Maybe Maisa had been right about the way Second Esperah Dorrado looked at me.

I knew I had to talk to Diakono Copperwith before I went to Second Esperah Dorrado's home. I needed his guidance and wished he could come as well. I would go find him in the kahall and see if that could be arranged.

#

Diakono Copperwith finished with his duties for Morrim Pomodore around 2:00, and I went to visit him in their room at the other end of the visitor's area of the kahall.

As I entered, I noticed how much larger their room was than mine. Well, their room was for both of them, and a woman needed as much space as she could get.

"Diondray," Diakono Copperwith said. He seemed pleased to see me. "It has been a few days. Morrim Pomodore has kept Annalisa and me busy. How are you doing?"

"A lot has happened since the last time we saw each other."

"I see," he replied, and the smile on his face evaporated. "Let's talk outside. I need some fresh air."

I followed Diakono Copperwith out of the room and into the hallway. Oval lamps on each side lit up the hall as we walked to the exit. It was still quite dark, and I wondered if the kahall saved on using electricity by using lamps instead of electric power.

We reached outside and turned left from the main entrance onto a walkway. The lawn was perfectly manicured, and the aroma from the grass was heady. I did not want to start sneezing.

The diakono didn't waste time getting to the point. "What has happened since our last time together?"

"I received an offer from Mr. Cortes and an invitation from Second Esperah Dorrado."

Diakono Copperwith stopped on the walkway. "What kind of offer from Mr. Cortes?"

"He wants to join us on the expedition in exchange for his help with Second Esperah Dorrado's upcoming marriage."

"Oh my word! Have you made a decision?

"No. He gave me until the day we leave Santa Teresa. And I have no idea what decision I'm going to make."

I started to pace when Diakono Copperwith grabbed my shoulders to stop me. His grip was firm and kept me in place. "You said you also received an invitation from Second Esperah Dorrado?"

"She has invited me to her home for dinner this evening. She has told her mother that I'm going to help her, and the mother wants to meet me. And . . ."

"Is there something else?"

"She wants me to bring Oscar Ortega's Book of Kammbi to dinner. Her mother wants to see it the book is real."

Diakono Copperwith released his grip, and he had a forlorn look on his face. "Let's go back inside to the congregation hall. Prayer is needed at this moment."

We turned back toward the kahall, and I had to trot to keep up with the diakono.

#

Diakono Copperwith and a couple of other diakonos from the kahall prayed for me in the congregation room for several hours. They placed their hands on my upper body for the entire time and chanted in a language I did not understand. I had not been prayed for in this fashion since my last day in Santa Sophia at the Festival of Sinquinta. I was still uncomfortable with prayer. I did not know what to do or how to react to it.

I tried to read Diakono Copperwith's face to see if I could sense why he felt prayer was needed so urgently. He still looked forlorn—sad. It was like he had forgotten my presence and stepped into his own world. I had not seen him like this before.

I returned to my room after that prayer session with just enough time to get dressed for my dinner with Second Esperah Dorrado and her parents. However, my thoughts remained on that prayer session and its importance. I wanted to flip through the Book of Kammbi to see if Oscar Ortega had ever prayed for someone like that, or if there was any kind of significant meaning for that type of prayer. Then I spotted a note placed on top of the book. It was from Second Esperah Dorrado.

Meet me in the congregation hall after you are dressed.

I folded the note and put it in the left pocket of my shorts. I grabbed the Book of Kammbi and left the room.

I arrived at the congregation hall a few minutes later. Second Esperah Dorrado was standing next to Diakono Copperwith and Annalisa. She seemed out of sorts in their presence.

"They wanted to pray for me before dinner," Second Esperah Dorrado said.

"How come?" I asked.

"We were not invited to go with you, Diondray. But we prayed that the Eternal Comforter's presence would be at that dinner," Diakono Copperwith said solemnly.

"I trust that Second Esperah Dorrado will stay within her boundaries," Annalisa added.

"We both believe from the Eternal Comforter's guidance that Second Esperah Dorrado's plight is important in order to fulfill Oscar's prophecy," Diakono Copperwith said.

I was not sure where Diakono Copperwith was going with that comment. Of course, I already knew her plight was important to our expedition and Oscar's prophecy.

"She is special like you, Diondray," Annalisa explained. "Remember in Teresa's section of the Book of Kammbi how she met Oscar Ortega and the circumstances surrounding them. Once the circle starts, it must come back around for completion."

The second esperah gave a thin smile to the Copperwiths, and I followed her out of the congregation hall. She did not seem pleased by their actions. I hoped they hadn't ruined the dinner before it actually happened.

#

We arrived at Second Esperah Dorrado's house about ten minutes later. She drove into the Teresa district of the city, and her home was in the southeastern part of the district. We did not have much conversation in the automobile. I could tell she was still bothered by the Copperwiths' prayer in the congregation hall. I thought she would have brought that up during the drive, but she didn't say a word.

The Dorrado house was the last one on the street, and as I got out of the automobile, I glanced at the Ortega Hills in the distance. As much as I loved to walk along the beach back home and look out at the Bay of Charlesville, these hills had begun to captivate me in the same fashion.

I grabbed the Book of Kammbi before closing the automobile's door and followed Second Esperah Dorrado into the home. She led me to the dining room, where I assumed her parents and a sibling sat at the dining table. They all smiled at me and dropped their eyes to my shorts. I had on gray shorts with a red shirt. I knew my clothes would be a topic of conversation at dinner.

"Evening, my daughter," the man at the table said as he rose to greet Second Esperah Dorrado. "You are on time for once. I guess I will have to thank our dinner guest for that."

The second esperah's father smiled and extended his hand for a greeting. "Morris Dorrado. Welcome to our home."

I shook his hand and felt the roughness of his skin. He must work outside or do something with physical labor. Mr. Dorrado released my hand, and I noticed where Second Esperah Dorrado got her nose and smile from.

"Thank you for coming, Diondray. What a pretty name. I'm Carla," the woman sitting next to Mr. Dorrado said.

"Mom, you don't tell a man that he has a pretty name," Second Esperah Dorrado replied.

The second esperah's mother rose from the table and motioned for me to sit across from her at the table. She was the same height as her daughter, and I could tell where Second Esperah Dorrado got her figure.

"Annika, if a man has a pretty name, I'm going to tell him. Diondray is different, and I like it a lot."

"Thank you, Mrs. Dorrado," I said and sat down.

The boy next to me giggled, and I glanced at him. He had the thickest hair I'd seen since being north of the Great Forest. It looked like he had his own version of the blow-out hairstyle. In both cities of the north, I'd only seen either brown or blond feathery hair, not thick and kinky hair like we had in Charlesville.

"Amos, don't be laughing at our guest," Second Esperah Dorrado said as she began serving dinner.

"How has your time in Santa Teresa been?" her mother asked.

"It has been good so far. I have not gone outside of the kahall of Santa Teresa much. Coming to your home is only my second trip away."

Carla raised an eyebrow, apparently not approving of my self-imposed exile. "I hope you get to see the city some more before you leave."

"I visited Cortes Holdings a few days ago," I replied and placed my bag on the floor next to my chair. "That was an impressive building."

"Mr. Cortes owns this city," Morris said. "It's his money that has kept the kahall of Santa Teresa going."

"Father, that's not true. Mr. Cortes is a big contributor, but his money cannot buy the influence of Morrim Pomodore and the diakonos," Second Esperah Dorrado countered.

Morris laughed. "My daughter, you are only twenty-one, and even though you are getting ready for marriage, you are still a little green about how things are run in this city."

"Morris! Don't be so condescending to your daughter," Carla cut in.

Morris pushed away from the table and humphed a little. "It's not condescending. It's the truth, and she has been blinded by her position as second esperah. She needs to know who really runs that kahall."

Amos's giggling got louder as the conversation continued. I guessed he didn't talk. I looked away from him to Second Esperah Dorrado. Hearing her challenge her father's assumptions about Mr. Cortes's influence returned my thoughts to Annalisa's comments. If Second Esperah Dorrado was special, would she be coming on the expedition with us? And was that the Eternal Comforter's reason for wanting her to remain single? Would that complete the circle as Annalisa suggested?

Second Esperah Dorrado rolled her eyes. "Let's eat before we get one of Dad's lectures on how this city really works."

Relieved that they weren't going to start arguing, I looked down at my plate and saw a huge piece of meat in the center, with vegetables and sliced cherries arranged above and beneath it. Admittedly, I'd hoped for some changas for dinner. I'd only seen them for breakfast, and I had to assume that was the only time the people of this city ate them. I was a little disappointed in that fact.

"We eat buffalo here in Santa Teresa," Morris said. "What kind of meat do you eat in Charlesville?"

I smiled. "Fish is what we eat in Charlesville. Fish and more fish."

Morris shook his head. "No buffalo or even chicken? The people in Charlesville don't know what they are missing. After eating buffalo, you will probably want to give up eating fish."

"Morris!"

Mr. Dorrado laughed and locked eyes on me. He was clearly waiting for me to eat, so uncomfortably, I placed a slice of the buffalo meat in my mouth. It was quite chewy. It took several chews before I could swallow it. The texture was grimy, and I knew I would not be a fan of buffalo despite Mr. Dorrado's proclamation. I smiled and nodded at him anyway.

"So are you going to be here to see Annika get married?" Carla asked.

I looked sharply up at her, but her face didn't betray what she was thinking. "I will be here. But it will be one of my last few days in Santa Teresa. So I'm not sure I will be able to attend," I said.

"That's too bad, Diondray. Just love that name. Morris and I would like you to come. Annika thinks highly of you, and she would like your presence at this biggest day in her life."

I swallowed a bite of buffalo meat and chose my words carefully. "I appreciate the invitation, Mrs. Dorrado. Do you think Second Esperah Dorrado is ready to get married?"

I cut my eyes to Second Esperah Dorrado and could see the color dissipating from her face.

"She's twenty-one, and it's our tradition in Santa Teresa that she get married," Morris interrupted.

"So she has no choice in the matter," I replied.

"Why should she have a choice? She is of age to get married, and it's our job as parents to find the right man to be her husband," Morris continued.

"I married Morris at the same age. It was the best decision of my life."

Their words made me angry, but I tried to stay calm and reasonable. "Mr. Dorrado, are you saying that Second Esperah Dorrado gets no chance to voice her opinion about the person you and Mrs. Dorrado are choosing for her in marriage? What if she doesn't love him?"

Mr. and Mrs. Dorrado's smiles evaporated. "Love!" Morris exclaimed. "Marriage is not just a decision about love. It's about selecting a life partner, and as her parents, we know her better than you or anyone else. So we can determine what type of man would be best suited for her in marriage. I guess in Charlesville people of your age are allowed to get married to whoever they want."

"Yes, we are. But we not do marry in the same fashion as you do here."

"What do you mean 'not in the same fashion'?" Carla asked.

"A man and woman can be together in a union. But they do not have to stay together for life."Amos finally stopped giggling. I knew I had said something against their beliefs.

"A union, not a marriage!" Morris erupted. "I can see why Oscar Ortega wanted to go south of the Great Forest! Your people are all committing acts of passha."

Second Esperah Dorrado laid her hand on her father's arm and tried to calm him down. "Dad, that was not a nice thing to say."

"How about forcing someone to get married when they do not get to choose the person?" I replied. I could feel the anger rising in me, but I could not be disrespectful in someone else's home. I could hear Diakono Copperwith now, telling me to honor my hosts.

Carla cut in, like her daughter trying to calm things down. "Our beliefs about marriage are different, Diondray. Annika tells me you have read the Book of Kammbi."

"I have, Mrs. Dorrado. One of the oldest copies there is, in fact. And it seems to me that it applies to all this. This tradition of marriage at twenty-one applies only to women, is that correct?"

Carla nodded reluctantly. "Men can get married at any age they want."

"Is that fair? The Book of Kammbi does not say a woman must marry by twenty-one. But I have read the Baramesa in its entirety, and Oscar Ortega, with guidance from the Eternal Comforter, believes in fairness."

Morris snorted. "You are green like my daughter. Maybe fairness works in Charlesville. But not here in Santa Teresa. And this custom has created families in our city. I know the Eternal Comforter, and Kammbi honors that. Anyway, what do you know about our Book of Kammbi?"

"Dad, that's why Diondray is here," Second Esperah Dorrado

said, looking anxiously over at me. "He has Oscar Ortega's Book of Kammbi. The one he took when he traveled south of the Great Forest. Diondray is a fourth-generation member of Oscar's family, the one by his son out of wedlock."

"Don't be lying to me, daughter."

"I'm not, Dad. Diondray, did you bring it?"

I pulled out the Book of Kammbi from my lap. Carefully, I lifted it so they could see it.

"This copy of the Book of Kammbi was hidden in Charlesville for many years until my Aunt Maxina showed it to me. I did not know it existed until a few months ago. Because of this book, I'm here north of the Great Forest."

I handed the book to Second Esperah Dorrado. Her parents stared at it. I saw the anger from the prior conversation leave their faces.

"May I?" Carla asked.

I nodded.

Second Esperah Dorrado handed the Book of Kammbi to her mother. She gently flipped the pages.

"Oh my . . . this is the one."

"Carla. Do you really believe that?"

Carla faced her husband. "Morris, this is the book."

Second Esperah Dorrado straightened her shoulders and steadied her voice. "Mom and Dad, I want to tell you that Diondray is here because he's the one to fulfill Oscar's prophecy. I believe it. As a result, I will not get married to Turner Perez."

Chapter 5

Ten days passed after the dinner at Second Esperah Dorrado's home. The diakonos assigned another second esperah to take care of my meals and my room. I looked throughout the kahall for Second Esperah Dorrado, but she was nowhere to be found. I'd thought I was acting with Morrim Pomodore's approval, but I could not get a meeting with him to discuss this reassignment, even with Diakono Copperwith's help. His request was denied by the other diakonos, and he was told to maintain his duties while he was still here in Santa Teresa.

I felt bad for Second Esperah Dorrado. If she had never met me, none of this would have happened to her. I was convinced that her parents did believe I had Oscar Ortega's copy of the Book of Kammbi, but it hadn't changed their minds about their daughter's marriage.

I got dressed and headed out of the room to meet Maisa. She was taking me to Cortes Holdings today. Mr. Cortes had requested my presence again. My time to make a decision about him was getting shorter. Besides, the businessman had offered his help with Second Esperah Dorrado, and now that she had become unavailable to me, I might have to take it.

Mr. Cortes sent an autobus for both of us, and we arrived at Cortes Holdings a few minutes later.

"Welcome back, Diondray," Felicia said as we reached the main entrance. She was wearing a green maxi dress that looked a size too large for her. Was she trying to cover up body parts that she found unappealing? Or was that one of Mr. Cortes's latest fashions? I hoped not, because that dress did not accentuate her figure.

"Hello, Felicia," Maisa said.

Felicia sneered at Maisa, who was wearing a fitted pink mid-thigh dress that looked wonderful. I sensed that Felicia wanted to change her dress just to get back at Maisa for wearing such a beautiful piece of clothing. "Welcome, Maisa," she replied with an edge in her voice.

We followed Felicia through the main lobby and past the elevators. The employees looked up from their work as we passed by, appraising my blue shorts and Maisa's dress.

"Are you enjoying our city, Diondray?" Felicia asked.

"I have not seen much of your city," I replied. "But it has reminded me a great deal of Santa Sophia."

Felicia gave me a sharp look. "We have nothing against our neighboring city to the north of us. But our city has its own identity."

"I did not mean to offend you with my comment. The scenery, with the Ortega Hills in the distance, and the buildings I have seen driving through the city looked similar to what I have seen in Santa Sophia. It's all different from where I come from."

Her face softened at me. "No offense taken, Diondray. The people of our city have heard that comparison most of our lives, and we can be somewhat sensitive about it."

"I have heard that comparison from our end in Santa Sophia too," Maisa added.

Felicia clenched her jaw as if she did not want acknowledge the truth in Maisa's comment. Why did she have such animosity towards Maisa?

We reached the far end of the main lobby, and Felicia opened the silver-plated double doors that allowed us to enter into a sizeable office. I noticed Mr. Cortes towering over his employees in the middle of the room. I was astonished by his size. However, he had an air of elegance about him that offset his massive appearance. Still, I could not shake my uneasiness whenever I was in his presence.

The employees' colorful clothing diverted my attention away from Mr. Cortes. The male employees wore either purple or orange one-piece jumpsuits. The female employees wore midi and maxi dresses that were just as colorful as the jumpsuits. Their shoes had four- or five-inch heels that made them seem almost as tall as me.

"Just in time," he said as he held up a pair of orange shorts. "Diondray, I want you to try these on. There is a changing room behind me. I hope they fit you well, because thanks to you, we may have the latest fashion trend here in Santa Teresa. I have to thank Kammbi for this wonderful and surprising gift for the business."

I grabbed the shorts and was escorted to the changing room by a female employee. I wasn't sure why I was going along with this request—there was something not right about this man. I could not put my finger on it. But I couldn't really refuse to try them on now.

I made it to the changing room and got dressed. The shorts were comfortable. I had plenty of room in them, and the fabric lay softly against my skin. I had to admit Cortes knew how to make clothing: they felt better than the ones I'd come in.

I exited the changing room and returned to the center of the office with that same employee. "They look good on you," Maisa said with a smile.

"I've already gotten approval from a woman. We have a new sensation," Mr. Cortes announced to everyone in the office. I saw all the employees smile. Their boss was pleased with his latest piece of clothing. So they were pleased too. He walked toward me, perhaps to shake my hand, and a shaking sensation started to come over me.

"Do you need some water?" Felicia asked.

"I have to leave."

"You can't leave," Cortes said with a frown. "You still have on my shorts. And I wanted to take you around the city to meet my suppliers. Diondray Azur will become one of my models as well as the one who will fulfill Oscar's prophecy. We are getting a two-for-one special with your arrival."

All I saw was the ceiling and heard a loud noise as I fell to the floor with a crash.

#

"Diondray!"

I heard my name being called, and my vision came back to me. My head was spinning, and I was not ready to stand up.

"Diondray!"

Maisa's pale face came into focus above me.

"Are you all right?" she asked. "You scared me. Felicia was going to get you some water, and you just hit the floor back first."

"I'm sorry, Diondray," Mr. Cortes said. He stood to my right. "I've never had a model faint. I would still like you to model these shorts for me. But I can postpone the meeting with the suppliers for today."

"That's obvious!" Maisa said.

I felt Maisa's soft hands on my shoulders as I rose up from the floor. "Easy, Diondray. Don't pop up quickly."

I followed her instructions and sat up slowly. My equilibrium was coming back, and the spinning sensation began to dissipate.

"Felicia, please cancel my appointments for today."

"Yes, Mr. Cortes."

I watched Felicia leave the room. Would my passing out cause a major inconvenience in the businessman's schedule? Why had he even been making plans for me without my permission?

"Drink this," Maisa said, handing me a glass of water.

I took a couple of sips and immediately felt my energy coming back. However, I still felt a shaking sensation while Mr. Cortes was squatting next to me.

"I heard that Second Esperah Dorrado was reassigned from your room," Mr. Cortes said.

I looked over at him. "How did you know that?"

"Diondray, there is nothing at the kahall of Santa Teresa that does get by me."

He smiled after that comment, and I believed him. "It's been ten days since I saw her," I said. "I don't know what happened to her."

"Well, I'm glad she's not taking care of you anymore," Maisa said.

Mr. Cortes laughed. "Do I hear a little jealousy in your voice, Ms. Merez?"

"She does not know him like I do."

"Wow, Diondray, you have two women who care about you. That's impressive. In any case, her parents demanded that she be removed from taking care of you. They felt your influence has caused her not to want to get married to Mr. Perez."

"Dinner did not go as well as I thought," I replied.

"That's okay, Diondray. I'm working on another way to keep her from getting married. I said I would help you, and with my money and influence in this city, there are always options."

The businessman and Maisa helped me up from the floor. I knew I had made Second Esperah Dorrado's parents angry, especially Mr. Dorrado. He was not going to let a stranger from south of the Great Forest keep his daughter from getting married. And that was going to be a hurdle to overcome. I didn't know what other plan Mr. Cortes had to keep the marriage from happening. But I sensed that Annalisa's comment about the circle needing to be complete would be involved with this issue. What was the connection between Second Esperah Dorrado and Teresa? And why did the Copperwiths believe she was special like me?

#

I returned to my room later that afternoon. My equilibrium was not all the way back, and I still felt lightheaded from passing out earlier in the day. I sat at my desk and stared at the word *decision* on the paper. I was going to start writing my latest themily using that word. But it didn't feel right, and I erased it off the paper.

I stared at the paper for a few more minutes, and words just came to me.

Does it matter if you are married or unmarried? Does a god treat married people better than unmarried people? If that's true, then he is only a god for one group of people and not for everyone. Should people follow and believe in a god like that?

I read the entire Baramesa of the Book of Kammbi, and through Oscar and Teresa and Issabella and Alicia's accounts, they never mention that Kammbi is a god for only one group of people. He was God for everyone. Didn't he allow Oscar to travel south of the Great Forest for that reason? Now, over two hundred seventy years later, I'm here north of the Great Forest—and for that same reason again. Kammbi still desires that all people worship him.

So why is there a custom that forces women to get married at twenty-one and not men? That seems to set apart one group of people amongst everyone else. That's not proper teaching from the sacred book you hold in such regard. It contradicts the God you believe in and follow.

I heard a knock on the door as I wrote that last sentence. I got up from the desk to answer it.

"Morrim Pomodore would like to see you." A second esperah said after I opened the door.

"When?"

"Now."

I followed the messenger to Morrim Pomodore's office. This second esperah was about my height and had blond hair. He wore a second esperah shawl that fitted snugly around well-muscled shoulders, like he was someone who exercised when he was off duty. He told me his last name was Rayfield and that he would be attending to the room for my remaining time at the kahall.

We reached Morrim Pomodore's office. I entered the office after Second Esperah Rayfield and saw the morrim, Diakono Copperwith, Annalisa Copperwith, and two other diakonos sitting at a table. They all had concerned looks on their faces except Morrim Pomodore.

"Welcome," Morrim Pomodore said. "I know this was short notice. But there is something that we must discuss."

Second Esperah Rayfield stood behind me against the wall as I sat down next to Diakono Copperwith at the table. I tried to read the diakono's face, but his stare was expressionless.

"Morris and Carla Dorrado have decided to renounce the kahall of Santa Teresa due to your influence, Diondray Azur," Morrim Pomodore continued. "They are going to seek to become parishioners elsewhere."

One of the two diakonos explained, "After the dinner at their house, they were alarmed that Second Esperah Dorrado had declared she would not get married to Turner Perez. Morris and Carla believed your presence has caused this change of heart. They wanted to cut off your influence before she commits an act of passha." The man's large nostrils flared out as he talked. Diakono Copperwith had a similar expression on his face. He clearly wasn't happy.

"Morrim Pomodore, I thought you were going to help me with

Second Esperah Dorrado's marriage. You could not convince her parents of her decision?" I replied.

"This custom has been around since Teresa's death," the second diakono said. "The women of this city are expected to get married when they turn twenty-one." Thick eyebrows were the dominant feature on the man's face. They were frowning at me.

"So, let me get this straight," I said. "In Teresa's section of the Book of Kammbi, she made a decision not to get married because she wanted to believe and follow Kammbi with no distractions. She wrote that it was her decision alone and that no other woman had to make the same decision. Then this custom was created after her death. It's not even written down in the book you all believe and follow literally."

"Diondray, we cannot go around changing a custom just because we disagree with it," Diakono Copperwith said.

"I was led to believe the people north of the Great Forest created their customs and traditions based on the Book of Kammbi, Diakono Copperwith. I could recognize that in Santa Sophia. The Festival of First Cherries and the Festival of Sinquinta linked directly to the Book of Kammbi. Is it different here in Santa Teresa?"

I cut my eyes to Morrim Pomodore after my comment. He had a slight smile on his face.

"Each city north of the Great Forest has its own customs," the diakono with the large nostrils replied.

"So they are not always based off the book you believe in and follow. And this custom was created out of thin air. What for? To make sure all women are married? And they are not allowed to choose their own husbands? That's not fair at all!"

I got up from the table and started to pace.

"Sit down, young man. We do not disrespect the morrim like that," the diakono with thick eyebrows said sharply.

But I couldn't calm myself, not even in the presence of my mentor. "I'm not sitting down until I get an understanding of why this custom exists. Because I've heard nothing in this discussion that makes any sense!"

"You will not come into our kahall and be disrespectful. Now sit down, or you will be asked to leave," the diakono with the thick eyebrows said and rose from his chair.

"Calm down, Diakono Paez. He is not going anywhere," Morrim Pomodore said. "Diondray, please return to your seat."

I caught the diakonos staring hard at the morrim as I sat down. And he returned the gesture. They lowered their eyes.

"Diondray, you have made a credible point that shows the inconsistency in our beliefs and customs. This is a lesson you will have to learn as you continue on your expedition here north of the Great Forest," Morrim Pomodore said.

"The morrim is correct," Diakono Copperwith added. "I did not get to discuss these inconsistencies with you when we were in Santa Sophia. I have learned in our short time together, Diondray, that you have a strong sense of fairness. That was evident from our first conversation. And I can understand why this custom would bother that sense of fairness."

Diakono Copperwith smiled after that comment. I could sense that both he and Morrim Pomodore wanted to have this discussion to see how I truly felt. I began to think this meeting was a teaching lesson for me.

"Morrim Pomodore, are you going to assist this stranger in changing our long-standing custom?" the diakono with the large nostrils said.

"Diakono Rivers, this man is not a stranger. If he is the one who will fulfill Oscar's prophecy, then he will find a way to keep Second Esperah Dorrado from getting married. And if that's the case, then we all know the Eternal Comforter has allowed it, and Kammbi will honor the change."

"What you are talking about, Morrim Pomodore?" Diakono Rivers shot back. "No one who is from south of the Great Forest could ever be the one to fulfill Oscar's prophecy!"

"I see that one of your diakonos has not completely read the book he is to believe in and follow," I replied.

Morrim Pomodore fixed his gaze on me and nodded. "Diakono Copperwith was correct about you. You are a perceptive young man."

"My husband and I felt the same way after we first met him, Morrim Pomodore," Annalisa added.

I had totally forgotten she was sitting at the table. Her comment pleased me, and I knew the morrim would hold it in high regard.

"The Copperwiths prayed before my dinner with Second Esperah Dorrado and her parents that she is special and the circle needed to be completed." I said.

Morrim Pomodore nodded like he knew where this entire conversation would end up. I glanced to see Diakonos Paez and Rivers with astonished looks on their faces. However, the Copperwiths had blank expressions.

"Second Esperah Dorrado is at Kahall Angelica in the Ortega district. You can see her there. I know she will be waiting for you," Morrim Pomodore said. "And you will find out why she is special."

"Thank you, Morrim Pomodore," I said, and I smiled at him. With the morrim's full approval, I was going to visit her.

Chapter 6

"When you arrived for the first time, I knew I was finally going to become my own woman. I hoped there would be other women who are allowed to make the same choice. I believe it will take someone like you in the future, telling another woman that she has the right to make her own choice about marriage. This woman will show that she can still be a believer and follower in Kammbi while remaining unwed. My choice will have to be taught for generation after generation until someone like you and that woman make it a reality once and for all."

Those words from Teresa stayed with me as I left for the final time. She had finally rejected Leopolde's proposal. This caused disappointment and outrage amongst her tribe. Some of the tribal members wanted me killed because of Kammbi's teachings. Teresa knew that what I taught was correct, and because of her influence, no one would attempt any act of violence against me. Also, I had Reuel the leopard as a companion, and that cat would protect me with its life.

I prayed to Kammbi for several days after my time with Teresa and her tribe. And the Eternal Comforter revealed through Teresa how the future was going to change.

Oscar's writing in chapter 6 of Teresa's section in the Book of Kammbi tossed and turned in my mind most of the next morning. I did not get much sleep, between thinking of the words I'd read and the events of the last few days. I had realized that Kammbi's teachings not only validated the belief that an unwedded woman could still be a believer and follower of Kammbi, but also that Oscar believed Teresa's words were the genesis of his prophecy.

Oscar wrote these words that he heard from the Eternal Comforter: Because of your obedience in leaving your homeland to come to a new land, I will continue to make your name great. Even though you have lost a child due to your act of passha, there will be a descendant who will unite the entire land. And the people will believe that Kammbi is the Lord of all. Those who have always believed in me and those who didn't believe in me will create a new people, establishing peace and sanctification throughout this land.

I flipped to the last page in the Baramesa, where Oscar's prophecy was written. Did it allow for more than one descendant? Was this why the Copperwiths, Morrim Pomodore, and even Mr. Cortes believed that Second Esperah was special?

#

"Was Teresa the reason for Oscar's prophecy?" I asked Diakono Copperwith as we walked on the grounds in the front of the kahall. It had been a while since we were by ourselves, and I had wanted to leave my room for a change of scenery.

The perfectly manicured grounds gave off a serene atmosphere that reminded me of all the time I had spent on the beach looking out at the Bay of Charlesville. I had to make sure that I got out of my room more often before our time in Santa Teresa came to an end.

"Her decision became the genesis of the prophecy," he answered. "Its importance can not be overstated. It revealed for the first time that Kammbi wants all people regardless of status: wed or unwed, man or woman, light or dark skin, to become a believer and follower of his."

I nodded. "I have clearly read that throughout the Book of Kammbi. It's fair and makes sense. So why did the people of this city create a custom that contradicts what you just said? Santa Sophia does not have any kind of custom or tradition like this."

Diakono Copperwith stopped walking abruptly and faced me. His blond hair glistened as he stood in front of me, and his diakono's shawl blew from west to east in the light breeze. I shivered; the breeze made it cooler than I'd expected for a morning in the sixth month of Une.

He frowned. "Unfortunately, there is still a belief amongst the men of this city as well as the other cities we will visit that a woman's only place is being a wife to a man and mother to their children. Even my Annalisa has not escaped the scorn of others around us because we decided not to have children."

"That's so unfair."

Diakono Copperwith's frown turned into a slight smile. "We both decided that children would not be the path for us. And by the guidance of the Eternal Comforter, it was the right choice. However, I know that her family has lamented our decision. Since women are the ones who bring life into our land, Teresa's decision angered her tribe, and they wanted to make sure after her death that the women of this city would get married with the ultimate goal of bearing children."

Diakono Copperwith grimaced after that comment. I sensed that he was admitting to something in his own beliefs, not just among the people of Santa Teresa.

"After Oscar's death, the morrims of this city at that time sent a petition to the konseho of Kammbi allowing for the custom of all women being married at twenty-one to be protected and upheld, with very few exceptions."

"Exceptions?" I asked.

He shrugged. "They are released from the custom if they are unable to bear children or have other health problems, if they are commit fornication before their twenty-first birthday, or if Oscar's prophecy becomes fulfilled."

I was stunned to hear Diakono Copperwith's description of the prescribed role of women in Santa Teresa. It seemed so unfair to me. Mother, Aunt Maxina, and other women I knew back home were encouraged to get married and have children, but there was no custom or law demanding that they do. As a matter of fact, I knew that both men and women were allowed to have more than one coupling as long as it was consensual.

"The konseho of Kammbi allowed their petition even though it contradicts the teachings from Kammbi. Why would they allow this to happen?" I asked.

"As you know from our earlier discussion, the konseho of Kammbi is the governing council for all the cities north of the Great Forest, and it meets in the city of Issabella. The konseho granted the tribe's petition because it fit in line with their own beliefs about what a woman's role in society should be."

"So if we help Second Esperah Dorrado escape this marriage, will her freedom to choose have to be recognized by the konseho of Kammbi?"

Diakono Copperwith and I reached a bench on the grounds. We both sat down. "Correct, Diondray. Also, there is a small group of unmarried women in this city who have lived outside of this custom secretly. They have refused to abide by it because of the correct interpretation of the Book of Kammbi. These women are called *resas*, a variation on Teresa's name. They have prayed that another woman would come along at the time when Oscar's prophecy is fulfilled. If such a woman does arise to challenge the custom, then they can convince the konseho of Kammbi to change the custom once and for all."

I stared at the ground during Diakono Copperwith's explanation. How would these women, the resas, convince the konseho of Kammbi to change this custom? Would they believe that I was the one who will fulfill Oscar's prophecy? And what would convince them that Second Esperah Dorrado was the woman Teresa had revealed to Oscar in her section of the Book of Kammbi—the woman the resas had been praying for?

#

It was the twenty-third day in the sixth month of Une, and we had already spent thirty days in Santa Teresa. Only twenty days remained before our time came to a close in this city. And it felt like I had not gotten any closer to helping Second Esperah Dorrado.

A few days before, Morrim Pomodore had told us that Second Esperah Dorrado awaited our arrival at Kahall Angelica. But the morrim of the kahall, Morrim Forde, denied our visit, and I learned from Diakono Copperwith that Morrim Forde got approval to do so from the konseho of Kammbi. Morrim Forde felt my presence would cause another disruption, and Second Esperah Dorrado's parents insisted that I stay away from their daughter. I had spent my time since that conversation learning about the resas. I attended learning sessions with both Morrim Pomodore and Diakono Copperwith. I had to learn everything I could about this entity in the time we had remaining in Santa Teresa.

The resas had been formed in the Year 36 A.O.A., a year before Teresa's death. Teresa's relationship with her tribe had become difficult, and the leadership had made sure that most of the tribe's women would not follow Teresa's choice. However, there was a small group of women who could not marry because of their inability to have children, because of fornication, or because they were deemed undesirable by the men of the tribe.

Teresa took this group of eleven women under her leadership and prepared them to become faithful believers and followers of Kammbi. They learned from Kammbi's teachings and assisted with the daily activities of the tribe. A short time before Teresa's death, she chose one of the women, Angelica Di Maria, to become madre of the group. Teresa believed the women needed a motherly presence, and Angelica fit that description. Teresa knew her death was imminent, and the women would need a leader to keep them together.

Angelica Di Maria came from the Mayza tribe of the northwestern hills. The Mayza tribe was the first tribe Oscar Ortega came to when he arrived in the land. Angelica knew that tribe had banished a pregnant Adrianna because of her illicit relationship with Oscar. Angelica had her own illicit relationships with several leaders of the Mayza tribe and decided to leave the tribe before they banished her as well. When she arrived amongst Teresa's tribe, Angelica revealed that part of her life to Teresa. Teresa had learned through Kammbi's teachings that forgiveness could be obtained upon confession for any act of passha. Angelica received the first recorded act of aphemmia, forgiveness, in the Baramesa of the Book of Kammbi.

After Teresa's death, the resas were ostracized from the tribe and began to work in the shadows with the married women who were having difficulties with their husbands. Angelica and the other resas made sure to pray for those women and give them the teachings they had learned from Teresa in secret.

The resas became an inspiration to the women of the tribe, and the leadership accepted their influence as long as they did not actively recruit women away from marriage and motherhood. Angelica accepted this compromise because it kept the resas around the tribe, even if they could only be active in a shadow status, and she was able to get the group officially sanctioned by the konseho of Kammbi. However, she believed what Oscar wrote in the Baramesa about Teresa's last words to him: that his prophecy would come to fruition and a new madre would bring the resas fulfillment and freedom.

After learning the history of the resas, I realized how unfairly these women had been treated over the years. The resas had been devoted believers and followers of Kammbi, and their unwed, barren status should not have placed them in the shadows of Santa Teresa's culture. Even if I was able to keep Second Esperah Dorrado from getting married, her freedom would likely not be sanctioned by the konseho of Kammbi, and this city's leadership would double down on the custom. Yet, I felt a growing passion to see justice done. And I wasn't alone. Diakono Copperwith and the other diakonos at the kahall would not have prayed for Second Esperah Dorrado before our dinner if they did not believe Kammbi was at work in this situation. Annalisa would not have told me that she was special. They were putting themselves out there for Second Esperah Dorrado, and I guessed it was due to my presence in this region and their belief in the pages of the Book of Kammbi.

I was still not sure about my role in fulfilling Oscar's prophecy, but I was compelled to help Second Esperah Dorrado and go to the konseho of Kammbi to get this custom revoked. I had never felt in my life like there was something to pursue that was bigger than me. However, since arriving in this region, I was starting to see that life was much bigger than myself, and I had to connect to that higher purpose whether I believed in it or not.

#

After two days of digesting as much information as I could about the resas, I wanted to gather the group together for dinner. I thought it was time that I shared about the decision I would have to make before we left Santa Teresa. We had dinner in the kahall's cafeteria. The staff had laid out a smorgasbord of changas, sliced meats, fruits, and vegetables. It was the most elaborate dinner we'd had so far during our stay.

I got up from the table and started to pace. "Diakono Copperwith and Annalisa, there is something else I need to discuss with you."

"You have our attention," Diakono Copperwith replied.

I glanced over at Maisa before I continued. She gave me a reassuring smile, and that stopped me from pacing. "Mr. Cortes has offered his help in getting Second Esperah Dorrado out of her upcoming marriage."

Annalisa frowned.

"What for?" Diakono Copperwith asked. "I doubt he's just doing it out of the goodness of his heart."

"He wants to join us on the second expedition."

"Oh my," Annalisa replied.

The color had drained from both their cheeks. I knew how they felt about Mr. Cortes's offer.

"That man does not belong on this expedition with us," Annalisa said. "I cannot believe he would make such an offer to Diondray."

"I can," Diakono Copperwith said flatly.

"My love, what you do mean by that?"

"Darling, Mr. Cortes is a businessman, and he reads the Book of Kammbi all the time. He has his own learning session with Morrim Pomodore once every seven days and believes that Diondray is the one who will fulfill Oscar's prophecy. And he's seizing on a role for himself with this expedition."

"We don't have to allow him, my love," Annalisa said dejectedly.

I watched them closely during this part of the discussion. It seemed like Annalisa was outraged by the offer, but to my surprise, Diakono Copperwith was not. Maisa was not bothered at all by Mr. Cortes's offer.

"You know why he's doing this?" Maisa added.

"Why is he?" I replied.

"Who came back from Guadharra with Oscar Ortega when he went to get Sophia?" Maisa continued.

I glanced at Diakono Copperwith, and I could tell he knew where she was going with her questions. "Diego Carranza, Santa Sophia's first businessman."

Maisa nodded.

"This man thinks he's the second coming of Diego Carranza!" Annalisa erupted. "What an ego he has!"

"Diakono Copperwith, you seemed resigned to something about this offer."

He looked over at me. "Because I know you are going to allow him to join us."

"How do you know that?" I replied. I was leaning in that direction. But I had not made up my mind yet.

"The Eternal Comforter."

"That's wrong, my love," Annalisa protested. "I do not believe the Eternal Comforter would allow such a thing to happen."

"Darling, has the Eternal Comforter ever lied to us?"

Annalisa did not reply.

"I have been waiting for Diondray to talk about this offer before we left. I knew Mr. Cortes was going to use Second Esperah Dorrado's marriage as a way to join us."

"Because the Eternal Comforter told you," I said.

"Correct, Diondray."

"So I'm supposed to take his offer, even though I have not made a decision?"

"Have you thought of refusing his offer?"

"No, I have not."

"More confirmation from the Eternal Comforter. If you had immediately refused his offer, then I would have to question my own belief in Kammbi."

"This was a predetermined decision when we arrived in Santa Teresa."

"You are perceptive, Diondray."

#

It felt like my decision to accept Mr. Cortes's offer had been predetermined as soon as I arrived in Santa Teresa. Diakono Copperwith's comments had dominated my thoughts for the past six days.

I tried to write a themily in order to express how I truly felt, but I could not write anything on paper. It was the first time since I'd started writing themilys that nothing came out of me. It was the first day in the seventh month of Yul, and six days before Second Esperah Dorrado's marriage. I had not written anything about how the marriage should not be allowed or expressed my apparently predetermined decision regarding Mr. Cortes.

Even though I had been led to come north of the Great Forest by the actions of Aunt Maxina, I had not felt like my arrival had been foreordained until now. I was not happy about that revelation. I much preferred to feel as though I had some control of my own! I would have to come to grips with things being predetermined by the Eternal Comforter as I continued on this expedition.

Speaking of the Eternal Comforter, I was starting to wonder when would I receive that presence in my life. I had read in Book 1 of the Baramesa that Oscar Ortega received the gift of the Eternal Comforter soon after he arrived from Guadharra and began his teaching to the Mayza tribe. In Book 4, Teresa received her gift of the Eternal Comforter just before she rejected her marriage proposal from Leopolde. In Books 5 and 6, Issabella and Alicia received the Eternal Comforter right before Oscar Ortega finished his teaching with each of them on his expedition. In each case, it seemed there was a major event followed by a declaration that the individual in question become a total follower and believer in Kammbi. Well, I had not made that declaration yet. But I felt this decision to accept Mr. Cortes's offer would be a major event. I could use the guidance of the Eternal Comforter right now.

"Are you ready?" Second Esperah Rayfield said after entering the room.

I nodded and followed him out of the room. I could not write a themily or get help from the Eternal Comforter. I hoped this decision was the right course, even though it would be difficult to be in Mr. Cortes's presence all the time.

Second Esperah Rayfield led to me to the autobus, where Maisa was already waiting for me. I got on and sat down next to her. She gave a wide smile, and I started to get lost in those piercing eyes.

"You are doing the right thing," she said softly and caressed my right thigh.

"I hope so, Maisa," I replied and looked straight ahead as the driver left the kahall.

#

"Diondray, have you made a decision?" Mr. Cortes asked as we entered his office. "We are getting closer to the end of your time here in the city."

"Actually, my decision was already made for me." I couldn't look at him straight on, but I said, "We would welcome your help. And your company."

"That's great to hear," he answered. "First of all, I would like you to drink some water. You are starting to look like you are going to faint again."

Felicia got up from her seat next to Mr. Cortes and gave me a glass of water. I gulped the water, trying to alleviate the uneasiness that had begun to come from my stomach again. If this was the right decision, why did it feel wrong to me?

Maisa pulled her chair closer and caressed my thigh like she had on the autobus. Her touch began to offset my uneasiness, and I did not want her to stop. I was glad that Annalisa was not here to see us in this position.

"I had a belief that you would accept my decision," Mr. Cortes started as he rose from his seat.

"The Eternal Comforter told you."

He glared at me momentarily. "Morrim Pomodore and Diakono Copperwith were right about you. Highly perceptive. Well, I have used my influence to help Second Esperah Dorrado."

Maisa continued to caress my thigh, and my confidence in being in this man's presence was gaining as he talked. I knew that from this moment on, I would need Maisa whenever I was around him.

"How have you helped?" Maisa asked. "The marriage is in six days, and the Copperwiths as well as Morrim Pomodore have tried to reach out to the resas unsuccessfully."

"Also, I'm not allowed to go to Kahall Angelica," I added. "Second Esperah Dorrado's parents demanded that as a condition from Morrim Pomodore in order for her to leave the kahall of Santa Teresa."

Mr. Cortes strutted toward our side of the office, and I could tell from his gait that he was a man used to getting his way. That kind of confidence was unsettling. "Don't worry, Diondray Azur," the businessman said as he whirled back to his chair. "I have heard that you write words of wisdom. Words that you have spoken in front of people in your home city of Charlesville."

I guessed that he had found out from Maisa, Diakono Copperwith, or even Morrim Pomodore about my background. Nothing got by him.

"Themilys," I replied.

"I like that name. Unusual. Anyway, you will need to write your best themily in six days. We will need those words of wisdom along with my help for Second Esperah Dorrado."

"What about the konseho of Kammbi?" Maisa interjected. "Even if we stop her marriage, her freedom to choose will still not be recognized by them."

Mr. Cortes sat back down in his chair and gave us an impish grin. "Maisa Merez, I know you have read your Book of Kammbi. And I know that Diondray has as well. More than the people of this city who claim to be believers and followers of Kammbi. If Diondray is the one to fulfill Oscar's prophecy and if Second Esperah Dorrado is the one Teresa spoke about to Oscar in her section of our sacred book, then the konseho of Kammbi will have to recognize what we are going to do for Second Esperah Dorrado."

"If they don't?" I said.

"That's why I'm coming on this expedition with you, Diondray Azur."

Those words rang true. I just hoped I could make it to the city of Issabella with Cortes in our presence.

Chapter 7

Inspiration returned as I spent the next four days writing themilys. It felt good to have the pencil in my left hand and watch words appear on the paper. I was glad that whatever kind of block I'd been suffering from writing had vanished as quickly as it had come. I hoped that I did not have any more of that again. Writing had become a release where I could express everything that had happened since I left my family home. I needed an area of my life where I could be unfiltered and not feel like I had to hold something back.

Love and *choice* were the first two words I wrote down on the paper. I had begun to realize that my entire time here so far was about those two words. *Love.* Second Esperah Dorrado's lack of love for Turner Perez. Teresa's lack of love for Leopolde. What about my love for Maisa? I did not know if I lacked it. But I felt that love had to be choice, and it could not be forced onto someone by a custom or tradition or even a belief system. Did Kammbi want us to love him by choosing him?

Choice. It seemed that Oscar Ortega's choice to leave Guadharra and come to the Ortega Hills had been predestined by Kammbi. However, Oscar still had the choice to share his teachings on his expedition many years ago, and he had the choice to become a believer and follower of Kammbi in the first place. Teresa had the choice to embrace Kammbi's teachings from Oscar. Because of that choice, she wanted to believe and follow Kammbi as an unwed woman. Now, Second Esperah Dorrado wanted the same choice. Because of that choice, could she become Teresa's descendant?

And what about me? It did not seem like I'd had a choice in leaving Charlesville or allowing Mr. Cortes to join us on this expedition. Every choice I had made so far was predetermined, as far as I could tell. However, I had not fully embraced becoming a believer and follower of Kammbi. I still had many questions about this unusual religion. And I had sensed so far that Kammbi wanted me to make this choice for myself. I could not explain why I felt that way. I just did.

I wrote all of that on paper as the beginning draft of the themily. It was time to reshape it into the themily that would keep Second Esperah Dorrado from getting married—the themily that would ultimately be read before the konseho of Kammbi.

#

Kahall Angelica was located in the Ortega district of the city. Diakono Copperwith explained to me on the drive over that this district was the poorest in the city, and Kahall Angelica had become the one place the people who lived here could rely on for assistance.

I found it interesting that the kahall was named after the first madre of the resas. Diakono Copperwith commented that the people of this district at the time the kahall was built had wanted it named after her, even demanding it when the city's leadership and the konseho of Kammbi did not like the idea. The resas' influence throughout the district and Madre Angelica's position after Teresa were so strong that the common people won the argument. The leadership and the konseho of Kammbi conceded the naming of the kahall to the people.

The building was half the size of the kahall of Santa Teresa, and its distinctive bright orange color caught my eye. I carried my bag with the Book of Kammbi and the themilys I'd worked on for the past few days. I had written and rewritten them until late last night, and I'd even contemplated prayer after I finally finished. I hoped these words would have the impact I wanted on today's event.

Mr. Cortes handed me a second esperah shawl on the autobus as we arrived at the kahall. It was all a part of his plan to get me access to Second Esperah Dorrado at the proper time during the wedding. I placed the shawl over my clothes before we exited the autobus. The fabric rubbed against my skin, causing my forearms and lower legs to itch. I wanted to take it off as soon as it touched my body. But I could not do that if we were going to pull off what we needed to today.

A tall broad-shouldered second esperah greeted us as we walked through the parking lot. "Welcome to Kahall Angelica, where everyone is welcomed to hear the teaching of Morrim Forde. His teaching is touched by the Eternal Comforter and inspired by Kammbi," he announced proudly while walking beside Mr. Cortes.

"Second Esperah," Mr Cortes said, "I have another one of your kind to help with today's special occasion."

Mr. Cortes and I stopped walking while the rest of the group and Felicia continued toward the entrance. The businessman had made arrangements with the morrim of the kahall to have the group minus myself attend the wedding. It was a good thing that Second Esperah Dorrado's parents had only met me and didn't know what my companions looked like.

"I did not know that extra assistance would be needed for today," the broad-shouldered second esperah said cautiously.

Cortes was undaunted. "I spoke to Morrim Forde about this several days ago, and he assured me that he could use all the second esperahs from other kahalls that he could get. Do I have to bring him out here in order to clear up this matter?"

"No, Mr. Cortes. I'm sure that you got approval from the morrim," he replied and bowed to the businessman. "I can take him through an alternate entrance where his assistance will be needed."

"Thank you, Second Esperah. You will be rewarded by Kammbi because of your duty," Mr. Cortes said warmly.

I followed the second esperah toward the alternate entrance, leaving Mr. Cortes in the parking lot. The itching got worse, but I had to endure it for a little while longer. I realized that I could not have been a second esperah if I had to wear this shawl at every kahall service.

"We've never had a second esperah dark-skinned like you at our kahall. I've heard that someone with your skin color had arrived in our city claiming to be the one who will fulfill Oscar's prophecy. What kahall are you from?" the second esperah asked as we reached the alternate entrance.

"Kahall Cinda," I replied. "I've heard about this person you mentioned as well. He's at the kahall of Santa Teresa with Morrim Pomodore. If this person was the one who will fulfill Oscar's prophecy, how would you feel about it?"

I did not like lying so easily. Mr. Cortes and Felicia had created a script for me for this occasion. Kahall Cinda was another kahall in this district where Mr. Cortes's influence had reached. I would have to be mindful of how easily he bent rules as he continued with us on the expedition.

"It's heresy," he shot back. "Oscar's words clearly state that no one knows what this descendant looks like. So I don't believe it could be someone as dark as you."

I found his comments problematic and wondered if this was a belief many people like him and throughout this city shared. Would the people of the city and entire region north of the Great Forest accept the fulfillment of Oscar's prophecy from someone who did not look like them?

We entered the kahall and headed up the stairs. The walls were white, and the age of the building showed through the cracks. I followed the Second Esperah to an area where there was seating.

"You will help the parishioners be seated and patrol this area," he instructed me. "After the wedding, you can join us for our second esperah meal provided by the kahall. Kammbi is grateful for your duty."

The second esperah bowed, and I returned the gesture. It felt unusual to bow to another human being. He left the area. I looked out at the kahall and realized I could see down to the main sanctuary beneath me. I hoped that Mr. Cortes's plan would work, because these parishioners would not be expecting what was going to happen shortly!

I looked down to the lower level of the congregation hall to see the rest of the group being seated. Maisa came first, followed by the Copperwiths, Felicia, and Mr. Cortes. They were seated on the right side of the congregation hall only a couple rows away from the podium. All eyes were on them. The parishioners knew the group was visitors, and their curiosity was piqued.

I glanced over to the podium at the white flower arrangement on both sides of where the morrim and the couple would stand for the marriage procession. A thick strip of white lace came from the podium through the middle of the congregation hall toward the main entrance of the kahall. I assumed that was where Second Esperah Dorrado and Turner Perez would walk as they made their entrance.

I found it all very interesting. We did not have elaborate marriage ceremonies like this in Charlesville. Marriages were not formal back home. If a man and woman decided to formalize their union, they declared it to each other and told their relatives. Nothing else was done. Seeing this kind of ceremony made me wonder if we had been doing wrong in Charlesville all of this time.

"Can we be seated up here?" a frail-looking woman wearing an oversized white maxi dress said as she approached.

I did the customary second esperah bow and led the woman to a seat. Another couple came in right after the frail-looking woman and sat down next to her. I was not going to be able to look down to the lower level for a few moments as more people came through the entrance to this upper level of the kahall. I searched the area for another second esperah—anyone who could interfere with the plan—and did not see anybody else. How did Mr. Cortes manage to get only one second esperah sent up for the whole upper level of the kahall? I had to admit, it was impressive. Even though I still had my misgivings about his presence on the expedition, I felt that his kind of influence would be needed when we traveled to the cities of Alicia and Issabella where the konseho of Kammbi resided.

"His skin is quite dark," I overheard the frail-looking woman say to the couple seated next to her. "I did not know our city had that kind of people here."

I stared at the woman as I passed by her seat. I wanted to respond to her comments. Plus, my forearms and legs were still itching from the shawl's fabric. However, I had to follow Mr. Cortes's plan, and it did not need me to bring any undue attention to myself. Not only that, but they reminded me that it was going to be an uphill climb to convince people like that woman and others that I was the one to fulfill Oscar's prophecy.

Soft music began to play. I heard it through the speakers as I returned to my area, where I stood able to look down to the lower level. This upper level had filled quickly with parishioners, and I noticed the looks I got as they were surprised to see someone like me serving as a second esperah.

"Welcome to this special service at Kahall Angelica." I heard that announcement through the speakers as a short, wrinkle-faced man wearing a morrim's shawl came up to the podium. It had to be the morrim of the kahall, Morrim Forde.

"One of the things I enjoy as a morrim is the celebration of a man and woman coming together in holy matrimony," the morrim continued. "Marriage is a special event in one's life and has been honored and blessed by Kammbi. So as believers and followers of Kammbi, we must treat it as something special as well."

I placed my hands inside the shawl to rub my arms while the morrim spoke. I was ready to get this shawl off me. I had to wait a little while longer.

"Today, we are celebrating the union of Annika Dorrado and Turner Perez. As you know, Annika Dorrado serves as a second esperah here at the kahall. Turner Perez is a member of the influential Perez family, whose contributions to this kahall have been warmly received."

The music got louder. It was a long, drawn-out piano song that I assumed was used for this type of ceremony. I watched the parishioners on the lower level turn their heads toward the white lace in the middle of the congregation hall. Moments later, I saw the back of a tall man wearing a dark suit as he headed to the podium. His gait was stiff and purposeful. He stood on the right side of Morrim Forde at the podium. This must be Turner Perez, I thought. His close-cropped haircut and stern facial expression belied what a joyous occasion this marriage ceremony was supposed to be.

Shortly after his entrance, the parishioners rose from their seats as the music finally got softer. Second Esperah Dorrado came down the center of the congregation hall slowly. She was wearing a beautiful white dress that flared at the hips. She walked alongside a man I assumed to be her father. However, there was some distance between the two, and their gait seemed awkward somehow. I did not know if he was supposed to assist her down the aisle or if this was some kind of coercion.

Second Esperah Dorrado made it to the podium and stood on the left side of the morrim. Her father lifted the veil over her face, and I saw her heavy eyes and swollen cheeks. She did not want to be here. I glanced at Turner Perez's blank expression and sensed that he might have been forced to go through the marriage ceremony as much as Second Esperah Dorrado. How many other marriages did this custom force upon people who did not want to go through with it?

"The bride and groom have made their way to the podium," the morrim continued. He was looking directly at the parishioners. I'm pretty sure he did not want to see the pain in either the bride or groom while performing the ceremony. "I have one question before we make this marriage between Turner Perez and Annika Dorrado official. Does anyone object to the marriage of these two wonderful people?"

I noticed Second Esperah Dorrado turn her head and look up to my level. Tears flowed over her cheeks. I didn't want to see her like this.

This was my moment.

"I object to this marriage," I announced. "Second Esperah Dorrado is being forced to marry someone she does not love due to a custom that is not written in the Book of Kammbi."

The congregation hall gasped. The morrim grimaced at their reaction.

"Who are you to object, Second Esperah?" A man in the front row on the left side of the congregation hall rose from his seat. "Morrim Forde, this heretic is no second esperah. He's the one who has been filling my daughter's head with nonsense about not getting married. He should not be here," Morris Dorrado proclaimed.

I took off my shawl and grabbed my bag off the floor. "Mr. Dorrado is correct when he said that I'm not a second esperah. My name is Diondray Azur, and I'm from Charlesville, south of the Great Forest. However, he is incorrect about me filling his daughter's head with nonsense. Your sacred book does not sanction a custom where a woman has to be married against her own wishes. The fact that it has been allowed and even mandated in this city is unfair."

The parishioners went into an uproar. I felt all their eyes as I paced.

"Silence!" the morrim shouted. I was surprised at how his voice carried throughout the congregation hall. "I do not like this kahall being disrupted in such a fashion. But this visitor has raised an objection, and it must be properly followed through."

"His objection has no grounds to be followed through," Mr. Dorrado retorted. "He does not belong here, Morrim. You know the terms of our agreement."

Mr. Cortes stood from his seat. "I have overridden those terms, Mr. Dorrado. You pulled your daughter out of the kahall of Santa Teresa for your own reasons and not because of her own choice."

"Your money cannot buy every kahall in this city," Morris Dorrado snapped back.

"Enough!" the morrim interrupted. "Diondray Azur has an objection to this marriage and has made a charge that is unfortunately true. And by the power vested in me as a morrim, I must hear the reasoning behind that objection. Please, Mr. Azur, come down to the podium."

I nodded and left the upper level.

"I don't like what you have done here, Mr. Cortes. And if this objection is just a way to throw your weight around, I will report you to the konseho of Kammbi," the morrim said sternly as I arrived at the podium.

"I assure you that what you are about to hear is not about throwing anyone's weight around," Mr. Cortes replied.

The morrim looked away from the businessman and glared at me. "Continue with your objection to this marriage." I tensed to speak, but before I could, someone else did—Turner Perez. "Morrim, I would like to address this man who has disrupted our ceremony."

The morrim turned away from me and faced Turner Perez. "Go ahead."

Turner Perez looked at me. "I don't know who you are or what words you have filled the woman I love with. But you cannot stop our wedding. You are not even from here. Annika is twenty-one and ready to be married, as has been our tradition for many years. Would you like it if I came to your city and did the same thing to the woman you loved?"

I felt the sincerity of his words. I knew he loved Second Esperah Dorrado. But she did not love him. Despite his feelings for her, this marriage could not be allowed.

I replied, "I would like to answer your words in kind. I wrote words of my own just for this occasion. These words are called a themily and are popular where I'm from. I ask you to give me an ear."

I opened my bag and pulled out the themily.

What is love? Is love one-sided or two-sided? Is love when you force a woman to choose your love against her will? Or is love when she is allowed to choose you out of her own beliefs and feelings?

What is belief? Is belief something that is passed from one generation to the next generation and followed literally? Is belief something taken from a sacred book that everyone reveres but does not actually read—at least not all of its words? Or is belief when someone can change a thing to suit his or her own needs, regardless of what has been passed down from prior generations or written in a sacred book to be believed or followed literally?

I have been trying to get answers to those questions since my arrival in this city. And the answers I keep getting are that love is one-sided and belief can be changed at random regardless of past generations or words from their sacred book. If those are the correct answers, then I must ask: are the people of Santa Teresa true believers and followers of Kammbi?

"Who are you to question our belief in Kammbi?" Turner Perez retorted.

"Mr. Perez, I would suggest you let Diondray Azur finish his themily," Mr. Cortes said as he stood next to me on the podium.

Morrim Forde placed a hand on Turner Perez's shoulder in an attempt to calm him. His gesture validated Mr. Dorrado's accusation—he was following whatever Cortes said.

I paced the stage in order to get some space from the businessman. I did not want to faint again, especially at this moment. Second Esperah Dorrado needed my help. I was still itching on my arms and legs from wearing that shawl, but I had to finish the themily.

The answers to those questions have created a contradiction I cannot embrace. If you don't believe me, here are words from people you revere:

"I chose not to get married as my own choice. I did not love Leopolde in that way. And when I met Oscar Ortega I knew my calling was not to be a wife or mother but to believe and follow in Kammbi as guided by the Eternal Comforter."

Or these words:

"My passion for Adrianna was not love. She loved me, and I desired her. She was beautiful, and since my Sophia was not with me . . . I acted on my passions and crossed a line that I have forever regretted. My act of passha cost me my son and forever changed my relationship with Kammbi, even though I asked for forgiveness and received it. Love has to be a choice of both people."

These words from Teresa and Oscar Ortega answered my questions satisfactorily. What will it be for the people of Santa Teresa? One-sided love and beliefs changed at random? Or will you actually follow what is written in the sacred book you all revere so much?

Sweat drenched my paper after I read the themily. It was so quiet in the congregation hall that I could hear the wind whizzing by my ear.

"Who are you?" the morrim asked.

Diakono Copperwith stood from his seat. "Morrim Forde, this is Diondray Azur. He is the one who will fulfill Oscar's prophecy."

The people in the congregation hall murmured after that last comment. I saw the disbelief on Morrim Forde's face. He wanted to speak, but I could tell he was trying to find the right words to say.

"Are these the words this stranger has been telling you?" Turner Perez said to Second Esperah Dorrado.

"He has. And are they not correct?" Second Esperah Dorrado answered. "I do not love you, Turner. You are a good man and belong to a great family. But my path is not to be your wife. I know our marriage would be an unhappy one. "

"How can you say that? Feelings of passion or desire don't create love or a marriage! Our common backgrounds and beliefs in Kammbi are what creates a marriage," he replied in exasperation.

"I can see you have not read the Book of Kammbi as closely as you should have. Teresa spoke of her calling to follow Kammbi with everything she had. And the tribe ignored her calling, even though they claimed to believe and follow Kammbi. We in Santa Teresa have done that ever since her time. You would rather marry a woman who doesn't love you in order to keep a tradition than wait for someone who does love you—someone who can be a good wife to you," Second Esperah Dorrado continued.

Turner Perez dropped to his knees and covered his face in anguish. While I did not agree with this tradition, I hated to see a man being rejected like this. I wished it could have been stopped well before the wedding.

"Morrim Forde, I apologize for having come this far with the wedding," Second Esperah Dorrado said. "I was forced into something I did not want. Diondray Azur's words have strengthened me, and I will not proceed with this marriage," Second Esperah Dorrado said.

"Oh yes, you will, my daughter. As long as you live under my roof, you will follow the tradition that has been set before us," Mr. Dorrado said. Menacingly, he began walking up to the stage.

Mr. Cortes turned away from everyone on the podium, pointing a large finger in the direction of the irate father. "Mr. Dorrado, you have wanted this marriage more for yourself than for Annika. A parent is always supposed to have a child's best interests at heart. But you have put your own interests above your daughter."

Mr. Dorrado pointed a finger of his own. "Your money and that unbeliever you have brought here will not stop my daughter from getting married!"

Turner Perez was still on the ground in anguish while the morrim tried to comfort him. Second Esperah Dorrado walked toward me, and I noticed the relief on her face. I felt more connected to her at that moment. Maybe she truly was special.

It was then that another voice rang out. "Mr. Dorrado, I would suggest that you stop trying to get your daughter married."

"Madre Harriet!" the morrim said with a stunned look. "What are you doing here?"

I turned to see a tiny woman wearing a sky-blue shawl and a headdress walking down the aisle. Three women dressed in the same fashion walked behind her. The congregation watched these women as they approached the stage. I could tell immediately how much respect they had amongst the people of this city.

"I was summoned by someone for this moment," Madre Harriet said as she stood at the podium next to the bride-to-be. She glanced at Mr. Cortes in acknowledgment of her arrival. "Second Esperah Annika Dorrado will be coming with us. She has been selected to be a resa."

"How could that be, Madre Harriet? Second Esperah Annika Dorrado has never been married before, and Mr. Perez finds her desirable and suitable for marriage," Morrim Forde countered.

"Morrim Forde, did you just hear those words from the one who will fulfill Oscar's prophecy? He was correct about this tradition and how we have made it up instead of following the actual words written in the Book of Kammbi. The resas have gone along with it since Madre Angelica. I believe it's time for a change, and my belief coincides with the guidance I've received from the Eternal Comforter," Madre Harriet answered.

Mr. Dorrado returned to his seat as Mr. Cortes met him. I knew he would not challenge Madre Harriet. Morrim Forde backed away from Turner Perez and looked at Madre Harriet and the other resas as they stood over him. They bowed and began praying for Turner Perez. I felt a tug on my left sleeve. It was Second Esperah Dorrado gesturing for me to bow as well.

The prayer was more of a chant than actual words. It did not last long, and I got another tug telling me to lift my head up. The resas circled him, and since they were just as tiny as Madre Harriet, I could see the pain in his face. He truly loved Second Esperah Dorrado.

Madre Harriet stood before Second Esperah Dorrado. "Second Esperah Annika Dorrado, you have been chosen to become one of us. All of the resas have heard the voice of the Eternal Comforter about who you will become. And as faithful believers and followers of Kammbi, we must obey the voice. You will serve this city and be guided by the Eternal Comforter like every resa has done before you. Do you accept this calling?"

Second Esperah Dorrado nodded firmly. "I do."

The other resas joined Madre Harriet after they escorted Turner Perez off the stage. I watched him walk up the aisle and exit the congregation hall. A couple got up from their seats and followed behind him. I believed that must have been his parents. I could imagine they were heartbroken by this just as much as their son.

Morrim Forde stepped away from the resas as they circled Second Esperah Dorrado. Madre Harriet stood in front of her. Second Esperah Dorrado bowed to Madre Harriet, and I knew the offer was sealed by that gesture.

"Diondray Azur, may Kammbi bless you on your expedition. I'm convinced you are the one to fulfill Oscar's prophecy," Madre Harriet said. She turned to face me.

I nodded in acknowledgment of her comment.

Moments later, the resas escorted Second Esperah Dorrado off the stage. She stared at me the entire time as she left the stage and walked past where the rest of the group was sitting. She had tears flowing over her cheeks and the biggest smile I had ever seen from her. Change was coming to Santa Teresa, and everybody here in Kahall Angelica knew it.

Part 2:
Alicia

Chapter 8

We spent our last six days in the city at the kahall of Santa Teresa. Morrim Pomodore advised that we stay at the kahall until it was time to leave for Alicia. It made me realize how fast fifty days had passed and how that short time period could cause an impact for the people of this city. Word had gotten out to the public about what happened at Kahall Angelica, and many people were upset at Second Esperah Dorrado's rejection of their custom for marriage.

I learned that Morrim Forde had reported to the konseho of Kammbi about what happened at the wedding, and the council had mandated that the rest of the city's morrims continue to reinforce the custom. Without the intervention of Madre Harriet and the resas, Second Esperah Dorrado would still have been forced to marry Turner Perez despite our intervention. Also, it was revealed that Second Esperah Dorrado's action would be dealt with at the appropriate time. I knew from this information that the konseho of Kammbi knew about me and that I would eventually be summoned to meet them in the city of Issabella.

I was still trying to get a grasp of everything that had happened in the last few days. The fact that Mr. Cortes was able to get Madre Harriet and the resas to appear in public and the realization of Second Esperah Dorrado's importance to our expedition were still making my head spin. Even though she was not going to join us on the expedition, her rejection of the custom had depended on my fulfillment of Oscar's prophecy. I had never had that kind of responsibility placed on my shoulders even as a member of a ruling family back home in Charlesville. Uncle Xavier and Mother had handled everything in running the city. Yes, I had been a child for most of my life, and only so much could be expected from me in dealing with the city's affairs. But I was never even asked to be responsible for anything other than appearing with the family at public events throughout Charlesville. Maybe that was why Uncle Xavier was so mad when I decided to move out of the family home three years ago. I had everything handed to me on a golden platter, and I did not appreciate it. This time, being in the center of changing a city's customs had made me think a little differently. I was starting to feel the weight of purpose and responsibility.

Maisa and Felicia had sneaked into the city over the last few days and found out that other women had been emboldened by Second Esperah Dorrado's decision and were choosing to reject marriage as well. Somehow, they had received a copy of my themily and used those words as inspiration along with Teresa's words in her section of the Book of Kammbi. The city's leadership tried to maintain enforcement of the custom; more women came to the forefront to reject it.

I was starting to make peace with my decision to allow Mr. Cortes to come with us on the expedition. Without his help, Second Esperah Dorrado would have been married now. I remembered seeing the unhappiness on her face at the wedding, and that marriage would have been in trouble from the start. I was grateful for his assistance, and even though I was still uncomfortable in his presence, I knew that having him along was the right thing to do.

I could tell that Diakono Copperwith and Annalisa still did not like my decision. But I knew they would honor it, and I hoped they would come around.

Mr. Cortes provided an autobus for our travels to Issabella and Alicia. The autobus was bigger than the ones I'd been in both in Santa Sophia and Santa Teresa. There were beds in the back for each of us, and it was equipped with a bathroom and kitchen as well. We were traveling high class, and I knew how pleased Maisa was with the arrangement. Diakono Copperwith and Annalisa, on the other hand, seemed out of sorts with this extravagance. I guessed they would probably need the Eternal Comforter's guidance more than ever.

"Three hours until we reach Alicia," the driver announced.

He looked up at the mirror to view us, and I noticed he had a gap between his two front teeth that seemed like it was natural. It made him disarming and friendly.

"I thought we were traveling to Issabella?" Diakono Copperwith asked.

"Mr. Cortes paid me to drive to Alicia," the driver answered. "And as long as he is paying, I will do exactly as he wants."

The driver smiled, showing his gap teeth. I thought he used that smile to diffuse passengers' anger.

Diakono Copperwith sat down next to me. "Diondray, I do not like this. Oscar Ortega went to the area where the city of Issabella is currently right after being in Santa Teresa. Mr. Cortes knows his Book of Kammbi. Why would he want us to not follow exactly in Oscar's footsteps?"

I understood his concern, but for some reason I couldn't explain, I didn't share it. "Diakono Copperwith, I believe going to Alicia is the right thing to do at this time."

He frowned at me. "How could you know that?"

"I don't know. I just do."

"The Eternal Comforter is guiding him," Maisa interrupted. She was sitting behind both of us.

I did not know if that was true. I just felt that going to Alicia was the right path to take. And if that turned out to be the case, then the Eternal Comforter would be more real to me than ever.

I watched Diakono Copperwith as he got up from his seat and walked to the back of the autobus to get into his bed. He looked solemn when he walked past me. I'd wanted to get his approval, but his silence gave me the opposite answer. I hoped Maisa was right that the Eternal Comforter was guiding my decision. I knew that would be the only way to get Diakono Copperwith's approval at this point.

"Driver, can you play some devotional music?" Annalisa said as she got up from her seat to join her husband at the back of the autobus.

"It's not the first day of the week. And that's the only time I play devotional music," the driver answered. I glanced at his pudgy face through his windshield mirror. His expression showed he was bothered by Annalisa's request.

"You only play devotional music on the first day of the week? Are you a believer and follower of Kammbi?"

The driver's face strained. "Mr. Cortes paid me to drive you all to Alicia and Issabella safely. Not to be questioned about what type of music I listen to."

"Annalisa!" Diakono Copperwith called from the back of the autobus.

"Coming, my love," she replied while glaring at the driver. I knew she wanted to press him more, but she turned her back to the driver and walked to the back of the autobus.

With Annalisa gone, Maisa gave the driver a sly smile. "Can you play some of the music you *do* have? I would like to know about your musical tastes." I knew she'd enjoyed the driver standing up to Annalisa.

"Of course, Ms. Merez," the driver replied. He pulled a cassette from the glove box. "I have Coltrain Hayes's latest song. I've been playing it for the past few days."

"Coltrain Hayes?" I asked. "Isn't he from Walter's Grove?"

The driver cut his eyes to me in the mirror, surprised. He smiled and seemed eager to converse. "You are from south of the Great Forest, Mr. Azur. You have probably heard of him before."

"Yes. My best friend, Trayvonne, played his music on occasion. How did you know about him? I did not think someone from the north would be interested in a musician from our region."

"My relative who lives in Alicia gets me all the guanamamma music from Walter's Grove. He works in the silver mines with people who came from that city. They have moved to Alicia for a better life. But they share their music and other aspects of their culture with the natives. I have music by John Jose Rollins, Delia Quintana, and the group Cinco. They have some great music in Walter's Grove! I would love to visit that place someday to hear them in person."

The driver's entire mood had changed from the conversation with Annalisa. He straightened his posture in the driver's seat. I could tell he was getting positive energy from our conversation. I reckoned he could drive to Alicia and back to Santa Sophia in one evening because of it. It was interesting to see how people reacted once they had common ground with you.

"Let me play a couple of tunes by Coltrain Hayes first. Then some John Jose Rollins. I like his music a lot as well." The driver placed the cassette into the stereo. "This song is called 'Anna.' I'm sure you know Coltrain Hayes named all of his songs after women. My relative told me he was quite the womanizer."

Maisa and the driver laughed at the same time. The song opened with a deep horn sound. It was mournful. I wondered if Coltrain Hayes had lost this woman he'd named the song after. It felt that way. Next, drums and a guitar played in rhythm with the horn. "Anna" was a sad song.

"I know you are probably wondering why a driver would want to hear a song like this while driving. It helps me focus on my job and takes my mind off my life at home."

He'd said it lightly, but I knew that comment had more meaning behind it. I would have to explore that with him sometime. Hopefully, I would be able to, since we had some common ground established. Maybe I could become a man of the people after all.

I leaned back in my seat and listened to the song. There were no words. "Does he play some Kammarice music?"

The driver bobbed his head to the music and replied, "Only guanamama music. I like music that makes you dance. The next Coltrane Hayes song, Wanda. Is for dancing."

"I hope that song is happier," Maisa said. She sounded a little put out.

The driver continued bobbing his head. He was entranced by the music. "It will be, Ms. Merez."

I closed my eyes as the song continued. "Anna" ended with a horn solo like the beginning of the song.

"Coltrain Hayes loved Anna more than any other woman he named a song after," the driver remarked. "You can tell from the music. None of his other songs are like it."

Seconds later, pounding drums announced the next song. I sat up in my seat and started bobbing my head to the music. Those drums were powerful.

"Coltrain Hayes plays drums and guitar on 'Wanda,'" the driver told us. His relative must have taught him about every song by Coltrain Hayes. He knew as much as someone who lived in Walter's Grove. I was impressed.

"Wanda, I saw you movin' on the floor. Shakin' everything your mama gave you. And I had to have you, Wanda. Come here, my love."

Maisa popped up from her seat. "I like this song."

The guitar played fast over those pounding drums. It was a song made for dancing. "Wanda" reminded me of a Ruben Davar song called "Mango Surprise," which was played a lot at Aliki Park in Charlesville before my themily readings. All the women at the park would dance to that song. It had the same pounding drums. I remembered Trayvonne trying to dance with every girl at the park when "Mango Surprise" came on.

"Come on, Diondray. Dance with me," Maisa said and pulled me out of my seat.

I moved my shoulders to the rhythm and watched Maisa twirl in front of her seat. She was enjoying herself.

It felt so good to move, to let loose a little. "I needed a song like this, driver. Keep playing Coltrain Hayes."

I felt Diakono Copperwith's hand on my left shoulder. I turned and saw the solemn face from earlier in the evening. He shook his head.

"Not for you, Diondray. This music is not for someone who will fulfill Oscar's prophecy." I stopped dancing. "Why not?"

"It does not glorify Kammbi," he replied, and he walked past me toward the driver.

"Diakono Copperwith," Maisa pleaded, "Diondray and I were having some fun. There's nothing wrong with fun!"

Diakono Copperwith leaned over the driver. "Please change that song."

"I'm not changing my music," the driver shot back. "I told your wife earlier, Mr. Cortes paid me to get everyone to Alicia and Issabella safely. I'm allowed to do everything else my way."

"No matter how much money you are getting from Mr. Cortes, our comfort should be your concern as well."

The driver turned slightly toward Diakono Copperwith. I

thought he was going to reply harshly, but the diakono bowed to him and placed his hands on the driver's right shoulder. Seconds later, the driver returned to his forward posture.

"Out of respect for you, Diakono Copperwith, I will change the music."

"Thank you."

Diakono Copperwith turned from the driver and walked toward the back of the autobus. He paused in front of me. "I may not agree fully with your decision to have Mr. Cortes on the expedition with us. However, I'm commanded by the Eternal Comforter to keep us on the right path in order for you to fulfill Oscar's prophecy. And I must do that, Diondray Azur."

I watched him continue his walk to the back of the autobus. I knew he was right about his role on this expedition. The music was gone.

#

Even though I knew Diakono Copperwith was right about the music, I had made a connection with the driver. I wanted to listen to more music by Coltrain Hayes. I still wanted to listen to Ruben Davar. If I fulfilled Oscar's prophecy, would I have to stop listening to music like that forever? Also, what was wrong with dancing? I'd enjoyed Maisa twirling around in front of me. Were you allowed to have fun as a believer and follower of Kammbi?

All those questions came to mind as I looked out the window at the cars passing by. The bubble-shaped automobiles were small compared to the autobus and fast. My RKV-100 was bigger than they were.

I turned away from the window and opened my bag to pull out the Book of Kammbi. I figured that reading would take my mind off the music I still wanted to hear. Maybe it would even give me answers to some of my questions.

"I didn't think Diakono Copperwith would react like that," Maisa huffed. She was sitting in her seat across from me. I saw the disappointment on her face.

I sighed. As much as I wanted to agree with her, I knew I needed to listen to the diakono. "He's right. I should not be listening to music like that anymore."

"Wrong, Diondray. That's the old way of thinking. Being a believer and follower of Kammbi does not mean you have to listen to glorifying music everyday. We should be able to listen to all kinds of music."

"I agree with Ms. Merez," the driver added. "That glorifying music is boring and simple. There's no depth to it. People like Coltrain Hayes, Bill O'Neal, and even an instrumentalist like Ruben Davar have more to offer than glorifying music."

Maisa nodded.

"I don't understand why you both feel that about glorifying music," I said. "Both of you are believers and followers of Kammbi. Since I'm on the path as well, shouldn't I be listening to glorifying music too?"

"Just because we are believers and followers of Kammbi does not mean we like every aspect of our beliefs. Music is one of the areas where we differ," the driver said.

"He's correct. I wish we had music like Coltrain Hayes in Santa Sophia. We could only listen to glorifying music about Kammbi most of my life. That's fine when you are a child. But you need something more when you reach adulthood. "

"Mr. Azur, if you are the one who fulfills Oscar's prophecy, I hope that you are allowed through the Eternal Comforter to let believers and followers of Kammbi listen to music other than glorifying music. Music reveals all types of experiences. I've read the Book of Kammbi, in the Ryianza, where Jorge lived life fully. That did not stop him from being a believer and follower in Kammbi. I believe that freedom is missing from our belief system."

The driver's words felt right. Music did reveal all types of experiences, and it was one of the best ways to tell stories. Why were believers and followers restricted to one type of music? Maybe I was going to change that for everyone on this second expedition.

I opened the Book of Kammbi and started reading in Alicia's section. Her account was in Book 6 of the Baramesa and was not as long as Teresa's section. She had a husband named Dexter, whom she loved a lot. They both met Oscar Ortega at a river that seemed important. Oscar stayed fifty days with Alicia, Dexter, and their tribe, just he did with Teresa.

At the end of Alicia's account, I read about the river god her people believed in. The river god acknowledged Oscar Ortega's presence and told Alicia and Dexter to begin believing in his god, Kammbi. Alicia believed the river god, but Dexter did not. That caused some tension between him and Oscar. However, Alicia knew from her spirit that the river god was right. Oscar Ortega's god, Kammbi, was to be followed.

Alicia's beliefs caused a split between her and Dexter. He refused to follow the god of this stranger and continued to pray to the river god. The river god explained that he must follow his wife and begin believing in Oscar Ortega's god, Kammbi. Dexter refused, and on the last day of Oscar Ortega's time with them, he was pulled into the river by the river god for his disobedience. This event was called the offering of Dexter. In the last chapter of Alicia's account, she wrote that her husband's sacrifice should always be remembered by her tribe and following generations. Dexter was a great husband and loyal to their tribe. But her command troubled me. It seemed they were remembering a man who did not obey his god's command. Was that worth remembering? If so, weren't these people of the city of Alicia honoring disobedience?

I had been made to believe that Kammbi wanted people to believe and follow him absolutely. Now, I had seen up-close an example in Santa Teresa of how believers and followers added their own tradition through a misreading of Teresa's words. And this, here in Alicia's section, was another example of the same issue. Could people of a belief system truly follow their writings literally? Or did it come down to one's interpretation of those writings?

"You are in deep thought," Maisa said.

I looked up from reading. "Yes, I am. This offering of Dexter concerns me. Alicia wrote loving words about her husband. I can understand that. But it seems he was disobedient to this river god's command. I don't think that is something worth being remembered for."

Maisa snorted. "I can tell you don't know much about love."

"What do you mean?"

"Dexter was a great husband to Alicia. And she was going to make sure that her people would always remember the man she loved. When a woman loves her husband, she will do anything for him."

Maisa sat up straighter after that comment. She had a distant look on her face, like she could identify with Alicia's sentiment about Dexter.

But I wasn't ready to let it go. "Because of her love for him, Alicia would overlook what he did? She would overlook the whole reason he was offered?"

"You are truly inexperienced about love," Maisa said sharply. She glared at me, and I felt her anger immediately. "I thought you were trying to keep distant from me because of this expedition. But you have never loved before."

I bristled. "How do you know that? I have not told anything about my past. It's best not to make assumptions you have no knowledge of."

"At least you have a pulse. Even though you are defensive. Maybe you *have* loved before," Maisa replied with a slight smile on her face.

Her accusation about my love life stung. I would not share my experience with Mara with her. That relationship had lasted two years and ended because I wanted to leave the family home and live on the west side of Charlesville. I'd wanted to live among the "ants," as Uncle Xavier called them. Mara felt the same way as Uncle Xavier about the people of the west side. I asked her to come with me, but she refused. She liked her life on the east side and would not give that up for me. But I had truly loved her.

The driver chuckled at our conversation. I assumed he agreed with Maisa.

"I can tell you've had some experience with love," Maisa told him.

"Yes, I have, Ms. Merez. Why do you think I like Coltrain Hayes's music so much?"

I turned my back to both of them and looked out the window. They were both chuckling at my expense. I wanted to respond to their comments, but I had nothing to say.

Chapter 9

We made it to Alicia in three hours, exactly like the driver said. The city's skyline stood in the distance as we entered the outskirts. Alicia was the second most populated city in the north, next to Santa Sophia. Diakono Copperwith and Annalisa got up from resting to tell me about the city. Alicia's economy was made from silver production and fishing in the Issabella River. The fishing part reminded me of Charlesville.

"Welcome to Alicia," the driver announced. "My home away from home. Mr. Cortes has reserved rooms for you all at Hotel Dexter in the Hill district."

"I would prefer to stay at a kahall," Annalisa said. She was sitting next to Diakono Copperwith, and both were sitting behind me.

"The kahalls in Alicia do not have accommodations for visitors like they do in Santa Teresa. Even the main kahall in the city is much smaller than you're used to. Everyone will be pleased at the accommodations Mr. Cortes has provided for you," the driver continued. Not for the first time, I wondered why Mr. Cortes hadn't come with us. Why make such an effort to join our expedition only to stay behind when we finally set out?

"First this autobus and now a hotel room. What else does Mr. Cortes plan to give us?"

"What's wrong with Mr. Cortes giving us a little luxury? We do not have to travel like Oscar Ortega did during his time," Maisa said. "Times have changed."

Annalisa glared at Maisa. "I bet you are loving this opulence. Being a believer and follower of Kammbi is not about the comforts of this land. Those will come and go. You should know that, Maisa Merez."

"Definitely," Maisa said, "I've heard that all my life. Where has that gotten us believers and followers of Kammbi? We do not have to live life like we are in Oscar Ortega's time. Those days have come and gone. And we do not have to believe and follow Kammbi like they did in the past. Diondray's arrival has shown that it will be a new way for everyone."

Annalisa's cheeks flushed red. Diakono Copperwith placed his right hand in Annalisa's lap, stopping her from responding to Maisa's proclamation.

"Driver, how soon will we arrive at Hotel Dexter?" Diakono Copperwith asked.

"Ten minutes."

"Thank you. We are looking forward to our accommodations at the hotel."

The driver nodded as he drove further into the city.

#

Hotel Dexter was huge. It must have been one of the buildings I saw in the skyline as we entered Alicia. I looked out the autobus's window as the driver drove into the waiting area. The manicured lawn, with perfectly placed sun-yellow flowers along the main walkway, gave the hotel beauty and warmth. Men dressed in black jumpsuits with yellow trim on the sleeves helped people with their luggage. The driver parked and got up. He faced us, his prominent stomach protruding over his pants.

"I hope everyone had a safe and enjoyable trip to Alicia. Mr. Cortes has your accommodations inside the hotel. I will be on call as needed when you wish to travel around the city."

The driver walked up the aisle and opened the overhead bins to pull our luggage out. I grabbed my bag and placed the Book of Kammbi inside. I was looking forward to getting into my hotel room so I could write a themily. I needed to get some words on paper. Our prior conversation about love was still on my mind.

The driver returned to his seat as we were exiting the autobus, stopping me for a moment. He smiled broadly, showing his tooth gap. "Mr. Azur, I still want play some Coltrain Hayes for you."

"I would like that . . ."

"Percival. Percival Arturo."

"I would like that, Percival," I replied and shook hands. Percival had a firm grip.

I exited the autobus after Maisa and the Copperwiths. Three hotel employees grabbed our travel bags.

"Welcome to Hotel Dexter, the best hotel in Alicia," the tallest of the three employees proclaimed.

"We know you are guests of Mr. Cortes. We have the best accommodations for all of you. The Hotel Dexter staff has made sure of that," the shortest of the three employees said. I noticed he wore the most silver of the three. He had several necklaces, bracelets, and rings. I had never seen that much jewelry on a man.

Maisa tugged gently on my sleeve and giggled as we entered the hotel. She was going to enjoy our stay. The two taller men placed our bags on a cart and pushed it into the hotel.

"Your rooms are on the fourteenth floor. The elevator is just ahead," the shortest employee said.

It had been a long time since I stayed at a hotel. I remembered as a child staying at one in the city of Terrance. Mother had finally decided to let me meet my father after I asked her repeatedly. I did not have any fond memories of the trip—my parents argued the entire time we met. My father brought some playing cards and said a few words to me. He was a professional card player, and those cards were the only thing that he could give me.

We entered the elevator after the hotel employees and were whisked up to the fourteenth floor.

"I can't believe Mr. Cortes would make accommodations for us here!" Maisa said, brushing against me in the elevator. "I've heard this is Alicia's best hotel."

"Where is he?" I asked.

"We will see him tomorrow morning at breakfast."

"I was wondering why he did not travel with us to Alicia."

"I was wondering that same thing, Diondray." Annalisa said. She stood on the other side of Diakono Copperwith, close to the panel for the elevator buttons and just behind the employees.

Maisa grabbed my hand and whispered, "It's because he knows how uncomfortable you get in his presence."

Her answer surprised me. "That's a nice gesture," I replied.

"Because you made the right decision to have him join us on the second expedition, Mr. Cortes wants to make sure that he honors your decision."

"We are all on this second expedition together, Maisa Merez. Any information from Mr. Cortes should be shared with all of us," Diakono Copperwith said sternly.

"There's nothing to hide from you or Annalisa," Maisa shot back. "Mr. Cortes just wants to make sure that Diondray is comfortable with his decision to allow him to join us."

The diakono frowned. "Secrets always leads to mistrust and will be eventually exposed by the light."

I squeezed Maisa's hand as the elevator doors opened. I knew she was going to say something out of turn, and I did not want my companions to have such tension amongst each other.

"No secrets, Diakono Copperwith," I answered before Maisa could comment. "She knows how uncomfortable I have been in Mr. Cortes's presence, and apparently so does he. He is trying to be respectful of that issue while we are together. That is all Maisa said."

Diakono Copperwith stared at me, and I thought he was searching my face to see if I was lying. He nodded and smiled slightly. I believed he thought I had told the truth.

I appreciated Mr. Cortes's consideration of me. His kind action strengthened my faith in my decision to allow him to come with us. Was the Eternal Comforter finally guiding me? I'd expected his guidance to feel more dramatic, but maybe it just felt like this—like making decisions the best that I could, guided by a sense of what was right or wrong. My belief in that possibility started to grow.

"Your rooms are this way," the shortest hotel employee said as the elevator doors opened. We followed them out of the elevator and turned right into the well-lit hallway. I began to read the room door numbers as we passed by.

"Room 1407 is for Diakono and Annalisa Copperwith. Room 1409 is for Diondray Azur. And Room 1411 is for Maisa Merez." The other two employees opened the doors to each of our rooms and placed our travel bags inside. We stood in the hallway with the shortest man, who seemed to be in charge. "We will give you a couple of hours to rest and freshen up. Dinner is at seven o'clock in our wonderful restaurant back down on the lobby floor. Each of you will get a buzz from your room phone, and that will be your signal for dinner. Enjoy your stay at Hotel Dexter, and we'll see you at dinner."

#

I arrived at the hotel's restaurant for dinner at seven o'clock. I had just started writing a themily when the phone buzzed, breaking my concentration and telling me it was time for dinner. I was writing about love, inspired by the conversation I'd had with Maisa and Percival on the bus. I had been thinking about it since our arrival in Alicia. To both of them, love made you do illogical things for a special person. Their beliefs were supported by Alicia's words in the last part of her section in the Book of Kammbi. I wondered if I would have to focus my themily on the apparent power of love to make you do the illogical.

"Welcome to Hotel Dexter Restaurant," a waitress said as she pulled out the chair for me to sit. Her dark-brown skin and cloud-white smile caught my attention. "I have some cherry juice to get you started."

The waitress wore a couple of shiny, thin silver necklaces and thick silver bracelets on both wrists. She was the first person I had seen with my complexion since I been in these cities north of the Great Forest.

"Are you from south of the Great Forest?" I asked as she poured the cherry juice into a glass for me.

"Walter's Grove," she answered and flashed her cloud-white smile. "And where are you from?"

"Charlesville."

"I heard about your city growing up. You usually get those huge tropical storms during this time of the year, don't you?"

"We do. I'm Diondray Azur."

"Bonita Golde." She continued to pour cherry juice into the other glasses at the table. "I would like to talk some more with you at a more convenient time."

"I would like that as well, Bonita."

Bonita flashed her smile at me again. "I will be back shortly to take everyone's orders for dinner." I watched her walk away from our table. The midi dress she wore showed off her full figure. She would have been Trayvonne's kind of woman.

"Diondray!"

I turned back to the table and saw Maisa's frown. "We have some things to discuss."

I nodded and looked away from her. I was in trouble.

Diakono Copperwith and Annalisa were sitting across from me, and Annalisa was frowning as well. I was in trouble with both women at the table. But it would be for a different reason with Annalisa.

"It's good to see you've met someone from south of the Great Forest. You looked so comfortable with that waitress," Diakono Copperwith said in order to break the tension at the table.

"That's because she was an attractive woman," Annalisa added sourly.

"Maybe so, my love, but I think something else was at work here. I've heard that many people from Walter's Grove migrated here to Alicia to work in the silver mines. I believe Diondray will see a lot of people here in this city with a complexion like his. Perhaps it will make him feel more at home."

"Percival, the driver, mentioned that while you both were resting. I did not know there were other people from south of the Great Forest who have come north. He surprised me with that comment— I thought I was the only one."

"Don't forget that your Aunt Maxina came before you," Diakono Copperwith added.

"She did. I'm the second person, then. Or so I thought. Apparently I'm one of many!"

"Those other people don't matter like you, Diondray," Maisa said. She was still bothered about the attention I'd paid to Bonita.

"That's a terrible thing to say, Maisa Merez. These people are made in Kammbi's image just like we are," Annalisa shot back.

Bonita returned to take our orders, and thankfully that stopped the conversation between Maisa and Annalisa. I did not want the dinner ruined with their usual tension.

"We have to discuss our time here in Alicia and what you are meant to do, Diondray." Diakono Copperwith continued. "As you know, we have the same fifty-day period we had in Santa Sophia and Santa Teresa."

"That is correct. And sir, I think I already know some of why we are here. From reading Alicia's section in the Book of Kammbi, it seems the river god is still a major part of the people's beliefs, even though Dexter was meant to learn from Oscar Ortega's teachings." Maisa seemed happy to be talking about something else. "The people here still believe in the river god even though Alicia's words are clear. How can we get them to see that Dexter disobeyed the river god?" she said.

"That's why we are here," I said as Bonita brought our food to the table. The diakono nodded in agreement. But just thinking of the task ahead made me feel overwhelmed. The offering of Dexter had made such a big impact. How would I be able to convince people of this city about Dexter's disobedience?

Chapter 10

How can people fully unite to believe in the same thing? How can people believe in something that's different than what is written in their sacred book? Does everyone have his or her own interpretation of the sacred book? If so, can people truly ever believe in the same thing? Or, if there is an actual true *interpretation of that sacred book, how do we know whose interpretation is correct?*

I started writing the themily in my hotel room on the fourth day of our time in Alicia. It was the seventeenth day in the month of Yul. I had forty-six more days to prepare a themily that would make the people of this city see how Dexter's disobedience had been misinterpreted because of his wife's love. But the people of this city were divided on Dexter, and my task here could be harder than keeping Second Esperah Dorrado from getting married.

Mr. Cortes joined us the day after we arrived and explained at breakfast that he had some business to take care of in Alicia and he wanted Maisa and I to join him. He wanted us to get a full view of the city and how the people lived on a day-to-day basis—I wouldn't be sequestered here like I had been in Santa Teresa. The businessman believed like Diakono Copperwith that Oscar Ortega's ability to connect with the people during his first expedition had been instrumental in getting them to become believers and followers in

Kammbi. I would have to do the same. Connection came before conversion.

I met the businessman, Felicia, and Maisa at the waiting area in front of the hotel. Felicia and Mr. Cortes stood out amongst the crowds of people who were coming to the hotel by wearing flower-patterned shorts. They must have been the latest fashion item he'd created. I watched how people stared at the businessman and his right-hand woman as they walked by.

"Where are Diakono Copperwith and Annalisa?" I asked.

"Percival took them to the kahall of Alicia earlier," Mr. Cortes replied. "Our business is elsewhere."

Maisa stood some distance away from Mr. Cortes and Felicia as people continued to stare at them. I knew that she did not like his latest style. The flowers were just a little too much. Percival arrived and parked right in front of us. On the bus, I made sure that I sat several seats away from the businessman. Yet, I could still feel his presence running through my body. I still had no idea why he affected me the way he did, and I wondered how long I could last on this expedition being in such close proximity to Mr. Cortes.

"Drink," Maisa said and opened her travel bag to hand me a water bottle. "You going to need this for today."

I took the water bottle from her as she sat down next to me. Her presence would be a shield between the businessman and me. The water sent a refreshing chill through my body. I would need a lot more of it if I was going to be around Mr. Cortes for the rest of this expedition.

"We have taken all precautions for you, Diondray," Felicia replied. She sat across from us, a few seats behind the driver. She opened up a large purse and handed Maisa another water bottle.

"She is correct, Diondray," Maisa added and grabbed the water container. "We have a city to explore, and you have to see all of it."

The frown from our first evening in Alicia was gone. Maisa was back to being herself around me. Bonita Golde had sent me a note last night saying she wanted to talk after work in a couple of days. If Maisa saw us together, it could become unpleasant. I did not know why I was so worried about her feelings, but I knew I'd have to find a way to keep our meeting from her. "Diondray, I have some Coltrain Hayes music with me," Percival said. "I can play it for you now."

"Go ahead."

Maisa giggled as Percival pushed play on the stereo.

"This song is called 'Tamara.' He had a wild time with this woman," Percival remarked.

"Tamara" was a faster song than "Wanda." The drums and guitar were in harmony, and I could not help but move my shoulders.

"This was Coltrain Hayes's most popular song," Percival told us. "It's probably one of the most popular songs ever recorded in Walter's Grove."

"Dance with me, Diondray."

Maisa got up from the seat and reached for my arms. She was striking, and I could not keep my eyes away from her. But I heard Annalisa's voice in my head.

"No dancing, Maisa," I said.

She pouted. "Diondray, don't be like that."

"No dancing. You know what I'm here for."

Maisa frowned and stopped dancing. "I know. But I don't want you to become like Diakono Copperwith and that wife of his. They are too straight-laced, and they never learned to live a little. Not everything has to be exactly by the Book of Kammbi." "I agree with you, Ms. Merez," Mr. Cortes chimed. "They are a little too much by the book. Times have changed, and we must change with them."

For some reason, the conversation was making me uncomfortable. "I understand that. But until I fully grasp everything

I'm doing, I will stick by the book. No dancing."

Maisa plopped into the seat and sighed. I knew I was doing the right thing by her reaction. The Copperwiths were not with us, but their reaction on the drive to Alicia resonated with me. I wanted to dance with Maisa, and it seemed like harmless fun to me. But with everything that had happened on the expedition so far, I needed to stay focused and not let my emotions get off track.

Percival explained on the drive that the city of Alicia had three districts: Silver, Hill, and River. Each district was named after a main feature of the city's landscape. I took the information in, my thoughts still distracted by Maisa. She was upset with me for not dancing with her. I began to realize that we were acting like a couple in a lot of ways. I knew that she loved me, and her actions so far had backed up her declaration. However, I was not ready to reciprocate. I could not shake the feeling that her true motivation for coming on this expedition had not been revealed. I would need to see that motivation before I could move forward with love.

Did I love her? I could not give a definitive answer, even to myself. She was striking and attractive. But I did not know her yet, and she did not know me. We still had a long way to go in finding out about one another. On top of that, I believed that Diakono Copperwith and Annalisa were right about my need to remain undistracted in order to fulfill Oscar's prophecy. I had to finish this second expedition without the distraction of love and learn what fulfilling Oscar's prophecy would do for everyone on both sides of the Great Forest.

I reached for Maisa's hand, and she pulled it away. "You are becoming just like them," she said with hurt in her voice.

"What do you mean?"

"You take the Book of Kammbi so literally. Every word written in the Book of Kammbi has to match and mean exactly what it says."

"Of course," I answered. "How else am I supposed to read it?"

Maisa turned her body away from me. "The Book of Kammbi was written by eight different people, and they all give their accounts of why they believe and follow Kammbi. Eight accounts and eight different interpretations."

"That's correct, Ms. Merez," Mr. Cortes remarked.

I looked away from Maisa to the businessman. Mr. Cortes's height made it look like he was standing in his seat.

But I didn't agree with either of them. I'd spent a lot of time pouring over that book, and I didn't see eight different interpretations—I saw one story. "These eight writers all share the same story about how they became a follower and believer in Kammbi. Of course, they all have a different experience as to how they came to conversion. But it still reads cohesively to me."

"But there are still different interpretations. And to Ms. Merez's point, you don't have to read the Book of Kammbi literally, do you?" Felicia added.

"You can have different experiences, even some different interpretations, and still come to the same conclusion." Frustration rose in me. Why was I even having this conversation? Shouldn't these people be teaching *me?* "I can't believe I'm saying this to all of you as an outsider to this belief system. When I arrived in Santa Sophia, I got the sense they were determined to follow the Book of Kammbi literally. It gave the impression that these people truly believed in this god Kammbi and the Eternal Comforter. Since, I've been to Santa Teresa, and it seems that literal interpretation is not the belief for those people. I don't understand why people have such a problem taking the words written in a sacred book at face value."

I turned away from everyone and looked out my seat's window.

"You are proving the need for the Eternal Comforter in our lives," Percival said.

"What do you mean?" I asked, turning toward the bus driver.

"A human being's mind and heart do not like to be forced into anything. We might declare literal interpretation and want to believe it. But we are rebellious by nature, and eventually we find ways or reasons against the literal interpretation of a belief system. We will even take our sacred book and read things into it for the sake of our rebellious nature. It's an act of passha to do that. Stay on the direct path, Diondray. Maybe this is your reason for being here to fulfill Oscar's prophecy. Kammbi wants us to return back to the literal interpretation of the words he had written in his book." Percival's words rang true. Mr. Cortes, Felicia, and Maisa did not respond, but I felt comforted by the driver's comments.

"Is that Reuel?" Maisa said while looking out the window over my left shoulder.

I looked to the right and noticed people in shock as the leopard ran in stride with the autobus on the sidewalk. I smiled. Reuel had made it to Alicia.

We stopped at a traffic light, and the leopard did the same. "It is," I said.

"Just like Oscar. The first Reuel was his companion," Felicia remarked as she came to our side of the autobus and looked wonderingly out the window at the leopard. "Thank you for letting Mr. Cortes and I come on this second expedition, Diondray. This is much more interesting than working at the office right now."

The leopard stared at me and roared as we drove away. I did not know the next time I would see the cat, but its presence comforted me.

We reached Silver district a few minutes later. Felicia and Maisa were still looking out their seat's window for Reuel, but the leopard had disappeared as quickly as it appeared. I began to wonder myself about Reuel. Was the animal's presence a sign that I was on the right path for this second expedition? When did the leopard decide to make an appearance? And how did it know to come at this time?

"Welcome to the Silver district," Percival announced. "Home to the silver mines and the hardest working people of the city."

"I will find out about that soon enough, driver," Mr. Cortes replied.

I looked over at Mr. Cortes as he rose from his seat. He smiled at me, but it didn't ease my discomfort. Why did I feel so uneasy around him? He had been gracious and helpful, but I could not stop feeling uneasy around him. It didn't help that I couldn't understand my own decisions. As much as I wanted to fulfill Oscar's prophecy, I needed to know why I had allowed someone to join us who made me feel in such a manner. Surely I could have helped Second Esperah Dorrado without him. I would have found a way. So why had I said yes?

"You are correct, Mr. Cortes. We have reached Silver Mine 12."

Percival parked the autobus. Silver Mine 12 appeared to me to be an old and rundown building. It had a faded entrance sign with missing letters, and the lawn around it was wild and uncut. Did all the silver mines in the city look like this one? I thought of my people, immigrants from the south, working in places like this. It made me feel uncomfortable all over again.

I followed Mr. Cortes and the women off of the autobus. Percival would wait for us until our tour of Silver Mine 12 was finished. He wore a satisfied look on his face as we exited the autobus. I felt he was at home here in Alicia.

A short, stocky man wearing thick silver bracelets on his wrists and silver rings on his pinky and index fingers greeted us beneath the entrance sign. "Mr. Cortes and guests, welcome to Silver Mine 12," he said with a deep voice.

"Jorge Feldman. We are glad to have finally made it your silver mine. I have my assistant, Felicia, Maisa Merez, and Diondray Azur with me."

The two men shook hands and embraced. Jorge Feldman stepped back from the embrace and stared at Maisa. A delighted smile appeared on his face, and I did not like it.

"Ms. Merez. I've heard wonderful things about you. Glad that you could come to see the silver mine."

Maisa giggled and embraced Mr. Feldman. I knew he enjoyed having his arms wrapped around her. I wanted to pull her away from him. Why did I feel that way all of a sudden?

"Hello, Felicia. Mr. Cortes speaks highly of you, and I look forward to doing business." Mr. Feldman continued with his greetings.

Felicia nodded and shook his hand. I knew she did not like being touched. That handshake looked uncomfortable for both of them.

"Mr. Azur. You are the first person from Charlesville here at Silver Mine 12. The workers will be interested in hearing your story of how you got here. As you know, most of our workers come from Walter's Grove south of the Great Forest. They have provided a tremendous benefit to the business and the city as a whole."

I shook his hand, still miffed about how he had embraced Maisa. But I was looking forward to meeting workers from Walter's Grove. It would be nice to see some people from my region, despite it being a different city than Charlesville.

We followed Jorge Feldman into the building, and I noticed he walked between Mr. Cortes and Maisa. "Silver Mine 12 is one of the biggest producers of silver in all the cities north of the Great Forest. There are a couple of silver mines that claim to produce more silver than us. But I do not trust the yearly data produce from the konseho of Kammbi for that claim."

"The konseho of Kammbi owns this silver mine?" Maisa asked.

Jorge Feldman smiled at Maisa. "They were granted ownership when the last members of the Merez family passed away a few years ago. Rudolfo and April Merez wrote into their will that the konseho of Kammbi would take over this mine and appoint an overseer to run it until a family member showed up to claim ownership. The konseho of Kammbi appointed me as the overseer, and I have to provide yearly data showing how much silver is actually being produced. But the konseho of Kammbi owns some of the big silver mines in Alicia, and I don't trust their yearly data to be as accurate as they claim."

Maisa clutched my left arm during Jorge Feldman's explanation. "I remember my parents teaching me about my relative who had left the Mayza tribe after Oscar Ortega's arrival and followed him east as he spread his teachings. Marco Phillip Merez was spoken about often in our home."

"Yes, Maisa. He was the original owner. Marco Phillip Merez came east with Oscar and discovered silver in this area. He decided to settle here for a time and built this mine. Marco Phillip established a connection with people south of the Great Forest and began the first migration route between our city and the city of Walter's Grove."

Jorge Feldman led us into an area where yellow coats and hats were hanging against the wall. He pulled out earplugs from his pocket. He handed each of us a coat, hat, and earplugs. "Everyone will need to wear these as we enter the mine. It gets dark, dusty, and noisy as we get deeper into the tunnel."

"This mine has been in my family for all of these years," Maisa marveled. "I knew my family had a bigger impact in this region than what it has been given credit for!"

I noticed a look of satisfaction on her face. I believed she'd had a reason for being on this expedition outside of her apparent love for me. She might have found it.

"You can claim this mine as a surviving member of the Merez family, Maisa," Jorge Feldman continued. "But you will have to provide proof of your birthright and file a petition with the konseho of Kammbi for a change in ownership."

Mr. Feldman stopped walking as we reached an open area. I was trying to get comfortable in the thick rubber yellow coat. It felt slimy on my body, and I did not like it. Feldman was glancing at Maisa as he talked. I decided to walk between them.

"That's why I wanted you to come here, Maisa," Mr. Cortes said proudly.

I had a sense there was another reason we had come here for our stop in the city of Alicia. Maybe I would learn why Mr. Cortes really wanted to come on this expedition as well.

"Can you help me with obtaining ownership of this mine?" Maisa asked as she faced Mr. Cortes.

He grinned. "Of course. I will have Felicia work on the petition while we are here in Alicia and be ready when we leave for Issabella. Because Diondray has allowed us to come on this expedition with the group, I want you to consider this as a gift from me."

Maisa hugged Mr. Cortes. "Thank you so much. This will mean so much to our family."

"There's another condition before you can claim ownership of this silver mine." Mr. Feldman replied.

"What is that?" Maisa said finally.

"Glad you asked, Maisa," Feldman said. To my surprise, he looked at me. "Your family since Marco Phillip's arrival have been staunch believers and followers of Kammbi. They believe the offering of Dexter is heretical. But the mineworkers believe in the offering of Dexter and the river god. I've been told that Mr. Azur is the one to fulfill Oscar's prophecy. He will have to convince these workers that Kammbi is the one they should follow and believe in. That will help in getting the konseho of Kammbi to give Maisa ownership of this mine."

"He will do that, Mr. Feldman," Mr. Cortes replied. He gave Mr. Feldman a handshake.

As for me, my mind was whirling. I'd just found out why I was here in Alicia.

Chapter 11

Jorge Feldman led us deeper into the silver mine. Even though I wore a headlamp, I felt the darkness of the silver mine surrounding me. Dust floated in the air from the ceiling, and the tunnel we were walking through became narrower. I started to feel claustrophobic and wished I could turn around and leave. Up ahead, Maisa sneezed, and the sound echoed through the tunnel. She was walking next to Mr. Feldman at the front of the group. Mr. Cortes and Felicia followed right behind them, and I was in the rear. I kept my headlamp beam aimed toward the ceiling, because there was enough light in the tunnel to see the rest of the group without it.

Mr. Feldman walked close to Maisa, and I kept a sharp eye on them. I wanted to make sure he didn't make an advance on her inside the silver mine. Did that mean I loved her? My feelings felt illogical because we were not in a relationship. But I sensed that Mr. Feldman wanted to have Maisa, and I was not going to let that happen in my presence.

I pondered whether Jorge Feldman had an alternative motivation for getting close to Maisa. I had to admit that I was surprised that she and her other family members had not known about this inheritance from Marco Phillip Merez. It seemed strange. Anyway, I believed that Jorge Feldman did not want to be out of a job if ownership did change hands, and getting close to Maisa could be his main strategy to keep his employment from now on.

The tunnel curved right, and we entered a relatively bright section of the cave, where Jorge pointed and explained to us about the hoisting pulley that carried workers back and forth throughout the mine to extract more silver. The hoisting pulley made a loud, droning noise that had me cover my ears, even though I was wearing earplugs. I wanted to leave this part of the mine as soon as possible.

We walked past the hoisting pulleys into another section of the mine, where several long benches occupied the area. They looked similar to the benches at Aliki Park back home. Jorge Feldman pointed for us to be seated on the first bench as he walked over to a second one. He returned to our bench and placed down food wrapped in silver packaging and a couple of pitchers of a drink that had a distinct aroma.

"What kind of drink is in those pitchers?" I asked before Jorge went back to grab more food and drink.

"Cherry cider does have a strong smell," he replied while looking at me over his shoulder. "But it is actually sweet and washes down the food easily."

"Quite early to have cherry cider." Mr. Cortes interjected.

Jorge Feldman smiled. "There is no alcohol in this cherry cider. We cannot have drunk workers inside the mine. Too dangerous of a job for that kind of pleasure."

Mr. Cortes grinned at Jorge in approval. I turned my head away from the smell of the pitchers of cherry cider as Jorge walked away from our bench. I'd only had alcohol on a couple of occasions back home at various functions, and I did not like the taste. I was never going to become inebriated and did not get why people would want to drink themselves into such a stupor.

Jorge placed paper plates and cups on the bench next to the food and cherry cider pitchers. "The workers will be coming for lunch, and you will get a chance to talk at that time. Our workers work from sunup to sundown, and lunch is the only time when they are really conversational."

"I would like to see more of the mine," Maisa said.

"You will, Ms. Merez," Jorge replied and pulled a small silver object out of his pocket. He blew into that object, and I covered my ears again at the shrill whistle.

Moments later, the workers joined us at the bench. They sat across from us—all men except one. She stood next to Jorge Feldman as they had a brief conversation. The workers did not even look at us as they grabbed food and poured cherry cider into their cups. I guessed that working in this mine could create quite an appetite.

"Mr. Feldman, you have a visitor here who looks like us," the female worker said as she turned her headlamp toward the ceiling and sat across from me.

"That's observant of you, Phyllis," Mr. Feldman answered. "This is Diondray Azur from Charlesville and the other visitors I told you about at the beginning of the shift."

Phyllis nodded while keeping her gaze on me, and the workers remained focused on eating like they only had a short time for lunch.

"We will talk," she replied and grabbed food for her plate.

I was starting to feel that Phyllis was examining me for some reason. What had Jorge Feldman told her and the workers about our visit today? I looked away from her and watched Jorge Feldman, Mr. Cortes, and Felicia leave the bench. Where were they going? I did not feel comfortable with this woman staring at me like this. I hoped they would return soon. I would not even have minded having Mr. Cortes seated next to me right now.

"Diondray is the one," Maisa said and stared at Phyllis.

"The one?" Phyllis replied and finally took her gaze off me to look at Maisa.

"To fulfill Oscar's prophecy. You do read the Book of Kammbi?"

I noticed the workers look up from eating at that comment.

"No one reads that book here," one of the workers interjected. He was the tallest of the workers and sat a couple of people away from Phyllis.

"Quiet, Clarence!" Phyllis shot back.

Clarence lowered his eyes and returned to eating his food. The rest of the workers followed suit.

"Your boyfriend is not eating," Phyllis continued. "He cannot be the one, if he does not like eating havannas."

Laughter erupted from the workers as they looked up from the food at us. Phyllis cut her eyes to the workers, and the laughter stopped.

"He is not my boyfriend," Maisa shot back. "It's not that type of relationship. Something you wouldn't understand."

What did Maisa mean by that?

"You are acting just like the rest of them," Phyllis countered.

"Acting like who?" I said before Maisa could respond.

"The believers and followers of Kammbi. They always judging us with comments like what your girlfriend just said."

"I'm not his girlfriend!"

Phyllis had a dour look on her face. "You two love each other and don't know it yet. That's the first thing I noticed when I saw you both." Despite her expression, I could tell she enjoyed interrogating us. "I don't remember reading about love in Oscar's prophecy."

"He's dark-skinned like us!"

Phyllis turned her head sharply at the workers. "The next person who speaks out of turn will be docked half a day's pay."

The workers lowered their heads and resumed eating. Her comment finally made me look down at the food on my plate. I opened the silver packaging to find a hard, thin, triangular piece of bread with a mixture of meat and green vegetables piled on top of it. It did not look pleasing for me to eat.

"You are correct, Phyllis. There is nothing about love in the prophecy," I said while taking a sip of cherry cider instead of eating that havannah. "Is that why you and the workers here don't believe in it?"

"You should know that we believe in the river god," Phyllis replied sharply.

"You believe that Dexter did what was right with his disobedience," Maisa added.

The workers looked up from eating again and stared at us.

"It was not disobedience." Phyllis scowled. "I see that you and your girlfriend have already been convinced of the literal interpretation of the Book of Kammbi."

"Is that not the correct interpretation?" I asked.

I felt the workers' stares as they rose from the bench. Lunch must have ended, because Jorge Feldman, Mr. Cortes, and Felicia returned. I knew it was not going to be easy to convince these people to reconsider their interpretation of Alicia's section in the book.

"It is the correct interpretation of our sacred book," Mr. Cortes said as he stood next to Phyllis.

She grimaced at Mr. Cortes, not intimidated in the slightest by his height or his wealth. "He will never be able to convince the people, especially in the River district, of that interpretation. Many morrims and diakonos have tried over the years. And they still treat us like second-class citizens of this city."

Mr. Feldman intervened. "Mr. Azur is here to prove that Dexter's offering was the wrong path to take."

"Boss, if Mr. Azur can prove that to us, then he is the one to fulfill Oscar's prophecy," Phyllis answered.

#

I spent the next five days after our time in Silver Mine 12 rereading Alicia's section in the Book of Kammbi and working on a new themily. The first chapter clearly stated that the river god came out of the river and told Alicia and Dexter to follow Oscar Ortega's teachings because he served someone greater than itself. Alicia agreed, and Dexter refused. Because of that decision, a water funnel from the river swallowed Dexter.

Dexter's death had clearly been a punishment for wrongdoing. I could not wrap my mind around how those workers could read the same section and come to a different conclusion. I wondered if they viewed Dexter being swallowed by that water funnel as a sacrifice—as something noble and good? Still, they were ignoring the river god's command to Dexter. Or had they been taught that the command to worship Kammbi instead of the river god only applied to Dexter?

Also, Phyllis had mentioned that they were treated like second-class citizens for their beliefs. I did not like anyone being treated like that regardless of what they believed in. My next themily had to address Dexter's offering and the mistreatment of those who believed in it. Also, I was starting to get the idea that something else was at work here. *Could* people follow a belief literally, or would they always interpret it to suit their own personal needs and comforts? If that was the case, then why believe in anything bigger than yourself?

I began rewriting what I'd started when I arrived in my hotel room.

The new version began like this:

Reading what is on the page and comprehending what you have read in your mind are two different actions. Sometimes those actions come together as one to create a proper interpretation of what a writer wrote. Much of the time, those two different actions create a miscommunication between the writer of those words and the reader.

How important is the correct understanding between a writer whose words are written in a sacred text and the reader of those words who is supposed to believe and follow them? Do you follow the writer's words literally, or do you read your own meaning into it? Especially if that writer's words are from the past? A distant past? How does a literal interpretation apply to the current time?

I stopped writing and lifted my pencil from the paper. I felt better about this version of the themily in addressing the issue of literal interpretation against each person's own interpretation. I hoped the final version would begin to change the minds of those workers at Silver Mine 12 and others here in Alicia about how something should be read in their sacred book. This issue had kept people in both Santa Teresa and Alicia from becoming true believers and followers of Kammbi, and I'd done it myself back home in Charlesville. I'd created my own interpretation of the life chart and refused to follow it literally like Mother and Uncle Xavier wanted me to. I was beginning to understand why that had to change.

I joined Diakono Copperwith and Annalisa at the kahall of Alicia. They wanted to get the perspective of the morrim about Dexter's disobedience and whether the believers and followers of Kammbi in Alicia believed in the correct interpretation. I'd talked with the Copperwiths a couple of days ago about my visit to Silver Mine 12 and how firm the workers were in their belief of their interpretation of Dexter's disobedience. Diakono Copperwith had to hear from the morrim of the kahall of Alicia how these two interpretations came about in this city.

The kahall of Alicia was half the size of the two I'd visited already in this region. It sat alone off of the main street in the Silver district. If you were driving through the city and did not know its exact location, you would drive right by it.

Two female second esperahs escorted us to the morrim's office. They had their customary solemn looks on their faces and did not speak upon our greeting them. I thought about Second Esperah Dorrado and wondered how she was doing as a resa. I knew she did not have to look like these second esperahs anymore.

The second esperah on our left side opened the door to the morrim's office. We entered the office, and the morrim for the kahall of Alicia greeted us with the same solemn look on his face. He stood about two inches shorter than both Diakono Copperwith and myself. The morrim's wrinkled face made him appear older than his actual age. I sensed that he had gone through a lot in his life.

"The kahall of Alicia welcomes you." the morrim said matter-of-factly and pointed for us to sit in chairs across from the desk.

Diakono Copperwith gave his customary bow to the morrim before taking his seat. I sat down at the right side of the desk, and Annalisa took a seat between her husband and myself.

"It has been made known to me that your other companions have made contact at Silver Mine 12," the morrim continued.

"That is correct, Morrim Paranga," Diakono Copperwith replied. "Mr. Cortes of Santa Teresa and Maisa Merez from Santa Sophia are spending much of their time at Silver Mine 12. Maisa Merez is a distant relative of Marco Phillip Merez and plans to take ownership of the mine. Mr. Cortes and his assistant, Felicia Hargrove, are assisting Maisa in that capacity."

Morrim Paranga's jet-black hair and reddish-brown complexion made him look like some of the workers at Silver Mine 12. He still had a solemn look on his face that I felt was more of his natural expression than an inhospitable greeting.

"She will have to prove her heritage with the konseho of Kammbi," Morrim Paranga remarked flatly. "And Mr. Cortes's reputation has been known around this city for some time."

"What do you mean by that, Morrim?" I asked.

Morrim Paranga stared at me momentarily. "It has been known that Mr. Cortes has wanted to buy a silver mine for quite some time. His attempts have failed, and he might see this opportunity with your companion as his best chance in achieving it."

I looked at the Copperwiths and sensed their disappointment. Annalisa's expression revealed that I should not have let Cortes come with us on this expedition. But Diakono Copperwith had said the Eternal Comforter wanted the businessman to join us. Now I would have to keep an eye on Mr. Cortes and figure out what his real agenda on the expedition was.

"Why should I believe that your companion here is the one who will fulfill Oscar's prophecy?" Morrim Paranga said to change the conversation.

"I had the same question when I first met Diondray in Santa Sophia. But the things that have happened since his arrival have convinced me that he is the one," Diakono Copperwith answered.

"Morrim Paranga, my husband is correct," Annalisa interjected. "Diondray Azur is the one who will fulfill Oscar's prophecy. As a woman, I have that special sense we've all received from Kammbi in order to tell if someone is truthful about who they are. Diondray and his actions on this second expedition have validated my sense that he is the one."

I turned my head to Annalisa, surprised at her comment. She nodded to me with a reassuring look on her face. She believed in the words she'd told Morrim Paranga.

Morrim Paranga replied, "Your womanly sense has guided you well, Mrs. Copperwith. I can tell your trust in Diondray Azur is genuine. Mr. Azur will have an opportunity to earn that same kind of trust from us here in Alicia."

I rose and started to pace behind my chair. "Morrim Paranga, I have a question for you. Are the silver mine workers the only ones who believe that Dexter's disobedience was justified and good? Do the believers and followers of this kahall and other kahalls in this city believe in that interpretation of the Book of Kammbi as well?"

"Please sit down, Mr. Azur," Morrim Paranga commanded.

"My apologies," I replied and returned to my seat.

"They are not the only ones, Mr. Azur. Many people of this city believed as those silver mine workers do. Even many parishioners of this kahall." He looked away. "The river god clearly stated that Alicia and Dexter should learn Oscar Ortega's teachings. And Dexter's disobedience got him swallowed up by the river. I do not understand how that can be misinterpreted."

Morrim Paranga sighed. "I am sure Diakono Copperwith and the morrims from the other cities here north of the Great Forest can tell you that people have read their own interpretations into the Book of Kammbi. People have wanted to add to the Book of Kammbi for years. They add their traditions, their own ideas, their teachings."

"The words from the Book of Kammbi are not enough for a lot of people. There has to be more to it," Diakono Copperwith added.

"Our imaginations have always desired more than what is in front of us or written down in a book," Morrim Paranga said.

"Why become a believer and follower in Kammbi, then, Morrim Paranga? "I asked.

"I hope your arrival in Alicia will finally answer that question."

#

I returned to my room later that evening. He seemed resigned to the fact that people in this city believed what they believed about Dexter's disobedience. I began to wonder: would my themily really be able to convince them of how they should read Alicia's section in the Book of Kammbi?

I received a knock on the door as I started writing. The hotel employee assigned to my room had already checked on me for the evening and brought me dinner. Diakono Copperwith and Annalisa had said good night earlier, and as far as I knew, Maisa, Mr. Cortes, and Felicia were out for the evening. Who could this be?

I got up from the desk and went to open the door. It was Bonita Golde. She wore a purple midi dress with a triangular pattern and high-heeled shoes that brought her to my eye level. Several silver necklaces dangled from her neck, and big silver earrings hung from her ears. She looked great.

"May I talk to you?" she said softly.

"Uh . . . come in," I replied. "I'm surprised to see you. That's a beautiful dress you have on."

Bonita smiled as she entered the room. "I would like you to come with me this evening."

"Come with you. Where?"

"I heard about your visit to Silver Mine 12. I heard you questioned the workers about their belief in Dexter's disobedience and the river god."

Bonita's smile was replaced by a circumspect look. But I'd settled in for the evening, and I did not want to leave the room. Plus, how did she know I had visited Silver Mine 12?

"Thanks for the offer, but I was writing a themily and planned to get some sleep once I finished."

"I know my request comes as a surprise. I assure you that where we are going will be relevant to your purpose in being in this city."

I tried to read her face to get a sense of why she wanted me to come with her, but she didn't give anything away. Then, unexpectedly, I got this feeling that said to go with her.

"All right, I will come."

Bonita smiled. "I can wait for you outside."

"No, that's fine. Let me put my themily away and we can leave."

"What's a themily?"

"Words written down on paper that I read to an audience. I hope those words will enlighten, inspire, or admonish those who listen to them. I started reading themilys back in Charlesville."

Bonita joined me at the desk. "I would like to hear some of these themilys. Can you bring some you have already written with you?"

"Uh . . . sure," I replied and turned the paper over on the desk. She was making me nervous, though not in a bad way. "Let me grab my travel bag."

Bonita walked away from the desk, and I caught a view of how that midi dress fitted on her. It hugged her curves, and I thought she'd worn that dress so she could see my reaction to it. Her prominent backside reminded me of the type Trayvonne liked. With a figure like that, Bonita would have been the next one he'd have on his arm. I grabbed my travel bag and followed her out. "You can read one of those themilys to me in the automobile," Bonita remarked as we started down the hallway. To my surprise, Maisa was standing in the hall just outside her room's door. She stared at us as we approached, and I knew this encounter would be uncomfortable.

"Where are you going, Diondray?"

I cleared my throat. "I've been asked by Bonita to come with her."

"You should stay in your room."

"I understand your concern, Maisa. But I was asked to see something important and relevant to the expedition. I'm going." How could I explain my sense that I was supposed to go? That maybe the Eternal Comforter was leading me again? I wasn't even sure about that myself, much less prepared to argue with Maisa about it.

"Diondray will be in good hands, Ms. Merez." Bonita added.

Maisa's stare pierced me. "I don't trust her with you."

"I've accepted the invitation, and I will talk with you tomorrow,"

I replied and walked away with Bonita. I must admit I was angry with Maisa at that moment. I knew she was staring at our backs as we walked down the hallway to the elevator. But she did not have a right to tell me not to go with Bonita Golde. I knew she loved me, but we were not attached to each other in that way. Still, I did feel some regret in seeing her expression.

Chapter 12

Bonita drove a Year 212 BU-12 automobile. She told me it was the only automobile she could afford on her hotel employee's salary. Bubble-shaped just like all the other automobiles I had seen in Alicia, it had wood paneling on the dashboard, steering wheel, and doors and was clearly an outdated version of the other cars zipping by us on the highway. Bonita explained that this version of the BU-12 was the first model built for purchase. She kept the automobile's interior clean, and it smelled like she had just bought it new.

We made it to the River district in about fifteen minutes. Bonita told me that the district was home to the working class of the city, along with most of the action—from nightlife to crime. Most of the silver workers who had emigrated from Walter's Grove lived in this district.

The cities north of the Great Forest segregated themselves amongst the wealthy and non-wealthy just like in Charlesville. I'd thought that since the majority of the people in these cities followed and believed in Kammbi, that type of segregation would be eliminated. I knew by now how wrong my assumption had been. But the Book of Kammbi did not teach or support that kind of division. Actually, the book didn't even talk about it.

Bonita parked in front of a building with a door on each side and turned off her engine. The building was tall and narrow and crammed in with many others along the street. "The people in this district live in duplexes. Only the well-off in this town live in houses."

"My home in Charlesville was a duplex."

Bonita gave me a sharp look and replied, "That's a surprise. You have an air of wealth and privilege."

"I moved out of the family home three years ago. I grew up in one of the wealthiest families in Charlesville. I hated it. When I became an adult, I moved into a duplex on the other side of the city as far away from my family home as I could."

"You wanted to live among the common folk."

I faced Bonita as anger rose throughout my body. "My Uncle Xavier called these people 'ants.' I hated that word. No people, regardless of their lack of wealth, should ever be called an insect."

"I can tell this is personal," Bonita said softly and placed her hand on my thigh. "Sounds like your Uncle Xavier has too much of himself stuck up his backside."

I laughed as Bonita patted my thigh to comfort me. She laughed as well, and tension from the conversation evaporated. I had never heard anyone make a joke about Uncle Xavier in my life. Bonita would be an ant in his eyes, of course. It was enjoyable to hear a comment about him that showed who was the real insect.

"Let's go inside," Bonita said.

We walked to the door on the left side of the duplex. Bonita knocked once and opened it. I followed with my travel bag over my shoulder and entered a long, narrow room where people in groups of four were sitting at tables, playing cards. There had to be at least ten tables stuffed into the space. What was Bonita going to show me in this setting that would be relevant to the expedition?

"Bonita!"

I looked to my left and saw an overweight man wearing numerous silver necklaces coming toward us. Those necklaces were thick and long enough to lie on his protruding stomach.

"Fat Vincent, you have another full house again tonight," Bonita replied. She hugged him as he reached us.

"Always on day five of the week. You know that, Miss Bonita."

"I do indeed."

Fat Vincent released Bonita from their hug and grinned at me. "I see that you brought a guest. I can tell that he's not from here. Men in Alicia don't wear pants that stop at the knee."

"Shorts," I replied as Fat Vincent stared at them. They were a pair made by Mr. Cortes. He'd brought several pairs of new ones for me to wear on the expedition. The businessman wanted to make sure I wore his clothes since he'd provided us with the autobus and hotel room. It was a fair exchange. I liked the way they fit on me. Better than the ones I wore back in Charlesville.

"Where are you from?"

"Charlesville. South of the Great Forest," I answered. "Are you from Walter's Grove?"

Fat Vincent gave me a big smile, revealing his enormous teeth. "I see you have done your homework. Yes, I am from Walter's Grove, like most of the people in here."

"Do you work at the silver mines?"

"We all do," he replied as Bonita snuggled next to him. "Do you play Blacks?"

I could barely hear Fat Vincent's baritone voice with the people talking at the tables and music in the background. "Not since my childhood. My father taught me how to play Blacks."

"I hope you remember your father's teachings well," Fat Vincent answered and began leading us through the tables.

I trailed Bonita and Fat Vincent. The people at each table we passed were focused on their card games. They did not even look up to see us walk by. These were serious players, and this establishment was similar to where my father played in Charlesville. Those duplexes were called Blacks Shacks back home on the west side, and my father had spent many evenings playing until the sun came up. I went along with him as an eight or nine-year-old-child. It was the only time we spent together. For the most part I was handed off to the lady at the Blacks Shack he played at. When Mother found out that I was going to the Blacks Shacks with my father, she put a stop to it and got my father removed from my life. I'd always wished she had never found out. I'd enjoyed spending time at those Blacks Shacks, and the people there treated me like one of their own children, not as a member of the most prominent family in Charlesville.

"Fat Vincent, I see you got your arms around the woman with the best backside in the house tonight," a man said as we stopped at the table where he was sitting. I recognized him from the silver mine.

Bonita smiled at the man, not at all embarrassed by his comment. "Be respectful of Miss Bonita," Fat Vincent replied and gave Bonita a pat on the backside as she sat down at the table. "She is playing at our table tonight, Clarence, and I want her sweet backside glued to that chair for the rest of the evening."

Clarence laughed and shuffled the cards as Fat Vincent and I sat down at the table. I sat across from Bonita and placed my travel bag between my legs. He seemed much more relaxed than at the silver mine. I could tell that Clarence was in his element, and while sitting, his towering height did not come off as intimidating, unlike Mr. Cortes.

"Where's your woman?" Clarence asked. "She would be the prettiest woman in the house tonight."

I glanced at Bonita as she rolled her eyes. "She is not my woman," I answered. "Just my companion."

"Companion. Is that what the young people call a man and

woman getting together these days? Whatever you are calling it, that's your woman. Keep her close to you."

Fat Vincent laughed as it took me a moment to realize that Clarence was the second person to believe that Maisa and I were together. Did it come off as that obvious to others? I looked at Bonita to get my mind off that observation, but her smile had disappeared. "Let's play," she said sharply.

I still had no idea why she had brought me here. I had not played Blacks since my childhood, and I knew how tough experienced players could be on novices. I did not know how well Bonita played Blacks or why she wanted me as her partner without asking if I knew how to play.

"Do you wear silver, Diondray?" Clarence asked.

"Never have."

"Well, you will need some silver to play Blacks."

Bonita's smile returned as Fat Vincent stared at her. "Okay, since you are with the most beautiful woman in the house tonight, I can get you some silver for tonight's game. Next time you have to bring your own. I will cover them both tonight, Clarence."

Fat Vincent motioned for a tall woman with black skin to come over to our table. She did, carrying a case. "Okay, Diondray and Bonita. Here's some silver for you. Make sure you can keep it." Fat Vincent said as she opened the case to reveal numerous silver necklaces. There were nearly as many as Clarence was wearing—I'd never seen so much jewelry in my life.

The woman pulled the necklaces out of the case and handed them to Fat Vincent. We placed them on the table and divided between Bonita and me. I just stared at how shiny they were.

"You have to wear them, Diondray," Bonita said.

I looked up from the silver and cut my eyes from Bonita to Fat Vincent. "You heard Miss Bonita," he said sternly.

I picked my portion and put them over my neck. I felt their weight immediately. My neck sunk into my shoulders, and I knew I could not wear these necklaces for the entire evening.

"No one should ever look that uncomfortable wearing silver." Clarence chimed in, laughing.

Bonita put on her portion of silver. She looked like she'd been wearing it all her life. "Clarence, my partner and I have to come to take some silver away from you and Fat Vincent." she remarked.

"Bonita, be glad you have a sweet backside. Because that is the only thing that will save you and your partner this evening."

Everyone at the table laughed at that comment. He started to deal the cards while I tried to think about those few times I'd played Blacks. I hoped that I could remember the rules of the game.

"Diondray, I have two rules in Blacks," Bonita said. "Play your suit if you have it in your hand is the first rule. Play Blacks if you don't have that suit and don't bang heads with your partner if they have won the hand is the second rule."

I nodded as Clarence finished dealing. I received thirteen cards that were divided into four colors: Blacks, Whites, Blues, and Reds. Blacks were always the wild cards and higher than any other color. Whoever played the first card led the hand, and you had to play that color unless you did not have it. Then you could play a Black to win the hand. The cards were numbered one to ten and included three face cards of each color. The face cards were Kammbi, Alicia, and Dexter. Kammbi was the highest face card, followed by Alicia and Dexter. I had six Blacks in my hand, including the Black Kammbi and Black Dexter cards. And I had four Whites and three Blues. No Reds.

"Place your silver bet in the center of the table," Fat Vincent said.

Everyone placed two silver chains in the middle of the table. I was grateful to get the weight off my neck. I felt like I could think more clearly without it.

"All right, Diondray, let's see you what you got," Clarence said. He placed a Red Kammbi down to start the hand.

Bonita played a Red Five next. Fat Vincent followed with a Red Seven. I played a Black Dexter card after him.

"Whoa! You don't have reds?" Clarence added.

"I don't," I replied.

Bonita smiled. "You don't have to answer him, Diondray. Follow my rules and play to win."

I nodded as Bonita collected the cards for that winning hand. I led the next hand and played a White Kammbi card.

"Your partner learns fast, Bonita," Fat Vincent said and played a White One card.

"Do you think I would not bring someone who did not know how to play?" Bonita replied and played a White Three card. I wondered again how she'd known I could do this.

Clarence stared hard at his cards. Then he played a White Ten, and Bonita collected the winning hand. I sensed that was the last White card he had, and I would lead with another color in the next hand.

"At the silver mine, your woman mentioned that you are the one," Clarence commented. "I will admit that she seemed believable and convinced about you."

"Only because she was pretty," Fat Vincent interjected. "You are fooling nobody with that comment."

Clarence grinned at Fat Vincent. I did not like him calling Maisa my woman. But I knew that was not going to change. "Maisa has been with me since we left Santa Sophia," I replied and played the Black Kammbi to start the next hand. "She believes I'm the one to fulfill Oscar's prophecy."

Fat Vincent gave me a sharp look. "I did not think a person from south of the Great Forest would believe in that prophecy." He played a Black Two card.

"I'm not sure if I totally believe in it. But I've made it this far on the expedition, and I want to see it through."

"I believe he is the one," Bonita said solemnly and played a Black Four card.

"You don't believe in that, Bonita," Clarence said sharply and played a Black Five card. "Heard that story all of my life. It's been over two hundred years since Oscar Ortega traveled throughout this land. Ain't no prophecy happening in my lifetime. Plus, the morrims and diakonos of the city keep treating Dexter like he did something wrong. It don't sit right with me or most of us."

Fat Vincent nodded at Clarence's comment. I led the next hand with a Blue Kammbi and said, "Dexter clearly disobeyed the river god's command to follow Oscar Ortega's teachings. Why do you treat him like he did the right thing?"

Fat Vincent played a Blue Five and said, "Because we were taught all our lives that he was a bad person for his disobedience. And that's not right. Alicia loved him and said as much in her section in the Book of Kammbi."

Bonita smiled and played her blue card. She knew I would have to convince Fat Vincent and Clarence that their belief in Dexter was wrong. I sensed that if I could do it here, then I would have a chance to change minds all over Alicia.

"No Blues!" Clarence erupted and played a Black Six to win the hand. "How are you, someone from south of the Great Forest, going to convince us that Dexter's disobedience was wrong? Have you even read the Book of Kammbi?"

Fat Vincent collected the winning hand. It was the first one of the game. I still had Blues in my hand, and I hoped Bonita did not. I was getting the hang of this, and all of my father's teachings were coming back to me. I wanted to win Fat Vincent's silver and stay for the rest of the evening.

"Maybe he can do it at the Festival of the River God." Fat Vincent said.

"How is that going to happen? The people are not going to let him speak about Dexter like that in front of them," Clarence countered as he played a White Kammbi card. I'd thought he was out of white cards. I was wrong.

"Diondray writes themilys," Bonita said as I played a White Eight card.

"Themilys?" Big Daddy Red said and played a White Seven card.

"Words of wisdom," Bonita answered and played a White Three card.

Fat Vincent collected their second winning hand. "Words of wisdom have been said by the morrims in this city for years. Doesn't work. They still treat Dexter like he did the worst thing in the entire land."

"An act of passha," Clarence added.

"Of course, everything is an act of passha. If I go to the bathroom wrong it's an act of passha."

Everyone at the table laughed as Clarence led with a White Alicia card for the next hand.

"Diondray, can you read one of your themilys right now?"

"Bonita! We are playing Blacks right now. Nothing comes before the cards," Fat Vincent said sternly.

Bonita got up from the table and started to move her hips seductively. "You said I have the sweetest backside in the house tonight. If you like it as much as you say you do, I hope you will honor my request."

Fat Vincent's expression instantly changed as he stared at Bonita's enormous backside. "All right, let me hear this themily, Diondray."

Bonita sat down and smiled at Fat Vincent. I guessed they did have a relationship after all.

I reached for my bag and pulled out a themily from the left pocket. The themilys in that pocket were some of the first I'd written when I'd just started reading at Aliki Park back home.

People can read into something whatever they want or whatever they hope for or whatever they wish for it to be. But can people read the truth and accept it? They say the truth cuts like a knife into butter. Actually, it can cut like a knife into flesh, and most people don't want the pain associated with the truth. However, pain can be our greatest lesson and teacher. Pleasure can numb your senses and make you sloppy. Pain can sharpen those senses and make you aware of what's happening in the moment. Pain transforms one into becoming what they are supposed to be. Pain, like truth, exposes who you really are and what you believe.

The entire house was silent as I finished reading. I felt everyone's eyes on me as I looked up. They all clapped. I was delighted at their response.

Bonita stood up from her seat and announced, "You will hear more words of wisdom at the Festival of the River God."

The crowd nodded, and I realized why Bonita had brought me here. I had to convince the right people to listen to my themilys in order for them to be receptive to changing their minds about Dexter and the river god. I was grateful for her gesture in bringing me here this evening.

"Diondray!"

I looked over my right shoulder and saw Maisa, Diakono Copperwith, and Annalisa coming toward our table. They didn't look happy.

"I found you!" Maisa said as she arrived at our table. "The hotel employee was right. He said you would be here because of her." She glared daggers at Bonita, who didn't seem to care.

"Yes, I'm here with Bonita. Everything is going well. I've made some new friends." I replied.

Fat Vincent and Clarence smiled at the new visitors. Clarence examined Maisa. "I told you she was pretty, Fat Vincent. She's got a backside almost as nice as Bonita's. Not quite as big. But nice and round."

Laughter erupted around us after his comment. Maisa smiled at his compliment despite herself. Annalisa, on the other hand, looked outraged.

"Let's go, Diondray. The one who is going to fulfill Oscar's prophecy should not be in a place like this. You probably committed an act of passha as soon as you came through the doors," Annalisa said in disgust.

Annalisa and Diakono Copperwith had been my spiritual mentors since this journey began, but this time, I didn't think she was right. I was sure I knew my purpose here. "Bonita brought me here as a guest, and I will leave with her," I replied.

"Diondray, I'm with my wife on this one. Being here could lead to trouble."

"Diakono Copperwith, did not Oscar Ortega relate to the tribes before he began with his teachings? Did he not take time to connect with them?"

"He did."

"And when Kammbi lived amongst us in the land, did he not spend his time amongst all the people of the tribes? Not just the elders and those who believed and followed him. So I'm following in the same manner. I'm relating to these people, and I just read them a themily everyone loved."

"Diondray is right about that, Diakono," Fat Vincent said. "He came here to play Blacks and not look down on us. The diakonos and morrims of this city have never treated the people here in this house like that. And if he is the one to fulfill Oscar's prophecy, then most of us in here could become believers and followers in Kammbi again."

Diakono Copperwith was silent and stared at Fat Vincent. Suddenly, he turned to Annalisa and Maisa. "Let's go," he said to them.

"What if Diondray commits an act of passha?" Annalisa protested.

"I believe something larger is at play here. Diondray has to make his own decisions."

Diakono Copperwith and Annalisa turned from the table and started to leave. Maisa remained at the table next to me and stared with sadness.

"I thought we were together on this expedition. I did not think you could be swayed so easily," she said and turned to leave.

I was not swayed as easily as Maisa thought. However, I could see how those who believed and follow Kammbi treated those who did not. If I was the one who was supposed to fulfill Oscar's prophecy, then that kind of behavior would have to change. I had learned in my reading of the Book of Kammbi that these teachings were meant for everyone. Believers could not treat those nonbelievers as second-class citizens. That would never work.

"Her backside is not as sweet as Bonita's. I would take it, though. You better not let that one go, Diondray. She loves you," Clarence said as I watched Maisa leave the house.

Chapter 13

I became a regular guest of Fat Vincent after winning his silver that first night. I never wore it outside of his duplex. It was gaudy and not to my taste. My playing got better, and I became one of the best players at the duplex. I also got to read some more themilys, and I talked with a lot of players about their interpretation of Dexter's disobedience and the worship of the river god.

Most of them still disagreed with me, citing the same reason that Fat Vincent had given on my first night here. The believers and followers of Kammbi in this city treated the players and the people throughout the River district as apostates, and they had criticized the sacred Festival of the River God as heretical. To the people of this district, that attitude toward them was unforgivable.

Despite their stance and objections to my interpretation of the Book of Kammbi, many of the players as well as the people of the district who came to the house because of Fat Vincent's influence listened to my story and how my life had changed since I arrived north of the Great Forest. A portion of them could not believe someone with my skin color could actually be the one to fulfill Oscar's prophecy. However, Bonita Golde spoke up for me, and she had a way of convincing people. I was surprised at how quickly she believed in my story, even though we had just met. Because of her, I could tell that I was starting to win some of them over. But they would reiterate that the Festival of the River God would reveal the truth about me, and they insisted that they wanted the konseho of Kammbi to accept the festival as one of the main traditions of this city.

It was the thirteenth day in the eight month of Gus and eighteen more days until the Festival of the River God. We had been in Alicia for thirty days, and I was really beginning to connect with some of the people here. Diakono Copperwith and Annalisa continued to work with the morrim of the kahall of Alicia on gaining the support of the other morrims in the city.

Mr. Cortes and Felicia spent their time between helping Maisa get ownership of Silver Mine 12 and returning to Santa Teresa to take care of matters with the company. I had not seen much of them in the last ten days. They might be members of our expedition, but it was clear that for them, business still came first. They would catch up with the rest of us by the Festival of the River God. That day would be our next to the last here in Alicia and my opportunity to show most of the city how they could correctly interpret the story of Dexter's disobedience. Maisa remained distant as I went with Bonita Golde to Fat Vincent's house. I assured her that Bonita's intentions were above board and that there was not any kind of relationship between us.

I explained all of that to Maisa even though I did not feel I had to do it. Still, I had to admit that Clarence's comments from the first night of playing Blacks resonated with me. Maisa *did* love me, and I could see that her intentions were true. Was I a fool because I didn't make a move to reciprocate? With the ownership of the mine as a real possibility, she had an opportunity to make sure her family name would finally be remembered. Would she want to stay in Alicia to run the mine? Would she want me to stay with her after we met with the konseho of Kammbi? Those questions came to me as I realized that her love was not the only motivation she had for being on this expedition. With all the tension between us, she'd begun spending her time between Mr. Cortes and Felicia and the Copperwiths.

I had all of those things on my mind as I continued writing my themily for the Festival of the River God. I knew this themily had to address the separation the people in the River district felt from the morrims, the diakonos, and other believers and followers of Kammbi. It had been made clear to me that the people like Fat Vincent, Clarence, and others at the duplex were treated like second-class citizens of the city. I thought back to how Annalisa had reacted when she was inside the duplex. Her look of disdain affirmed the people's feelings about how the religious establishment of the city treated them. And that contradicted everything I read in the Book of Kammbi. Kammbi believed his teachings were for everyone and reiterated that during his time in the land. He chose Oscar Ortega from Guadharra to be his most prominent disciple as a result of that belief. Now, over two hundred fifty years later, I had been chosen to continue on spreading one of Kammbi's strongest teachings—that everyone was equal and valuable.

This themily had to capture that belief to make people like Fat Vincent and Clarence feel welcome and to gain the attention of the morrims, diakonos, and others of the religious establishment. It needed to help them see that the teachings of Kammbi were truly for everyone. I hoped that having a man from south of the Great Forest telling them so would make that realization clear.

#

I attended the kahall service at the kahall of Alicia three days later with the Copperwiths and Maisa. Diakono Copperwith wanted me to hear Morrim Paranga teach about choices. Morrim Paranga gave a matter-of-fact teaching about the subject, and my attention was elsewhere during the service. I'd spent the past three days writing and rewriting that themily and trying to nail the division between the religious establishment and the people of the River district. It brought to mind the division back home between the east side and west side residents. I would get so angry at how Uncle Xavier and Mother viewed the west side residents as inferior and not worthy of discussion. The anger from those thoughts rose within me and gave enough inspiration to finish writing the latest version of my themily.

The service ended a couple of hours later, and we were invited to Morrim Paranga's favorite restaurant, where he went to eat after every kahall service. The restaurant was a short drive from the kahall of Alicia, and the owner had the morrim's preferred spot ready when we arrived.

We were seated at a long table in the middle of the restaurant. I noticed how the other patrons bowed their heads as the morrim and diakonos walked through the restaurant toward the table.

I caught people starting at my shorts and could tell they were trying to understand how a man could wear a piece of clothing that stopped at the knee. Their bemused looks made me feel a little uncomfortable. I clutched the travel bag over my right shoulder, wanting to pace. Diakono Copperwith had asked me to bring the Book of Kammbi, because he felt it would be needed today.

"Welcome Morrim Paranga, diakonos, and other guests," the restaurant owner said. "I will get the usual meal for the morrim and diakonos. Today's special is roasted beef over brown rice and corn. Any takers?"

"Actually, I will take today's special, Don Carlo," Morrim Paranga replied and sat down at the head of the table. "I want to thank you for getting our table ready to add some more guests."

"Of course, Morrim Paranga. Don Carlo's is your home for food away from the kahall. Any guests of yours are welcome guests as well," he replied and bowed to the morrim.

Don Carlo's jet-black ponytail extended to the middle of his back. I hoped that hair didn't get into any food while he served his patrons.

"I will do the same, Don Carlo," the diakono sitting on the left of the morrim said. He had a prominent nose that covered most of his face. Even though his reddish-brown complexion was like the morrim's and most of the people I had seen so far in Alicia, his nose made me think he had some connection with people south of the Great Forest as well.

Don Carlo took the rest of the orders at the table. "I would like to order havannahs," I said.

Don Carlo smiled. "Good choice, young man. We make the best havannahs in the city. How many would you like? Three, six, or nine?"

I remembered how small those havannahs were at lunch with the silver miners, and I was hungry. "Six," I answered.

"Got it," Don Carlo replied and left the table.

"Diondray, I've heard you have been spending time in the River district amongst the people, trying to convince them that their view of Dexter and the river god is incorrect," Morrim Paranga said as he raised his glass to take a drink.

I appreciated the fact that he did not waste time with small talk. "I have been spending time playing Blacks with Fat Vincent and Clarence in the River district. I've learned a lot in the short time we've been together."

The diakono to the right of the morrim gave a contemptuous look. His complexion was closer to Maisa's and Annalisa's, and his bald head and piercing eyes gave off an unapproachable presence.

"What have you learned?" the diakono with the prominent nose said. Unlike his compatriot, he seemed genuinely interested.

"I've learned that there is quite a division between people like Fat Vincent and Clarence and those like yourself and the morrim who believe and follow Kammbi."

"There is supposed to be," the baldhead diakono interjected. "It has been clear since the Book of Kammbi was written and published in the city of Issabella that Dexter's disobedience was an act of passha."

"Diakono Ayala is correct. And we have attempted for years to educate those people to see it the correct way. But they have refused." Morrim Paranga added.

I pushed back from the table slightly. "Here's the problem. Both you and Diakono Ayala have addressed people like Fat Vincent and Clarence as 'those people.' Diakono Ayala just said that Dexter committed an act of passha—no discussion allowed. You have already created separation with that kind of talk. I do agree with you about the words of the Book of Kammbi, but Alicia did love her husband and wrote glowing words about him throughout her section. The people in the River district feel that version of Dexter has never been taught by any morrim in this city."

Don Carlo brought our food and served everyone. Morrim Paranga and the diakono with the prominent nose nodded. Diakono Ayala still had a contemptuous look on his face.

"Diakono Ayala's face adds credence to Diondray's analysis," Maisa added.

Diakono Ayala gave Maisa a piercing stare. She returned it. I'd been surprised at how quiet she was since we left the hotel for the kahall service. I'd thought she would talk to me about Bonita Golde and my time at Fat Vincent's duplex, but she had remained silent until now.

"I will admit there has been a severing between the people you've mentioned and ourselves," Morrim Paranga said, trying to cut the tension. "However, we've tried to bridge the divide, and they still cling to that incorrect belief. It's not a small matter, Diondray; they actually worship the river god! That's a huge division from us. We cannot force people to the truth."

I had eaten a couple of havannahs. They were delicious. I was not sure about Don Carlo's claim of them being the best in the city, but they were much better than the ones I'd eaten at the silver mine. The aroma from the meal seeped into my nostrils, and I wanted to eat the rest of the havannahs before we continued with this discussion. Unfortunately, everyone was waiting for me to respond.

"People have to feel their viewpoint is listened to and considered before they will consider another," I said. "It seems to me that morrims and diakonos in Alicia throughout the years have dismissed their concerns and do not even consider why they are holding on to an incorrect belief." "Why should we?" the diakono with the prominent nose retorted. "Their belief is clearly wrong."

"Diakono Parra is correct. Why should we? The truth divides and excludes," Diakono Ayala added.

"The truth heals as well. Until you as the religious establishment actually listen to the people, the divide will continue. I have read the Book of Kammbi from the Ryianza to the Baramesa, and it is clear that the teachings of Kammbi are for everyone. Including people like Fat Vincent and Clarence."

"Oh, have you? I find that hard to believe," Diakono Ayala said defiantly. "From south of the Great Forest, have you ever even *seen* a copy of the Book of Kammbi?"

I looked over at Diakono Copperwith. He said, "It's time, Diondray."

I grabbed my travel bag from underneath the chair and pulled out the Book of Kammbi. I held it up at the table. "This is the Book of Kammbi that Oscar Ortega brought with him when he tried to reconcile with his son, Charles. I found out about it in the third month of Carm from my Aunt Maxina. This copy of the Book of Kammbi had been stored in my city ever since Oscar Ortega left after being rejected by Charles. And in the past five months, I have read this Book of Kammbi almost every night, trying to understand why I am the one being chosen to fulfill Oscar's prophecy. I have studied and pored over it. There is much I don't understand, but what I *do* understand, more then anything, is that these teachings are for everyone. Having someone from south of the Great Forest be the carrier of that message is just more evidence of that fact."

Morrim Paranga and the diakonos were silent. They stared at the Book of Kammbi. Their faces looked like they had seen someone who was dead and came back to life.

"My Kammbi, it is actually going to happen," Morrim Paranga replied softly.

#

Mr. Cortes and Felicia returned to Alicia earlier than I'd expected. It was fourteen days until the Festival of the River God. They planned to stay in the city to help Maisa with the final paperwork needed in order for the konseho of Kammbi to transfer ownership of Silver Mine 12 to her.

Diakono Copperwith and Annalisa continued to work with Morrim Paranga and Diakonos Parra and Ayala to get their support at the Festival of the River God. I had begun to convince Morrim Paranga and the diakonos of the rightness of my cause after showing them the Book of Kammbi. At first, the diakonos did not believe it was the actual copy that Oscar Ortega had carried with him south of the Great Forest all those years ago. However, I handed it to them during dinner at Don Carlo's Restaurant, and by the end of the meal Morrim Paranga and Diakono Parra were convinced it was real.

Diakono Ayala held onto his disbelief while I told them about my family history and how I'd found out that I was a descendant of Oscar Ortega. He started to come around when Diakono Copperwith explained how he had met me in Santa Sophia and the Eternal Comforter had orchestrated everything so far on our journey. Annalisa added her comments about my character, and I could tell that convinced Diakono Ayala to believe in who I was. I thought Annalisa had seen me in a different light after that first night at Fat Vincent's duplex and my newfound love for playing Blacks.

Those were the thoughts on my mind when I arrived at Silver Mine 12 with Mr. Cortes, Felicia, and Maisa. Jorge Feldman greeted us like he had during our first visit. Maisa occupied most of his attention, and she seemed more receptive to his flirtations since that prior visit.

"I wanted to take everyone into another section of the mine where we have found a new silver deposit," Jorge Feldman said after leading us for several minutes down a different tunnel than the one from our first visit. Your presence, Mr. Cortes, along with Maisa's, has brought the blessing of the Eternal Comforter with you."

Maisa giggled at Jorge Feldman's flattery. I was not amused and wanted to leave the mine as soon as possible. Both Mr. Cortes and Jorge Feldman made me uncomfortable, though for different reasons.

"We have Diondray to thank for any blessing from the Eternal Comforter," Mr. Cortes said.

I appreciated his compliment, and I had to admit he had done everything he could to help me feel comfortable around him since I'd passed out in his office. But I could not shake that sick, unnerved feeling I had in his presence. I pondered that thought and followed our group into an open area where workers were sifting through gravel for silver.

"Indeed, Diondray has been a blessing," Jorge Feldman said and whistled to get the workers' attention. "So much that our workers wanted to see him again."

The workers looked up from the conveyor belt and joined us in the center of the room. I glanced at Maisa. Jorge Feldman had a mischievous smile on his face while he checked her out. She turned away from his ogling and smiled at me. I hoped that would begin our road to recovery for whatever was going on between us.

"I've heard you have become quite the player at Blacks," Phyllis asked and took off her helmet.

"I have," I replied. "Word gets around." Clarence grinned as he looked at me and then cut his eyes to Maisa. I wanted to laugh as I thought about his comments on my first night at Fat Vincent's.

"Word does get around. We all live in the River district and know about Fat Vincent's duplex. It gets talked about when you take his silver."

"I did not know he was that good of a player at Blacks." Clarence interjected.

Phyllis whirled her head at him. Clarence looked away, not wanting to face her wrath.

I glanced at Mr. Cortes and Felicia, who seemed taken aback by Phyllis's gesture toward Clarence.

"I have won quite a bit of Fat Vincent's silver," I said. "If I'd known I was coming here today, I would have brought some of it for you."

Phyllis gave a slight smile. "Nice offer. No thanks. I don't wear it either. Only work for it. Plus, there is another reason we wanted to see you today."

I nodded for her to go on.

"Fat Vincent has spread word throughout the River district that you are going to be reading some words of wisdom at the Festival of the River God on the first day of Berm."

"Correct. It is called a themily."

"He believes you are the one to fulfill Oscar's prophecy. And this themily of yours will prove it."

"I hope so."

She nodded. "We will all be there as well and looking forward to hearing this themily."

I scanned the workers and saw their reddish-brown and black faces nod in agreement with Phyllis.

"You have gained the support of the people in the River district. I did not think that would happen so quickly. I hope your themily proves their support was right," Phyllis continued.

Chapter 14

With five days until the Festival of the River God, I had been spending my time between working on the themily in the mornings and playing at Fat Vincent's duplex in the evenings. Some nights he invited me over outside of playing Blacks, and we just sat and talked. Maisa went with me to keep an eye on Bonita. We had talked quite a bit since that last visit to Silver Mine 12, and she finally understood that Bonita Golde was only trying to help our cause for the second expedition—but she still didn't like to leave me alone with her.

I began to learn from Fat Vincent about the Festival of the River God. Nothing about it was written in the Book of Kammbi. A member of Dexter's family had started the festival a few years after his death. That family member felt Dexter was being ignored for his contributions to the creation of the city of Alicia. Dexter's leadership had gotten the tribe back then to start the city, even though, he did not believe in Kammbi and would not follow Oscar Ortega's teachings. The family member believed that the tribe had ostracized Dexter for continuing to believe in the river god and not Kammbi. Over the years, that belief about Dexter had disseminated even among those who believed and followed Kammbi up to the current time.

Fat Vincent guided me through the River district, and I learned how much influence he had here. Blacks was an important part of the culture, and the one who controlled how it was played in the district earned the respect of the people.

I also found out that not everyone in the city attended the Festival of the River God. Mostly people of the River district and some from the Hill district attended the festival. The majority of the people in Alicia stayed away from the Festival of the River God because they did not want to promote a false teaching that was not from the Book of Kammbi. But that had only made the division between the people worse.

I felt it would be crucial to have Morrim Paranga and the other morrims of the city at the Festival of the River God. Diakono Copperwith and Annalisa spent their time convincing the morrims of the city to come. I had gained an advocate in Morrim Paranga after our dinner at Don Carlo's. He began telling the other morrims throughout the city about me. He told them I had Oscar Ortega's copy of the Book of Kammbi. I let Diakono Copperwith take it to show those other morrims that it actually existed. They were stunned to see it in front of their faces after reading and studying about it most of their lives. Like Morrim Paranga, they became convinced that Oscar's prophecy could be fulfilled in their lifetimes.

I knew all the morrims of the city had to be at the Festival of the River God. The only way the city of Alicia could unite as one would be to have everyone represented there. My themily had to address the truth about what was written in the Book of Kammbi as well as the sentiment of the people who thought Dexter had been treated poorly over the years. I needed to make everyone feel that they were being heard, while still upholding the truth.

I had written several versions in the last few days, and Maisa heard me read them as practice sessions. She offered suggestions, and they made sense. I made those changes until I finally felt this version of the themily would be the one I would read at the festival.

As I finished penning the last line of the themily in the evening, I decided to kneel and pray to the Eternal Comforter. It was the first time I had prayed since being in these cities north of the Great Forest. I thought it was the right thing to do, and if I were to become a believer and follower of Kammbi, then prayer would soon become an essential part of my life.

#

"I have shown you everything you need to know about the silver mine," Jorge Feldman announced to Maisa during breakfast.

Everyone at the table clapped at his announcement. We were in the hotel's restaurant for breakfast. "Mr. Cortes and Felicia have helped you with the ownership transfer paperwork. If you get approval from the konseho of Kammbi, they will effectively take my place as the administrators of Silver Mine 12."

I sat between Maisa and Felicia, with Mr. Cortes and Jorge Feldman at the opposite ends of the table. The hotel restaurant staff had opened just for us and brought an elaborate breakfast of eggs, bacon, sweet bread with jelly, cherries, and cherry juice.

Maisa's smile while clapping was gone from her face. "That was not the agreement. I wanted you to stay on after the ownership transfer."

Jorge Feldman looked flushed and lowered his eyes.

"Jorge will be reassigned to another part of my business," Mr Cortes interjected. "Even though Felicia will take over his role upon approval from the konseho, I did not want to lose someone like him."

Maisa gave a dagger stare to Mr. Cortes. "Is this the reason you wanted to come on the expedition?"

Mr. Cortes seemed taken aback by Maisa's accusation. "You know why I came on the expedition. I believe just like you that

Diondray is the one to fulfill Oscar's prophecy. And I want to help him to fulfill this prophecy in any way I can. Helping you with the ownership of this mine came with good intentions. As Felicia delved into the complexities with Jorge on how to operate the mine, we felt that more of a hands-on approach would be needed."

"There's no guarantee of the approval from the konseho of Kammbi," Felicia added coldly. "And if you don't get it, then Mr. Cortes and I will have basically done this work for free."

Maisa glared at Felicia. The two women had made a truce after their initial meeting. But I felt that had come to an end after Jorge's announcement. I had been kept out of the discussions about the ownership transfer of the mine, and clearly whatever had been discussed between the three of them had been deliberately misinterpreted.

"Being honest about your intentions, Mr. Cortes, would have been the first place to start," Maisa replied and got up from the table.

"Don't leave. We are looking out for your interests," Mr. Cortes replied and rose from the table.

I got up from the table as well because I did not want to be in his presence without Maisa. Maybe the uneasiness I had about him was starting to come to fruition. The problem was that *I* had allowed him to come along on this expedition. There had to be a reason why I had allowed him to come despite my discomfort. I just wasn't sure what it was.

"I now have Annalisa's belief that you are trying to become the second coming of Diego Carranza," Maisa shot back and left. I glanced at the look of disappointment on Mr Cortes's face, and I followed her.

Bonita met Maisa and I as we exited the restaurant. I had not seen her since my last visit to Fat Vincent's house. I wanted to thank her for helping me connect with the people of the River district.

"I'm off at three o'clock. Can we talk?" she said while looking at me.

"You can talk to both of us."

"Maisa!"

"I know what you have told me, Diondray," Maisa said, standing next to me. Bonita had a surprised look on her face. "But I want to be with you for any conversations with her."

"All right, I can talk to both of you," Bonita replied in exasperation.

I walked away with Maisa, realizing her suspicion of Bonita had not gone away. I guessed I still did not know what love was truly about.

#

Bonita wanted to meet Maisa and me in the hotel's lobby. There were some oversized chairs in the back corner. She was sitting in one of those chairs when Maisa and I arrived.

"Is there something wrong?" I asked Bonita as I sat down next to her.

"Some people in the River district want to back out of the festival," she replied and looked away.

"Why?"

"They've heard about how many morrims and their parishioners are coming to the festival. We have never had any of them come before. They feel the festival is our way of honoring people in the Book of Kammbi, and they do not want to be lectured about how inaccurate our account is."

"Do the people of the River district want to change and honor the correct version?" Maisa asked from a seat across from Bonita. I wished she had not asked that.

Bonita grimaced. "You have not spent any time amongst the people of the River district. We know all too well what the correct version is. The Festival of the River God is bigger than that. And having most of the city's morrims and their parishioners at the festival will remind us of how incorrect we are."

"Can Fat Vincent invite those who want to back out to his duplex tonight?" I asked.

Bonita's expression changed from a grimace to a slight chuckle. "Fat Vincent's duplex is not that big. Not everybody could fit inside."

"Not everyone. The leaders, or those who are the most opposed to it. I want to speak to them."

"I can call Fat Vincent to see if he can get them."

"Great," I replied. "Let me know as soon as you hear." "What are you going to do, Diondray?" Maisa asked.

I smiled. "I have some words of wisdom to share just for this situation."

Bonita leaned forward with an earnest expression on her face. "I believe you are the one who will fulfill Oscar's prophecy," she said. "Because of you, I started reading the Book of Kammbi again. It has been the first time since I was a child that I've read it. I believe you are related to Oscar Ortega."

"I am."

#

I spent the next few hours going through my travel bag, trying to find a themily that would address the River district people. They did not want the morrims and parishioners reminding them that they believed in the wrong god. I had to find a way to address their concern while validating the authentic version of the story that was written in the Book of Kammbi. Regardless of how those River district people felt about it, I was here to fulfill Oscar's prophecy and ultimately become a believer and follower of Kammbi. I had to honor that position no matter what happened at the Festival of the River God.

I pulled out one of my earliest themilys. I'd written it when I first left the family home. No one would have stopped or objected to a member of the Azur family reading a themily at Aliki Park, but even so, back then I was still considered an outsider. I knew quite a few of those westsiders resented me being at the park at all.

I had finally gained some acceptance with this themily, and I believed it would be appropriate for tonight.

After I had made some corrections to it, I phoned Diakono Copperwith in his room and asked him to come with me to Fat Vincent's duplex.

Diakono Copperwith paused before he gave me an answer. "They want to back out because they feel threatened by the morrims."

"Yes," I answered. "And it would remind them that what they believe is incorrect."

"My presence tonight with you would remind them of the same thing."

I could hear the reluctance in his voice. He did not want to go to Fat Vincent's duplex for a second time. But I needed him.

"That's possible," I said. "However, I want to show them that there are those who believe and follow Kammbi who are willing to put aside their differences for unity. I believe this kind of gesture would be beneficial for our work at the Festival of the River God."

"That is a persuasive point, Diondray. However, I do not feel a Diakono should be in a place like that. I felt extremely uncomfortable when I was there the last time."

I held back a sigh. So that was the real reason he didn't want to come. "I could tell that you were uncomfortable . . . and that you think it is inappropriate for a diakono to be in an establishment like that."

"Yes. Annalisa does not want me to go back there either."

I heard Annalisa in the background telling Diakono Copperwith not to go. How was I going to convince him to put aside his hesitations?

Inspiration came to me suddenly. "Remember the last chapter in the Ryianza, where Kammbi tells the story of the lost animal? A man owned a big house and a bunch of land where he raised all types of animals. That man kept a good watch over them. However, one day he lost one of those animals, and he looked everywhere on his land, trying to find it. The man was distraught but determined to find where that lost animal had gone. It took several days, but the man found it on the other side of town, where it had been caught by another landowner who was preparing to kill it for food. The man pleaded with the landowner to give him back that animal. The landowner refused and said, 'What was lost to you has been found by me. And the finder gets to keep.' If you remember, the man made an offer to buy that animal at whatever price the landowner wanted. The landowner was surprised by the man's offer and decided to sell the animal to him for quite a few pieces of silver. The man got his lost animal and brought him back home. He embraced that lost animal in front of the others and told them, 'I would go anywhere and do anything to bring something that was lost back home.'"

Diakono Copperwith was silent on the other end of the phone.

"Diakono Copperwith, are you there?" I asked.

"Yes, Diondray," he finally replied. "I will go with you tonight."

I tried to hide the sound of my grin. "See you downstairs at the autobus."

"Thank you for reminding me of that story," he replied and ended the phone call.

I'd read that lost animal story several times since I'd been in the city of Alicia. I'd had no idea why I was drawn to it so strongly. But I knew why now. I began to believe this was another sign of the presence of the Eternal Comforter in my life.

#

The drive from the hotel was quiet. It seemed like everyone was trying to gather their thoughts and get ready. Maisa and Annalisa had chosen to come as well. I glanced at all three, wanting to give them some reassurance, but they were focused on their thoughts and did not return my look.

I knocked on Fat Vincent's door and entered the duplex. Maisa and the Copperwiths followed. I saw Fat Vincent, Bonita Golde, Phyllis, and four other people sitting on the same chairs we used for playing Blacks in the middle of the living room. They looked up as we approached.

"You are on time, Diondray," Fat Vincent said. He pointed to some chairs opposite of him. "That is a great quality to have. A lot of people treat time like it's flexible rather than fixed."

"When you are invited to someone's home, it's important to be there on time," I replied and sat down.

Diakono Copperwith, Annalisa, and Maisa sat in the chairs next to me. There was a glass of cherry juice in the armrest of each chair. I grabbed my glass and took a couple of swallows.

"I thought this man with the words of wisdom was coming by himself tonight," one of the others remarked.

I looked at the man. He had a pudgy face and bloodshot eyes that made me wonder if he'd had any alcohol before coming to Fat Vincent's duplex. I did not want anyone to be inebriated for this meeting. He sat next to two other men and a woman on the left side of Fat Vincent.

"Diakono Copperwith, Annalisa Copperwith, and Maisa Merez are my companions. They have been with me since my arrival here north of the Great Forest. I asked them to come with me," I answered.

"I saw the pretty one twice at the silver mine. I have not seen the diakono and the other woman before," Phyllis said. "But I don't sense anything wrong with them being here."

Maisa blushed at her compliment. I knew I had Phyllis on my side. I believed that would be needed tonight.

"I have no problem with the diakono and his wife in my house," Fat Vincent said. "I know they do not approve of my card playing. But I believe their presence tonight shows they are willing to step outside of their normal view to hear from those they disagree with." He smiled at me.

"Your card playing is gambling," Annalisa snapped.

Diakono Copperwith placed his right hand over his wife's hands and remained silent. The thin smiles on their faces revealed something else.

"Yes, it is gambling, Mrs. Copperwith. I know that is an act of passha from your view. I still appreciate you coming tonight."

I saw no reason to avoid the topic of the night, so I jumped right in. "I understand that you all have objections to having most of the morrims and their parishioners at the Festival of the River God four days from now. But I believe the only way the division in the city can be bridged is by having them attend."

"You requested for the morrims and their parishioners to attend the Festival of the River God?" Bonita Golde asked.

"He did," Maisa shot back. Her disapproval of Bonita Golde was still apparent. "Diakono Copperwith, Annalisa, and I have been working with the morrims to get them to attend."

"They were reluctant to come just as much as you all are to have them. However, they have come to believe that Diondray Azur is the one who will fulfill Oscar's prophecy. As morrims, they want to do the will of Kammbi and the Eternal Comforter instead of their own," Diakono Copperwith said.

Fat Vincent, Bonita Golde, and Phyllis seemed to have embraced Diakono Copperwith's comment. I knew they were on board. But the other four were going to be a harder sell.

"After all of these years and the many Festivals of the River God that have passed, the morrims have finally decided to come," the second of them, a woman, said. "All it took was this young man from south of the Great Forest to say a few words of wisdom. Seems too convenient for the rest of us here." I finished my glass of cherry juice and faced the woman. She had a similar complexion to myself and wore large silver earrings that dangled from her ears. "Are you a believer and follower of Kammbi?" I asked.

"Not anymore," she replied tersely. "I read the Book of Kammbi as a child. But all I heard over the years is how wrong Dexter was for his belief in the river god. Dexter has been treated like a criminal—just like the rest of us."

"Do you believe in the river god?"

The woman started to reply but was silenced momentarily by my question. "I do," she answered softly. "And seeing his presence each year at the festival has strengthened my belief in him."

I glanced at the other three objectors, and they nodded in approval.

"The river god's presence in our lives gives all of us something that the morrims and diakonos do not want to understand," the third person of the four added.

I turned my attention to this objector. He had a long ponytail going down his back and wore several silver necklaces. He could have been someone who played Blacks here at the duplex.

"What understanding should we have?" Diakono Copperwith asked.

I turned my head to the diakono, surprised that he had asked a question. I'd thought he would remain silent as a show of support for me.

"That everyone needs to believe in something bigger than themselves, even if it seems wrong to those in power," the fourth person answered.

I glanced at the final objector and noticed his large reddish-brown hands, which he held close to his face.

"I do understand that quite clearly," Diakono Copperwith replied. "I want to apologize on behalf of the morrims and diakonos of this city for treating all the people of this district unfairly. There should have been dialogue and understanding of why you believe in the river god. Instead, there has been division and mistrust. The river god is in the Book of Kammbi for a reason, and that should have started a dialogue for discussion."

The four objectors were taken aback by the diakono's words. I could tell they had never heard someone in his position speak to them like that. I'd known his presence would be needed.

"Are you concerned that the morrims' attendance at the festival will cause people like yourselves to become believers and followers of Kammbi?" Diakono Copperwith asked.

"We are not concerned about that possibility," the first objector answered sharply. "All of us are adults and should be allowed to make up our own minds." The other three looked at him in disgust.

"What your answer reveals, and their demeanors tell me, is that the Book of Kammbi is true—and you know it. And you would all rather remain in opposition to that belief than accept it?" I added.

"You do not know how those who don't believe and follow Kammbi have been treated in this city," the woman snapped. "However, the diakono's apology felt sincere, and getting that kind of acknowledgment from the other morrims and diakonos could be the first step in coming together. That's why it's important for the morrims and their parishioners to attend the festival. They need to understand the real division between both sides and begin to bridge that divide. We all live in the same city and should be united."

"United. That's like having a dream of finding silver in your backyard," the third objector said. "It will never happen."

"I agree on that point," Fat Vincent interjected. "I don't believe the city of Alicia can ever be united."

I got up from the chair and started pacing. I had to find the right words to get them to see that having the morrims and their parishioners would be the best thing for the city at this particular time. I felt that my old themily that I had brought would not help with this discussion.

"Are you okay?" Phyllis asked me.

I stopped pacing and went back to my seat. "There is a divide in my city of Charlesville as well. The divide is between my family, which rules the city, and the people who live on the west side. I grew up with this division. It is one of the main reasons I moved out of my family home when I became an adult. I went to go live on the west side of the city in a place similar to this one. My Uncle Xavier and mother hated my decision. They believed that an Azur should never live amongst the people. Those people on the west side work for people like my family and others who live on the east side of the city. We are not to have a relationship with them. As a matter of fact, Uncle Xavier called the west side people ants. I hated that term. No human being deserves to be called an ant."

The second objector stiffened in her seat while her earrings dangled from her ears.

"You grew up wealthy?" Phyllis asked me.

"Yes. My family is the wealthiest in Charlesville. I never lacked for anything growing up."

"I knew there was something different about you," Bonita Golde added. "You seemed unfazed by the silver when you were at Fat Vincent's for the first time."

"We have gold in Charlesville. And I've seen plenty of that as a child. Seeing that silver was not a big deal."

"Has your city bridged the divide?" the first objector asked.

"No, but some are trying. I hung out at Aliki Park amongst the west siders and learned how to write themilys. At first, they did not accept me because of my name and family. However, when they saw when I left the park that I lived in the same neighborhood, I began to be accepted."

"What about your uncle and mother?" the second objector asked.

"They begged me to return to the family home many times. I refused. There was going to be someone in the Azur family who treated all the people of our city with respect. Do you see? I believe this first outreach from the morrims and parishioners of this city can start bridging that divide here. If each group stays on their side, the division will continue and common ground will remain elusive for everyone. But if you are willing to reach across, I believe the morrims will listen to your perspective and reach out, like I did to the west siders in Charlesville. People want to be listened to before they can actually care about each other. This Festival of the River God will be the first step toward that unity. I ask you four to come and bring your supporters. I can promise that the themily I have prepared for the festival will start bridging the divide."

The four objectors looked at each other. I could sense that they took my words seriously.

The first man spoke slowly. "Fat Vincent, you were right about this young man. He has a way with words and sincerity that bolster those words. We will attend the festival."

I smiled at them as Maisa squeezed my hand. I knew that my themily for the Festival of the River God had to deliver.

Chapter 15

The Festival of the River God was here. It was the second day in the ninth month of Berm. I had spent the last three days getting my themily ready, and I even did a couple of prayer sessions with Diakono Copperwith. I still had my misgivings about prayer, but I had to admit that I felt better after those prayer sessions, and Diakono Copperwith encouraged me to reveal everything that was going on in my mind. I began to learn that prayer was good for getting all the thoughts out of your mind and out into the universe.

Maisa came to my room each day to become the first listener to my themily. She offered suggestions for word selection and delivery. I decided to incorporate her suggestions, along with the one I was supposed to read at Fat Vincent's duplex a couple of nights ago. I had not gotten a chance to read that themily for the objectors, and once again I thought I saw the Eternal Comforter's presence in my life. I never had to convince or persuade anyone from their position by having a regular conversation. I knew that the themilys I read had some effect. It wasn't like a regular discussion where I took the lead. Diakono Copperwith had told me after our last prayer session that he sensed the Eternal Comforter in my life now. But I had not become a believer and follower in Kammbi yet, had I? Was I receiving the gift of the Eternal Comforter prematurely? Or did the Comforter know what my eventual direction was going to be?

I got dressed in a new outfit that Mr. Cortes had brought for me last night. He and Felicia had gone back to Santa Teresa again and brought Maisa and I some new clothes to wear. This was my first jumpsuit. It was sky-blue with dark blue trimming on the sleeves, collar, and the edge of my pants. The fabric felt scratchy against my skin when I put it on, but it grew a little more comfortable the longer I wrote it. Mr. Cortes had got me some glossy black leather shoes that made me an inch or so taller. He'd wanted me to wear some of those shoes that had three-inch heels, but I had refused. I did not want to be that high off of the ground. Plus, I thought only women wore those types of shoes.

Maisa refused the businessman's gift. The tension between them was still evident after Jorge Feldman's announcement. She felt betrayed by the position Cortes had angled with the mine, and to have Felicia named as the administrator was a double blow. Outside of this gesture, Mr. Cortes had not shown any remorse for his actions. It seemed like he expected this kind of response from Maisa and knew he was not going to win back her trust overnight. I wondered if Maisa still wanted to get approval from the konseho of Kammbi for the ownership transfer. She had not spoken about it since the announcement, but I got the sense that if the konseho declined the transfer, she would accept it.

I remembered Maisa's comment about Mr. Cortes wanting to become the descendant or second coming of Diego Carranza, the first magnate of this region. I had read in Oscar Ortega's section of the Book of Kammbi that Diego returned with him from Guadharra after Oscar confessed to his wife, Sophia, about his tryst with Mother Adrianna. Diego Carranza wanted to leave Guadharra and create a new life for himself. Oscar had allowed him to come with one condition. Diego Carranza became his first convert to the teachings of Kammbi. He believed that decision allowed him to become Santa Sophia's greatest businessman, and the Carranza Tower at the marperia, in the center of the city, was a representation of his legacy. Did Mr. Cortes believe the same thing would happen to him because he was coming on this expedition? I did not see him as a friend, definitely not a best friend. That was Trayvonne back home in Charlesville. And those two could not have been more different. I did not see Mr. Cortes as a mentor like I did with the Copperwiths. It was like our relationship would exist for a certain period of time and would end appropriately. Maybe that was why I had been uneasy around him. I knew deep down that he would not have a permanent place in my life, and I had to figure out why I had allowed him to come with us. Yes, we had needed his help with Second Esperah Dorrado, but that wasn't the whole story. I had accepted his presence on this journey for some other reason—a reason I didn't understand. What was the real reason for his presence?

I grabbed my travel bag and kneeled for prayer before I left the room. The time had come for unity in the city of Alicia. My themily had to bring that forth.

I was the last one on the autobus. Mr. Cortes and Felicia sat in their usual spot on the left side behind the driver. They both looked at me with wide smiles on their faces. Maisa and the Copperwiths were on the right side, and they smiled at me too.

"You look sharp, Diondray," Felicia commented.

I nodded and sat down next to Maisa. She squeezed my thigh and grinned at me. I sensed she was in a good mood and ready for the festival.

"If your themily does not convince the people of this city to unite, that Cortes sky-blue jumpsuit will do it," Mr. Cortes declared.

I laughed. "Thanks for the jumpsuit. My first time wearing something like this."

"It's a time for firsts of many things, Diondray. Better to be first than last."

"I agree with you, Mr. Cortes."

The autobus driver pulled away from the hotel as Diakono Copperwith squeezed my left shoulder. I smiled and hoped that the Eternal Comforter would be present at the Festival of the River God.

#

We made it to the River district about ten minutes later. The driver explained that the Issabella River was on the other side of the district, and we still had a little bit of a drive to get there. He continued with his explanation about the river and its importance to the city. I was reading my themily and not really listening. Maisa patted my thigh and said encouraging words to me. I could tell she was trying to keep her mind off the ownership transfer issue with Mr. Cortes by making sure I was ready for the festival.

I looked over my shoulder at Diakono Copperwith and Annalisa. Their eyes were closed and hands clasped together in prayer. I felt comforted by their prayers and sensed that my reading would go well because of them. I turned back around to see Mr. Cortes and Felicia sitting next to each other. They smiled at me and remained quiet. It seemed like the entire group understood the importance of this moment and wanted to be ready for it.

We arrived at the Issabella River on the eastern end of the River district. I looked out my window and saw people lined up next to the water in three or four rows. I did not think the Festival of First Cherries in Santa Sophia had this many people.

I took a deep breath and mentally prepared to meet with them. I knew from my readings at Aliki Park that you don't focus on the entire audience. You find a couple of people to place your attention on and gain confidence from their reaction to your reading.

The driver parked the autobus a distance away from the crowd. We got off the bus and began our walk toward the crowd. I could feel the nervous energy in my stomach, and I wanted to start pacing to relieve that feeling.

Maisa grabbed my hand and I looked at her. She gave me a reassuring smile. "The Eternal Comforter is with you. I can feel it."

I returned a smile and believed her proclamation.

"Diondray!"

I knew that voice. I turned to see Bonita Golde and Fat Vincent walking towards us. I glanced at Maisa to see how she was going to react. She had a weak smile on her face, and I felt she was going to be okay. Bonita had a perfectly shaped treetop hairstyle and wore a pink jumpsuit that flattered her figure. Fat Vincent was dressed in a gray jumpsuit and shiny black shoes. I had never seen him dressed like that while playing Blacks at his duplex.

"Follow us," he said. "We have a spot for all of you."

Bonita Golde and Fat Vincent led the way as we reached the crowd. Everywhere we looked, people turned their attention to us while we walked past them. I noticed that everyone was dressed in jumpsuits and wore silver over their necks, on their ears, and on top of their heads. The River district people loved silver, and I got positive energy from them. They seemed to know that our group belonged here.

Fat Vincent led us to a spot where a podium waited next to the river. The podium stood several feet off the ground, high enough that whoever stood there could see over the crowd. "C'mon with us, Diondray." Bonita Golde said and reached for my hand. Maisa nodded and released my hand so that I could go with Bonita.

I climbed the stairs behind Bonita and Fat Vincent.

Bonita and I went to the back of the podium while Fat Vincent walked to the front, where a couple of people were standing. Music pounded from behind the podium as we stood at our spot. Bonita reached in her jumpsuit pocket and handed me some earplugs. I needed them to block out some of the music that was blaring behind me.

"Let's get this Festival of the River God started!" Fat Vincent announced. I believed he had a microphone attached to him, because I heard his voice reverberate over the entire area.

I still heard the music clearly with the earplugs on. The music began with pounding drums, and then I heard a piano coming over the top of it.

I found myself at the river
I looked into the water
And saw my reflection
I knew I had to be purified
But my mind was on Wanda, Tamara, Anita, and Cassandra
So purity would not happen tonight
I wanted to stay
Because I knew I needed to be there
At the river.

I heard the crowd singing along with the lyrics, and Bonita told me it was a Coltrain Hayes song titled "At the River." Coltrain Hayes had wanted to change from his womanizing ways, and he came to the Issabella River to get himself right. But he returned to Walter's Grove a few days later and continued his womanizing. He wrote this song while spending a few days next to the river. Bonita explained that this song always opened the Festival of the River God. The people loved it, and I realized there was a bigger connection between both regions of the Great Forest than I had thought.

The song faded out, and Bonita grabbed my left hand as we

moved to the front of the podium. I stood to the right of her and Fat Vincent, and then I noticed the long ponytail from one of the objectors at Fat Vincent's duplex the other night. He was directing the crowd with his hands to face the river. Most of the crowd followed his instructions, except a large section at the end. I knew that section were the morrims and their parishioners from the other kahalls in the city. They looked directly at the podium, and I could sense their uneasiness with the rest of the crowd.

"We want to honor the one who lives in this river," the long-haired man started. "This river gave life to our city, and the one we all worship allowed that to happen. Everyone bow your heads at the river to honor our master."

Suddenly, I saw water from the river rise in the air. The water turned into a funnel, and a glow came from the center. I was mesmerized by it. I heard the crowd yell out unintelligible words as the water funnel split itself in two. Then an image of a man appeared from the split. It glowed silver.

I glanced at the morrims and parishioners. The image had surely gotten their attention!

"Welcome, worshippers!" the image said in a deep baritone voice.

All the people of the district dropped to their knees and extended their arms out wide in submission to the river god, while the morrims and parishioners were in stunned silence. I had never seen people react like this before to a god.

"Something special has brought me out of the river after a very long time," the image continued. "Something that validates that change will be coming to this land. Something that has been predicted since the first traveler passed away. The one who is greater than me has revealed his plan on this day."

I could feel the image's presence come over me. I looked at my hands and saw a glowing light over them. I followed that glowing light toward my wrists, up my arms, and realized it had covered my entire body. The glowing light did not blind me, and it felt like I was being lifted off the ground.

"This visitor has arrived in our city to fulfill Oscar's prophecy. He is the reason I have risen from the river. And he should treated with respect as he fulfills the proclamation that the One who is greater than me has declared."

The glowing light vanished from my eyes, and I could see that I had been lifted over the river. I heard unintelligible words and weeping from the people of the district below me. I could sense that many of them were responding that way since it was the first time they had seen a god in the flesh. I understood why these people reacted the way they did.

"How can unity happen when most of these people here worship you instead of Kammbi?" someone from the crowd said.

Even though I was some distance away from the crowd, I heard that comment like the person stood right in front of me. How could that person's voice project itself to be heard by everyone? The image's other hand reached down into the crowd and lifted someone over the river. The light dissipated to reveal Morrim Paranga.

"Morrim, the time has come for everyone to worship the One who is greater than myself. I said that to Alicia and Dexter when Oscar Ortega came to the river. Now I will say it again, since this visitor has arrived. It has come full circle. I'm not here to honor your understanding of the Book of Kammbi. I'm here to honor the One who is higher."

"So are you saying you allowed these people to believe in you and Dexter's disobedience for so many years because it was not your place to convince them otherwise?" Morrim Paranga asked.

The image was holding Morrim Paranga face-first toward the funnel. He did not look over at me. It seemed like the morrim was oblivious to my presence. "It is written in the Book of Kammbi that the One who is higher than I has a different perspective. Since I come under his authority, I must obey that perspective."

The morrim was some distance from me as he talked with the river god. I sensed that this conversation needed to happen for everyone's benefit. Like it was orchestrated for the people of the district to understand that their reverence and worship of the river god had been misplaced for all of these years.

"Your understanding of the Book of Kammbi is correct," Morrim Paranga replied. "You have correctly revealed that Kammbi's perspective is higher than yours or mine. So how can that perspective be reiterated to the people of this district?" The morrim extended his right hand toward the people, who were still on their knees with their arms outstretched in reverence.

The glow returned around Morrim Paranga, and the image extended him back down to the crowd. "The One who is higher than me will be honored despite anyone's misgivings about what has happened in the past. His perspective will be revealed in the essence of his time. The visitor will elaborate on why the time has come," the image stated. I felt a burst of wind at my back, and it pushed me downward to the podium. I knew the light still encircled my entire body, but I felt protected by its presence. My feet landed on the podium, and I could see everyone looking at me. I had the audience at my command.

People want to know you care about them before they can care about you.
And if we all are to believe and follow that One who created us
We must honor the Creator first and then honor each other.
And the proof of that is my presence here amongst you.
I'm from south of the Great Forest
And my life has been forever changed

When I found out months back that I'm a descendant of Oscar Ortega.

Oscar Ortega did not look like me
Oscar Ortega did not think like me
Oscar Ortega believed differently than me
However, the one he serves still wanted someone like me to fulfill Oscar's prophecy.
That tells me the One who created us will use anyone for his purposes at any time.
And he will use my differences in thought and belief to get that message across to everyone throughout both regions of the Great Forest.
I would like the morrims and parishioners here at the Festival of the River God today to bring those who have worshipped the river god into your fold. Listen to them. Break bread with them. And let them know you care.
I would like those who worship the river god to understand that there is one whom the river god honors as higher than itself. And if you believe and worship the river god, then you must believe and follow the One higher than that god. And you must acknowledge the accurate account of what Alicia wrote in her section of the Book of Kammbi. Truth must rise above emotion.
If truth can rise above emotion, then Unity will arrive in this city.

"Unity has arrived in this city," the image said. "The visitor has spoken the appropriate words for us all. And from this festival forward, we will all serve the One higher than me."

I turned around to see the image transform into a funnel as the water came out of the river. A strong wind ripped through the area as the funnel descended into the water. I knew that the city of Alicia would finally be united.

Part 3:
Issabella

Chapter 16

We spent our last day in Alicia with Morrim Paranga.

Morrim Paranga spoke to me before we got on the autobus to leave the city. He praised my themily and told me he sensed from the Eternal Comforter that unity had become a real possibility in Alicia.

Tears welled up in his eyes as we talked. I was touched by his show of emotion. His last words to me were that he would send a letter to the konseho of Kammbi in Issabella on my behalf. Morrim Paranga believed my themily about unity should be added to the Book of Kammbi for all believers and followers of Kammbi.

I did not know how additional writings could be added to the Book of Kammbi. Was it possible? Diakono Copperwith had never spoken of such a thing since we had been together. Either way, the morrim's comments got me focused on Issabella and the konseho of Kammbi. What would be my purpose in the final city north of the Great Forest? I said a prayer in my seat before we left and hoped the Eternal Comforter would answer that prayer.

#

The drive to Issabella took three hours. The city was southeast of Alicia and built next to the southern part of the Issabella River. I found out from Percival that Issabella was the least populated of the four cities north of the Great Forest. The city was split into two districts: Issa and Bella. The Issa district was on the west side of the city, and the Bella district was on the east. The marperia intersected where the two districts met, and the kahall of Issabella was the main building there.

Percival further explained on the drive to Issabella that because of its size, everybody in the city was connected. Unlike Alicia, mostly everyone in Issabella was a believer and follower of Kammbi. The konseho of Kammbi governed the city, and because of their authority, the citizens here were the most dogmatic about the Book of Kammbi. I pondered how the citizens would welcome me. If they were all like Second Esperah Dorrado's father, then we would have to deal with them alongside the konseho of Kammbi.

I had gotten enough information about the konseho of Kammbi since Santa Teresa to know what to expect. Diakono Copperwith had explained that I would have to speak in front of the council by the end of our time in Issabella. They would have to examine me to determine if I was the one who would fulfill Oscar's prophecy. I did not know what kind of themily I would need to write in order to get their acceptance. I had a sense that everything I had written and spoken to the people of this region so far would not be enough to sway their determination of me.

Perhaps I should simply tell my own story. But how? Would I start with the story of the Festival of Sinquinta in Santa Sophia? How I kept Second Esperah Dorrado from getting married in Santa Teresa? How about speaking at the Festival of the River God in Alicia? All these experiences had affected me differently since my arrival in this region. Also, I did not know if the konseho of Kammbi would readily embrace what had happened in each of those cities, unlike the morrims of each kahall. I hoped the letter Morrim Paranga had said he was going to write would help in that regard.

Also, Maisa would have to make her case for ownership of Silver Mine 12. I knew she was proud that her family owned something of significance. However, there was still tension between her and Mr. Cortes and Felicia. She did not participate in our conversation on the way to Issabella or even look over at Mr. Cortes and Felicia on the autobus. I did not realize until then how betrayed she felt about how Mr. Cortes had forced Felicia into Jorge Feldman's position. It seemed there had been some kind of agreement between her and the businessman that was broken in Maisa's view. But neither person would talk about it. I hoped their tension did not cause the konseho of Kammbi to decline the ownership transfer. Even though she would be relieved to be done with Cortes, I knew that ultimately, Maisa would be highly disappointed if that was the decision.

Mr. Cortes and Felicia spoke with the Copperwiths and myself on the drive to Issabella. Despite the tension with Maisa, the businessman seemed pleased at being with us. I had not had that queasy feeling in my stomach since Santa Teresa. I was still wary of his presence, and with the silver mine ownership issue, I knew I needed to learn more about his intentions for wanting to come on this expedition. But his presence at least wasn't unpleasant for now.

All of us were affected by what had happened at the Festival of the River God. That topic took up the majority of our conversation. Percival joined us and commented on how the people of the River district seemed different after the festival. He said those people would usually continue in a festive mood for several days after the Festival of the River God. But driving around in this district for the past two days, he had noticed their somber mood. People seemed in a daze, and he knew something different had happened at the Festival of the River God.

The Copperwiths spoke about seeing the image of the river god, and the diakono stated that he could understand why the people of the River district would believe in something like that even though it was not in line with the Book of Kammbi. Diakono Copperwith was amazed at how those people had submitted to worshipping the image on sight, and it made him question his own obedience to the Book of Kammbi and the guidance of the Eternal Comforter. I watched Annalisa as she listened to her husband speak about those feelings, and I knew she had never heard him talk like that before. Even without Maisa's participation, I believed we all needed the entire conversation. The words spoken brought us closer together, and that closeness would be needed for our appearance at the konseho of Kammbi.

#

Percival drove us to the kahall of Issabella. It was smaller than the kahalls in the other cities north of the Great Forest, and it lacked a dome-shaped roof to show its status. If Percival had not told me this was the kahall of Issabella, I would have thought it to be just another building in this city's marperia.

In contrast, another building across the street got my attention right away. It was the largest building I had ever seen in my life, covering several blocks of the marperia.

"The konseho of Kammbi," Percival announced as he made a right turn away from it.

"I will have to speak in that building before I leave Issabella," I said.

"You will," Diakono Copperwith added. "And you will be prepared when the time comes."

"I will make sure of that," Maisa said and patted my thigh.

I smiled at her as she made her first comment since leaving Alicia. I would need to support her just as much as she had supported me so far on this expedition.

"You should know from Issabella's section in the Book of Kammbi that her second husband, Paulo, had the konseho of Kammbi built in her honor," Diakono Copperwith said as Percival parked in front of the kahall of Issabella.

I grabbed my travel bag and replied, "Indeed I do. It seems that husbands still played an important role despite what happened in Santa Teresa."

Diakono Copperwith grinned. "They still do, Diondray. I believe that Annalisa can validate your perceptive comment." The diakono stared at his wife lovingly as she smiled and clasped his hand. Even though she had supported Second Esperah Dorrado's decision about marriage, I could tell that Annalisa had not regretted her marriage to Diakono Copperwith. Their unity and affection had been lovely to witness on this expedition, and it gave me hope for myself as well.

We were greeted by a couple of second esperahs at the entrance to the kahall. They gave their customary bow to Diakono Copperwith and led us into the kahall.

"Morrim Sperrie will see you, Diakono Copperwith, and your guests tomorrow morning in the morrim's office," the taller of the second esperahs announced. "We will show you to your rooms."

We followed the second esperahs to our rooms. I was looking forward to meeting Morrim Sperrie and seeing if he would respond to my arrival like the other morrims did previously. Also, I wanted to know how closely the morrim worked with the konseho of Kammbi and whether we could use that relationship to our advantage in preparation for our hearing. I felt I would need every advantage I could get while I was in this city.

#

He was different. I knew it from the moment I saw him. His olive skin and thick dark-brown hair drew me in. The man had a presence about him that told me his God had sent him here. I had to take him to the river to get my first impressions validated.

I led him to the river and knew that Victor did not approve of that course of action. Victor viewed him as a threat for my affections. However, I did not have that kind of feeling for Oscar Ortega. It was not lustful or sexual. It went beyond that kind of attraction. Oscar Ortega was different.

I had to make sure that Victor understood he was no threat to our marriage. Otherwise, Victor would kill him. I had married a good man who would do anything to protect me. And I could not let Victor do something wrong out of anger that would affect us forever.

I remembered his first words to me. "Hello, I'm Oscar Ortega. I came from the hills of the northwest, and I want to meet other people where I can share my beliefs in Kammbi. Have you heard of Kammbi?"

I answered his question, and that began a fifty-day period of getting to know about Kammbi and the Eternal Comforter. Those fifty days changed my life.

I read that opening chapter from Issabella's section in the Book of Kammbi shortly after I arrived in my room. I was intrigued by Issabella's confession that she was drawn to Oscar Ortega even though she did not have a lustful or sexual desire for him. Both Teresa's and Alicia's accounts said similar things. Oscar Ortega had a magnetism that these women were drawn toward. It made sense that Mother Adrianna had been drawn to Oscar as well. I wondered if that magnetism had helped him convert these people to becoming followers and believers of Kammbi. And what about me? Did I have any magnetism in getting the River district people of Alicia to trust? Did I have any magnetism to Second Esperah Dorrado that kept her from getting married to Turner Perez in Santa Teresa? If I did, how would that help me at the hearing with the konseho of Kammbi?

I continued reading in Issabella's section before the second esperahs could call us to dinner. I wanted to get as much of this section deeply into my heart and mind before I met with Morrim Sperrie in the morning.

#

I finished reading Issabella's section of the Book of Kammbi last night after dinner. I learned from reading that Issabella had led her tribe just like Teresa and Alicia did in their parts of this region. She was the only child of the tribe's leader and rose to her position after her father's death. Her father had no other children, and her mother was not allowed by the tribe's customs to take over his role after his death. Leadership came to Issabella at the age of nineteen.

She fell in love with Victor, a man ten years older than her, soon after becoming chief. Victor's experience and guidance helped Issabella through the transitioning period of becoming the tribe's leader. She relied on him quite a bit, and with Victor's presence, she eventually got support from the other elders of the tribe. Issabella had a natural instinct for leadership and bringing people together. Victor became the enforcer during her leadership, and the two made a great team.

Issabella took immediately to Oscar's teachings about Kammbi. She became a follower and believer in Kammbi only a few days after meeting with him. That quick conversion troubled Victor, and he addressed his concerns to her. Issabella tried to convince him that he should start from Oscar's teachings and become a follower and believer in Kammbi. Victor refused because he believed in the river god like the rest of the tribe did.

Victor thought he was going to lose her to Oscar Ortega. The man had a natural charm and ease around women that made Victor uncomfortable. Most of the tribe's women took to Oscar's teachings rather quickly. Victor wanted Oscar gone before his customary fifty-day period ended. Issabella knew Oscar Ortega had to stay in order for them to receive their blessing from Kammbi because of his disciple's arrival.

She began to pray in the manner that she had learned from Oscar's teachings, and a few nights later a water funnel came from the river and scooped up Victor and some other men of the tribe who were fishing at that time. Some of the tribe believed it was the river god claiming those who worshipped it. Issabella knew from her prayers that the Eternal Comforter had caused the river to erupt and that her husband had become the first sacrifice for her new beliefs.

Issabella was heartbroken by the loss of Victor. She even thought about renouncing her beliefs in Kammbi. However, she relied on Oscar Ortega's teachings to get through her grief. She learned from Kammbi's wisdom on how to deal with losing someone close to you. She allowed Oscar to stay his customary fifty-day period and gained the strength to continue as leader of the tribe.

After Oscar left, she started receiving the attention of Paulo. He became her official assistant and started filling Victor's role. Issabella grew to love him and got married only after a few months of courtship. She shared with her new husband about a journal she had kept since becoming leader of the tribe at nineteen years old. Paulo read her journal and began chronicling her life until she died at age eighty-one. He was the one who wrote her section of the Book of Kammbi and helped form the council that would turn into the konseho of Kammbi. Paulo made sure her life would be printed in the Book of Kammbi.

Though I had read the story before, this time as I read, I realized the power of women. Both Oscar Ortega and Paulo understood that once they had the women behind them, the men would follow later. I sensed I would have to rely on that same model if I was truly going to fulfill Oscar's prophecy.

The second esperahs took Diakono Copperwith and me to Morrim Sperrie's office first thing in the morning. Mr. Cortes and Felicia had gone to check on the business back in Santa Teresa, and they would return later in the day to look for additional business opportunities in Issabella. Maisa called me before the Copperwiths came to my room and let me know that she was going with the businessman and his right hand woman. I was surprised by her decision to join them. But she explained that she wanted to keep watch on them and have a discussion outside of my presence. Plus, she wanted to see Issabella for herself.

We walked some distance from our rooms and reached the opposite side of the kahall of Issabella. On the walk, Diakono Copperwith explained to me about Morrim Sperrie. She was the first woman morrim in all the cities north of the Great Forest. I should have known better than to assume she would be a man. Her ascension into becoming a morrim was groundbreaking. There were many believers and followers of Kammbi who were against her becoming a morrim. They believed that the teachings of the Book of Kammbi prohibited a woman from becoming a morrim. Morrim Sperrie countered that resistance by explaining to the konseho of Kammbi upon her nomination for morrim that Teresa was essentially the same thing.

Most of the members of the konseho were initially against her nomination, but after Morrim Sperrie explained her reasoning about Teresa, she convinced them that she was worthy of the position. Diakono Copperwith believed Morrim Sperrie would be the perfect person to help me prepare for my hearing with the konseho on the twenty-third day in the tenth month of Coter. I had forty-eight days of preparation time. We entered the office, and Morrim Sperrie greeted us immediately. She wore a morrim's shawl that was white with red trim on the collar and sleeves, accented by her long brown hair and small-rimmed glasses. She came off as more of a university professor than a morrim. Standing next to her was a diakono whose height towered over everyone in the room. I thought he might have been the same height as Mr. Cortes or even an inch taller.

Diakono Copperwith gave his customary bows to both Morrim Sperrie and the other diakono. They returned his greeting and led us to an oval-shaped table near the back of the morrim's office.

"The morrim from your kahall in Santa Sophia sends his regards," Morrim Sperrie said as she took her seat across from Diakono Copperwith.

I sat to the right of Diakono Copperwith and across from the other diakono. Annalisa, on the other side of her husband, sat the farthest away from everyone. She was smiling at Morrim Sperrie, seeming almost inspired by her. I looked away from Annalisa and took a sip of cherry juice from the glass on the table.

"Thank you, Morrim Sperrie," Diakono Copperwith replied after taking a sip of cherry juice as well. "I have maintained contact with the morrim from the kahall of Santa Sophia on a regular basis."

"Diakono Prescott and I have awaited your arrival," the morrim continued. "And you are Diondray Azur from Charlesville?"

"Yes."

"We have a lot to discuss with you and the rest of your group. I thought there were more of you?"

"Mr. Cortes, the businessman from Santa Teresa, his assistant Felicia, and Maisa Merez from Santa Sophia did arrive in Issabella with us. They are attending to some other matters in regards to our visit," Diakono Copperwith answered.

Morrim Sperrie nodded and continued. "I received a letter from Morrim Paranga of the kahall of Alicia. He truly believes that Diondray is the one who will fulfill Oscar's prophecy."

Did Morrim Paranga write two letters? I wondered as I took another sip of cherry juice and felt that Diakono Prescott was watching me. I glanced toward him to confirm my suspicion. He stared at me with a blank look that was unnerving. I wished Maisa were here sitting next to me. Her presence would have deflected my attention from Diakono's stare and kept me from wanting to pace the room.

"Why should we believe you are the one who will fulfill Oscar's prophecy?" Diakono Prescott asked me pointedly.

I took a deep breath and faced Diakono Prescott in response to his question. His pointed nose and angular jaw added intensity to his face that made him intimidating. I found I couldn't hold his stare. Instead, I looked away from him and grabbed my travel bag. I pulled out the Book of Kammbi and laid it gently in the middle of the table. Morrim Sperrie gasped, and Diakono Prescott stared at it.

"When I saw this copy of the Book of Kammbi in Charlesville, my Aunt Maxina revealed it had been inside of Ama's Faddar, our city's spiritual home, for years. Oscar Ortega left this copy of the Book of Kammbi in the south after his failed attempt for reconciliation with his son. Ever since the discovery of this book, my life has drastically changed."

Diakono Prescott looked up from the Book of Kammbi. "It is not just a book."

"You are correct, Diakono Prescott," I replied quickly. I forced myself to stay seated and calm, no matter how much I wanted to jump up and escape his ire. "It is far more than just a book."

"I can assure you that Diondray has treated the Book of Kammbi with the respect it deserves," Annalisa interjected.

Diakono Prescott turned to Annalisa, and I could tell that he accepted her comment. I would not get anymore of his opposition. For now.

"May I?" Morrim Sperrie said. She had not taken her eyes away from the book.

"Yes."

Morrim Sperrie gently took the Book of Kammbi from the table and opened its pages. "Oh, dear Kammbi! This is his copy. This is the one. By Kammbi and the Eternal Comforter, will this prophecy be fulfilled in my lifetime?"

"Morrim Sperrie," Diakono Prescott said. He reached for the Book of Kammbi.

She handed him the book, and he flipped the pages carefully. Diakono Prescott did not display the same sense of awe, but I knew that seeing Oscar's Book of Kammbi had gotten his attention.

"Diondray's aunt came to me a month before I met him and told me about Oscar's Book of Kammbi," Diakono Copperwith said. "She explained that she'd seen a vision of her nephew coming north of the Great Forest to show our people Oscar's Book of Kammbi. His arrival would change everything in our land. It would fulfill the prophecy. It would have been easy to dismiss this woman as someone out of her mind. However, when Diondray came to Santa Sophia in the month of Lir and brought that Book of Kammbi with him, I knew he was the one."

"This is authentic," Diakono Prescott said. He placed the Book of Kammbi back in the middle of the table. "You need this Book of Kammbi as proof for the hearing with the konseho of Kammbi in forty-eight days."

"He will need this indeed," Morrim Sperrie added. "However, it might not be enough to convince them of his claim."

"I believe the things that have happened in the other cities north of the Great Forest will back up his claim," Diakono Copperwith interjected.

Diakono Prescott frowned. "What things, Diakono?"

"The letter Morrim Sperrie received from Morrim Paranga in Alicia explains one of the things. And what happened at the Festival of Sinquinta in Santa Sophia is another," Diakono Copperwith replied.

"And helping a young second esperah escape marriage in order to become a resa in Santa Teresa is the other event," Annalisa added.

Morrim Sperrie shot a look at Annalisa. "A young woman who turned twenty-one in Santa Teresa avoided marriage? In order to become a resa?"

"Correct, Morrim," Annalisa answered.

Morrim Sperrie seemed taken aback by Annalisa's revelation, while Diakono Prescott remained frowning. "I'm looking forward to making sure that you will be ready for your hearing with the konseho of Kammbi," Morrim Sperrie concluded.

Chapter 17

Eight days passed. I was getting ready for our first study session today and looking forward to spending time with the morrim. Meanwhile, I spent my time reading and rereading the Book of Kammbi. I wanted to make sure I knew every inch of it. I went through both the Ryianza, covering the time when Kammbi walked among us, and the Baramesa, the story of Oscar Ortega's journey and impact, carefully. I knew I had to familiarize myself with as much detail as possible.

At the same time, I also started writing a new themily that I wanted to read at the hearing. This themily had to address the konseho of Kammbi in a way that would get their attention. I needed words that would make them realize that believing and following Kammbi was for everyone. The Book of Kammbi made that fact clear. Kammbi wanted his teachings to be spread across the land for everyone. I had to relay that message. I had just finished eating breakfast when I heard a knock on my door. I got up and opened the door.

"I hope I'm not disturbing your writing time," Maisa said and entered the room. She wore a fitted yellow jumpsuit with a blue triangle pattern that got my attention. She looked gorgeous—on purpose, I was sure. But I had to keep my mind on track.

"I finished a few minutes ago," I replied as I closed the door. "Is that new clothing from Mr. Cortes?"

She sat down in the chair next to the desk in the room and smiled at me as I grabbed the themily from the desk. I did not want her to read what I had started writing yet.

"It is. He got Percival to bring new clothing from Santa Teresa. Mr. Cortes wants to introduce his clothing to the people of this city. He feels Issabella's clothing is outdated and needs to reflect the times."

"Are you two on better grounds with each other?"

Maisa's smile vanished from her face as a frown emerged. "I don't know if I can say that, yet. I thought in the couple of days since we arrived in Issabella that we would discuss the ownership transfer of the mine and talk about why he wants Felicia to take over for Jorge Feldman if we get approval from the konseho of Kammbi. However, he apologized for how it happened but did not want to discuss it any further."

"Did he say why?"

"He did not," Maisa continued. "He suggested that we focus on the hearing and getting acquainted with this city. I explained to him how important this silver mine is to my family. I did not know this mine existed before coming to Alicia, and I do not want it belonging to someone else. It belongs to the Merez family, and I will do everything I can to keep it that way."

I heard the determination in Maisa's voice at that comment. I knew she had found her reason from coming on the expedition, and she was not going to let Mr. Cortes and Felicia take it away from her.

"I learned from Jorge Feldman before we left Alicia that the mine exports silver to all the cities south of the Great Forest except your home city of Charlesville. The mine makes more of its money from those exports than it does in the city of Alicia. That's why Jorge Feldman did not believe the reports from the konseho of Kammbi about how much silver was actually produced from that mine. He knew those reports were wrong," Maisa explained.

"Mr. Cortes knows that as well," I replied. "But why would the konseho of Kammbi create false reports for the mine? Also, that mine brought workers from Walter's Grove. So there has been a connection established between both regions of the Great Forest. Why not celebrate that fact?"

"I don't know," Maisa answered as a small smile returned to her face. "It means my family, specifically Marco Phillip Merez, established a connection to people south of the Great Forest after Oscar Ortega attempted to reconcile with his son in your home city. My family will have to be recognized for their contribution along with the Ortega and Carranza families in this region. That's why I have to see this ownership transfer of the mine all the way through. I've been wanting answers all of my life, and finally in the last few months, being with you has started to provide those answers."

She got up from her seat and walked over to me. We embraced and kissed. I stiffened. It was not the right time for this—but I wanted to keep her in my arms, and we continued kissing.

"I'm sorry, Diondray," she said with an embarrassed look, pulling away. "I got ahead of myself. The time is not right for us."

She released from our embrace and looked away. I nodded as I watched her return to the chair. I was so close to losing my self-control and resuming the embrace.

"I believe that Mr. Cortes knew all of this information about the mine and wants to put himself in a position to buy it from you," I said as I tried to refocus our attention to our prior conversation.

"Annalisa might have been right when she said he wants to be the second coming of Diego Carranza," Maisa replied as she sat down.

"I'm beginning to believe that Annalisa's assertion might be true as well. However, Diego Carranza did not travel throughout the region with Oscar Ortega. He built his business in Santa Sophia."

"He did, and the Carranza family influence is all over that city. I grew up with it."

"What shall we do?" I asked.

Maisa frowned. "I found out from Percival before I came to your room that he dropped off Mr. Cortes and Felicia at the konseho of Kammbi yesterday."

"What for?"

"I don't know. I have the paperwork for the ownership transfer in my room, and they were at the konseho for several hours."

Maisa went silent, and I could tell she was lost in thought. I walked over and reached for her. Even though I was not going to kiss her again, I did caress her hand. She gave me a warm smile.

"We will need to have a discussion with the Copperwiths and Morrim Sperrie," I said.

#

The next morning, I ate breakfast with the Copperwiths in the kahall's dining room. I told them about my conversation with Maisa, and they went into prayer immediately. I thought Annalisa was going to admonish me for allowing the businessman and his assistant to come on the expedition. I had braced myself for that admonishment. However, she embraced me and did not mention her position on that decision. I was pleased at the gesture and really felt connected to her at that moment. She might be the most dogmatic about her beliefs amongst all of us, even more than her husband. However, I was beginning to see that she really cared about me and wanted to make sure that I fulfilled Oscar's prophecy.

After prayer and breakfast, Annalisa left with a couple of second esperahs to assist with providing food for the less fortunate who lived close to the kahall. The kahall of Issabella prepared meals on every third day of the week for the entire Bella district.

Diakono Copperwith and I arrived in Morrim Sperrie's office shortly after breakfast. Morrim Sperrie and Diakono Prescott sat on each side of the table. Diakono Copperwith sat next to Diakono Prescott.

"What year did Oscar Ortega begin his first expedition?" Morrim Sperrie asked without preamble.

"Year 10," I answered and sat down at the table next to Morrim Sperrie.

"What does A.O.A. mean?"

"After Oscar Arrived in the land from Guadharra. Because he obeyed Kammbi and left his home to come to this unknown land, that reference of time was established in the Book of Kammbi and has been used ever since."

"How many elders were in the Mayza tribe?" Diakono Prescott asked.

"Six."

"Please look at me when you are answering questions. The konseho of Kammbi will want to see your facial reactions at the hearing."

I winced. Without realizing it, I'd been looking at Diakono Copperwith when I answered Diakono Prescott's question. The big man still intimidated me. "How many books in the Ryianza?" Morrim Sperrie asked.

"Seven," I answered and turned to face her. "All seven books were written by Kammbi's disciples, covering the six years when he lived with humanity. Three disciples wrote their versions of Kammbi's time amongst us, starting with Gregory in Books 1 and 2, then Jorge in Books 3 and 4, and finally Carlos in Books 5 and 6."

I glanced at Diakono Copperwith. He gave me his reassuring smile, and I knew I was doing well so far.

"Where was Jorge from?" Diakono Prescott asked.

I faced the diakono and tried not to flinch. "Kammbi arrived in

Guadharra, where Jorge first saw him and touched his garment. No one had ever touched Kammbi before that moment, and Jorge was selected to chronicle Kammbi's time in Guadharra."

"A stranger," Morrim Sperrie said, shaking her head. "Someone from south of the Great Forest can answer questions from the Book of Kammbi without going into deep thought. A lot of parishioners at this kahall could not have answered those questions as quickly as he did."

Morrim Sperrie gave me a smile that made me feel like I had just passed a test at the university that the professor did not expect. "I'm impressed as well," Diakono Prescott added. "I wish our parishioners knew the Book of Kammbi as it appears that Diondray Azur does."

I looked over at Diakono Prescott, and while he did not smile at me, he seemed genuine. I sensed that he was staring to accept that I could be the one to fulfill Oscar's prophecy.

"I wanted to test your basic knowledge of the Book of Kammbi in this first study session," Morrim Sperrie continued, "because you will be asked these same kinds of questions during the hearing. They will test your knowledge, and I want to make sure you are prepared for any kind of question they might ask. Diakono Copperwith was right when he said you had read the Book of Kammbi a lot since you have been here in these cities north of the Great Forest. I will see you in two days as we deepen your knowledge in the next study session.

Percival came for me a few hours after my study session with Morrim Sperrie. I was summoned by Maisa and Mr. Cortes to meet them at a restaurant in the Bella district of the city. Maisa explained that Mr. Cortes wanted to talk about what was going to happen at the konseho of Kammbi for my hearing. He wanted me to spend a little time in the city as well. Maisa's voice sounded a little better when we talked. However, I did not believe the tension between her and Mr. Cortes was resolved at all.

Before the driver picked me up, I spent some time with Diakono Copperwith and Annalisa as Morrim Sperrie gave us access to her personal library next to her office. The morrim wanted me learn about the origins of the Book of Kammbi and the konseho of Kammbi before our next study session. She felt this information would give me a fuller picture of how this whole religious system came together, and my understanding the origins of it would be well received by the konseho at the hearing.

I learned that Issabella and Paulo had created the konseho of Kammbi in the Year 40 A.O.A., a couple of years after Oscar Ortega's death. Paulo had spent quite a bit of time with Oscar before he passed away. He was able to get all of Oscar's writings about his travels throughout this region north of the Great Forest, Oscar's homeland of Guadharra, and his travels south of the Great Forest when he attempted to reconcile with his son, Charles. Paulo also obtained the teachings of Kammbi that Oscar shared with the people he visited on his travels. Oscar gave Paulo his blessing to have the writings put together in a book for all believers and followers of Kammbi. Oscar Ortega wanted these believers and followers to learn about Kammbi and the disciples who came before him, as well as the people like Teresa and Alicia who became disciples during his travels.

Paulo and Issabella got Oscar's writings published in a book and formed the council that became the konseho of Kammbi around these writings. The council would readily publish copies of this book, called the Book of Kammbi, and disseminate it throughout the region for all believers and followers of Kammbi. Also, the konseho of Kammbi would govern all aspects of this religious system for the people of the region.

Moreover, I found out that Oscar had allowed his writings to be published only under one condition: that the first copy of the Book of Kammbi be sent to his son, Charles, as a gift. Paulo arranged a secret trip south of the Great Forest to deliver the first copy of the Book of Kammbi to him.

I now had that copy in my possession.

Diakono Copperwith and Annalisa prayed for me as soon as we discovered this information. I began to understand that the old adage, what goes around comes around, had been applied in this situation. In my case, everything was coming around indeed.

#

Percival parked the autobus in a parking lot next to the restaurant, where I saw people waiting at the entrance. It seemed to be popular and a good place for my first real excursion into the city.

I grabbed my travel bag from underneath the seat as I rose to get off the autobus. I felt a hand on my left shoulder. "Be mindful of your surroundings, Diondray. People will be watching you," Percival said with a circumspect look on his face.

I started to speak, and he raised the hand that had just touched my shoulder before words could come out of my mouth. "You're not in any danger. The Eternal Comforter is protecting you. However, the patrons in this restaurant know about you and your claim."

I nodded and exited the autobus. I knew that the konseho of Kammbi had learned about me considering that I had been traveling throughout this region since the fourth month of Lir. It would be naïve of me not to think that the morrims of each kahall in their respective cities had not reported to the konseho of Kammbi about my presence. And the fact that Percival had taken Mr. Cortes and Felicia to the konseho of Kammbi for several hours recently would add to their knowledge. However, I felt unnerved by his comment that the patrons in this restaurant knew about my claim. Would that include everyone in this restaurant? Were there members from the konseho of Kammbi inside? Would they tell the rest of the patrons about me? I did not like entering a situation where the flow of information was one-sided. However, I would not have been on this expedition if that was the main issue.

A short, wiry man with a close-cropped beard approached me as I stood at the end of the line waiting to get into the restaurant. "Diondray Azur," he said sharply. "Follow me."

I felt the patrons' eyes looking at me as I followed the man. I knew they were displeased about me getting preferential treatment, and I was still pondering how much they knew about me. The people here were dressed in monochromatic jumpsuits accessorized with silver necklaces, bracelets, and on the women, earrings. "How does he get to enter wearing an outfit like that?" a male voice shouted as I passed by. I had on a new pair of gray shorts from Mr. Cortes with a red shirt with thin gray stripes. I might have been underdressed for this occasion, and I could sympathize with the man's outburst.

The wiry man ignored it and announced, "Welcome to Tavares, the best restaurant in Issabella."

I had no point of reference to judge that claim, but the restaurant's appearance grabbed my attention as I walked further inside. Chandeliers in a flowerbud style brightened the entire restaurant, and smaller replicas attached to the maroon walls glowed dimly over each table. All the tables and chairs were placed next to the walls, creating a U-shape around the stage that occupied the center of the restaurant. The restaurant staff dressed in white jumpsuits with black trim. I assumed the wiry man must be the owner of the restaurant, because his red jumpsuit with gold trim was different from how the rest of the restaurant staff dressed, and they all nodded at him in deference as we passed by. Tavares gave off an elegant atmosphere that would have impressed Mother and Uncle Xavier.

Maisa smiled as I arrived at the table where she was sitting with

Mr. Cortes and Felicia. I noticed that she sat as far away as she could from the businessman and his assistant. I took the chair between her and Mr. Cortes and hoped that I did not get queasy sitting next to him.

"Thank you, Andres," Mr. Cortes said and gave the wiry man a handshake. "I'm pleased to see that your patrons have lined up for my show. It looks like we can do a lot of business tonight."

"Exactly, Mr. Cortes," Andres replied as he looked up at the businessman. "As you see, I have set up the stage in the center of the restaurant. The models will enter the stage from the rear, and my patrons are positioned on both sides of the stage to get a view of the clothing. I will introduce each model and describe what they are wearing as you have instructed. The patrons who want to buy clothing will write on a note that is placed facedown on their tables, and my waitstaff will collect those notes at the end of the show."

"Perfect!" Mr. Cortes said. "Felicia will handle everything from there."

Andres nodded and continued. "At the end of the show, I will make an announcement that we will have Diondray Azur from Charlesville give a reading for the crowd. I hope these words of wisdom are as extraordinary as you have been telling me. My patrons are well-educated and will not take lightly to second-class readings."

I sat up straighter in surprise. I did not know I was going to give a reading tonight! Maisa had not mentioned it earlier. I had not prepared for a themily reading, especially since my mind was thinking about how many patrons knew me and were there members of the konseho of Kammbi here as well.

Maisa reached over to pat my left thigh and smiled. Her gesture indicated that she knew how I was feeling. She looked away from me to Andres. "His themily will get their attention,"

Andres gave her a sharp look and then smiled immediately. "Well, because of your endorsement, I believe it now."

I appreciated her confidence as Maisa giggled at his comment while he continued to smile at her. Andres looked her up and down, and I knew this was another one I'd have to keep an eye on. "I hope our meal will give you the same kind of satisfaction," Andres continued as he reluctantly looked away from Maisa.

Our seats were on the left side of the stage, close to the back entrance. We would get the first look at the models coming out for the show. I glanced at Mr. Cortes as he sat down across from me. He smirked in anticipation that most of the patrons in the restaurant would buy his clothing. I knew he believed he would begin to change the fashion sense of this city tonight.

Felicia sat next to him and began writing on her notepad. She seemed oblivious to her surroundings. I assumed she had been to numerous shows like this in Santa Teresa. Even though we were in a new city, this latest outing was like all the rest for her.

I was trying to compose myself for my themily reading. I went over several themilies that came to the top of my mind, but they did not feel like the right ones.

Maisa continued to pat my thigh as Andres left our table and headed toward the back of the restaurant. "I'm so glad you are here," she whispered to me. "I'm looking forward to your themily."

I nodded as a waitress came to our table dressed in her white jumpsuit. She stared blankly as she poured cherry juice into our glasses on the table.

"A woman should not be wearing white before the first day of the month of Coter," Mr. Cortes proclaimed. "It's still too early for that color."

"It's her uniform," Felicia replied sharply. "Andres has both men and women wearing the same thing. Is that a problem?"

"My objection has nothing to do with her being female," Mr.

Cortes retorted. "I will have to buy this restaurant from Andres and have these uniforms changed. This city definitely needs a fashion lesson."

"It looks good on her," Felicia added.

Maisa cut in. "I agree with Felicia. I believe she looks nice and professional. Maybe you should add that look to your show tonight, Mr. Cortes."

The woman continued to set our table and did not look at us while we were talking about her attire. I could tell she had been well trained not to respond to comments from the patrons.

"Thanks, Maisa," Felicia replied with a thin smile.

The woman finished setting our table and headed to the stage's back entrance. She did not seem embarrassed about the conversation. If I owned a restaurant like this one, I thought, I would make sure that I hired people like her.

I turned from the conversation and watched the patrons on our side of the restaurant. I was still trying to settle on which themily I would read to these well-dressed and educated patrons. I wished I could have talked with a few of them to see what they were interested in and how much they believed in the Book of Kammbi or something like that.

"Oh gods. These patrons look like they belong in the past. The men are wearing loose-fitted jumpsuits, and the women are wearing dresses that fall to the floor. They don't show off their figures. This city needs a serious clothing makeover," Mr. Cortes continued his rant as he watched the patrons as well. "It's a good thing I'm here."

The waitress returned to our table with our food. The spicy aroma filled my nostrils and diverted my attention from the patrons back to the dinner.

I leaned over as she set my plate on the table and said softly in her ear, "Sorry about my companions. They are interested in clothing.

They shouldn't have talked about you like that."

"No worries, Mr. Azur. I've learned how to block it out," the woman replied and smiled. "Enjoy your dinner."

She served the rest of the group as I took a bite into the meat that covered most of my plate. It was cooked medium well and tender. Delicious.

"What did you tell her?"

"What?" I replied and looked at Maisa. She had a concerned look on her face.

"You heard me. What did you say to her?"

"I apologized about our earlier conversation regarding her clothing," I answered, taken by surprise. "Is there a problem?"

"No," Maisa answered and looked away from me.

"Welcome to Tavares," Andres said over a microphone, opening the show just in time. I could focus on the show instead of on Maisa. "We have a special event this evening that takes place in two parts. The first part is a clothing show featuring the work of Mr. Frederic Cortes of Santa Teresa. His clothing has changed fashion in his city, and he wants to bring that fashion here to our beloved Issabella," Andres said.

The patrons clapped.

"The second part will be a reading from Diondray Azur of Charlesville. He will read a themily, a common form of wisdom literature among people south of the Great Forest. I'm looking forward to that as well."

The patrons clapped again.

"Let's get started with the first part of the show."

Background music played until the first model arrived on the stage. She was a tall, reddish-brown skinned woman with pouty lips and a determined look on her face.

"Marena is wearing a deep pink jumpsuit with two-inch platform shoes. You can wear this jumpsuit at work or for a night on the town," Andres announced and stood just off the right of the stage.

The jumpsuit was loose on Marena's body, and her walk made it move from side to side like there was wind in the restaurant. She reached the front of the stage and stood for several seconds in an aggressive pose, facing the patrons. Marena turned her back to them and walked toward the stage's back entrance.

"Marena in a deep pink jumpsuit," Andres finished.

The patrons clapped halfheartedly.

I looked at Mr. Cortes. He still had a smirk on his face. He wasn't going to let a lukewarm response to his first model take that look away.

"Chelsea is wearing a geometric midi dress that flares out over the hips. This type of dress is for those women who want to hide that troublesome trio of backside, hips, and stomach."

The patrons laughed at Andres's announcement as Chelsea came onto the stage after Marena exited. She was blonde with fair skin and had the same body type as the first model, less a couple of inches. She walked with a big smile that made the patrons receive her warmly.

I glanced at Mr. Cortes and Felicia. They both seemed engrossed in the show. They genuinely loved their clothing. Whatever Mr. Cortes's agenda was concerning the expedition did not change the fact that clothing was the business he truly enjoyed.

I overheard a waitstaff person tell Felicia that patrons were writing on the notes placed at the tables. Chelsea had broken the ice. Maisa whispered in my ear that she wished she could have been modeling tonight. I had to admit I could have seen on her stage.

Andres introduced a couple more models, and the patrons clapped louder as each one of them presented their clothing. The drinks they were having before dinner probably weren't hurting either.

"I have one more model for the first part of the show," Andres announced. "This model is wearing a new type of clothing that Mr. Cortes recently discovered. It has taken the cities of Santa Teresa and Alicia by storm. And he believes it will do the same for us here in Issabella. Let's bring out Bonita."

"Bonita?" I blurted out.

Mr. Cortes looked at me, and I knew why he'd had the smirk on his face all evening.

"Bonita is wearing sun-yellow shorts and a dark blue blouse with a yellow flower pattern. Bonita is from the city of Alicia and has been wearing Cortes clothing since Mr. Cortes arrived in their city a couple of months ago."

Bonita Golde was here. I hadn't thought I would see her again. Maisa's face had gone pale.

"Excuse me, I have to go freshen up," she said, rising suddenly from the table. I watched her leave, escorted away by the waitstaff, before looking distractedly back at the stage where Bonita was modeling for the patrons.

"Shorts are the latest fashion sensation from Mr. Cortes. He discovered this clothing as worn by Diondray Azur of Charlesville when he first arrived in Santa Teresa. Shorts are popular in the cities South of the Great Forest and have now made their way to our region," Andres continued.

Bonita's treetop hairstyle and full-shaped figure got all the patrons' attention. She was not shaped like the other models and knew it. Bonita looked at me as she made it to the front of the stage. I knew she'd come here tonight for me.

"That ends the first part of our show," Andres continued as the patrons clapped. "Our second part will begin in fifteen minutes. Please place those notes at the edge of the table so the waitstaff can collect them quickly."

Bonita smiled at me as she walked to the stage's back entrance. I watched her walk away, still in disbelief that she was here.

"She loves you." Maisa said as she returned to the table. "I knew that being Fat Vincent's girlfriend was a ruse."

"How did you know that?"

"No woman would be attracted to a man like him," Maisa continued. "Also, to leave their city to be in a clothing show after what she and those people witnessed at the river. I'm sure she got in touch with Mr. Cortes. But she came here for you, Diondray."

I did not know how to respond. Bonita was here for me. I knew that. I just needed to know why.

"Please come with me," a waiter whispered in my ear. "Time to get ready for your reading."

I nodded and got up from my seat to follow him.

"She will never love you like I can," Maisa said and grabbed my hand that had the themily.

Maisa's comment was on my mind as I walked to the stage's back entrance. I'd really thought the Festival of the River God would be the last time I saw Bonita. I could not be the only reason she was here in Issabella!

Bonita was waiting for me by the back entrance. "I had to see you," she said as I approached her. "Your presence at the Festival of the River God has everyone still talking about it."

"What are you doing here?"

"Mr. Cortes told me you would be here tonight," she replied and touched my shoulder. "I know you cannot return to Alicia because the fifty-day period has passed. So I had to see you."

I still didn't understand what she was trying to say, but her touch almost made me angry. "I need to prepare for my reading."

"I love you."

I stared at Bonita. I could not believe what she had just said.

The waiter approached me. "Diondray, it's time."

Bonita caressed my shoulder and said, "Fat Vincent knows how I feel about you."

I turned away from Bonita and followed the waiter to the stage.

I heard Andres's introduction for my arrival, and the audience clapped as I reached the front of the stage. I searched the audience and saw looks of anticipation on their faces. At least the crowd was not hostile—most of them, anyway. I noticed one patron sitting at a table on the left side of the stage. He had a fatherly presence as he glared at me. It seemed that he was looking down at me through his thin-rimmed glasses. I sensed he had a position of importance, and I instantly felt he was in attendance to judge my themily reading. I looked away from him and began to feel a nervous energy running through my body as I got ready to speak.

I glanced at our table before I began and saw smiles on all faces except Maisa's. She looked distant. She'd known all along that Bonita Golde loved me. Now, Maisa was afraid that she was going to lose me—even though I had not declared myself to any woman.

I had to get my mind off of that situation and focus on my reading. I lifted the paper to eye level.

What can an outsider tell those who know what they believe?

What can an outsider tell those who have read the Book of Kammbi every day of their lives?

What can an outsider tell those who are governed by a council on how they should believe and follow Kammbi?

What can an outsider tell those who are used to knowing where they stand with their god?

This outsider can tell you that he has seen those who have believed in their own interpretation of the Book of Kammbi.

This outsider can tell you that he has seen those who believed that women should not be unmarried like Teresa and feel the call to believe and follow in Kammbi in their own way.

This outsider can tell you that he has seen those who believe and follow Kammbi who dismissed those who believe in the God of the River.

This outsider can tell you that he has seen someone predestinated to become a morrim be redirected by the guidance of the Eternal Comforter.

This outsider can tell you that he has seen the discovery of a book that has been in his city for years and has changed his life forever.

This outsider can tell you he has to learn to embrace this journey in order to fulfill Oscar's prophecy.

This outsider can tell you that he will have to find out in the next thirty-nine days why he is in the city of Issabella.

This outsider can tell you that by the time he leaves this city, you will all be changed.

I dropped the paper by my side and looked out at the audience. Silence. My themily had not reached them. I turned my back and began to walk to the stage's back entrance.

Then I heard a clap to my left. I stopped walking and turned around to see the patron with the thin-rimmed glasses clapping. He did not smile, but I knew he liked my reading. Moments later, the rest of patrons clapped. The entire audience rose from their seats and continued with their applause.

I had been wrong. My themily did reach them after all.

Chapter 18

Mr. Cortes told me at breakfast two days later that I had become the talk of Issabella. My themily reading at Tavares had been on everyone's lips throughout the city. They were amazed that a stranger from south of the Great Forest could read with such intelligence and wisdom that the patrons who attended did not even mention Mr. Cortes's clothes.

Andres reached out to me through Mr. Cortes and asked if I would give another reading at the restaurant. His patrons had asked for me ever since my visit, and I was good for business. I would not have to share the stage with anyone. I accepted the invitation and began revising one of the themilys I had read back in Aliki Park. I would go back to Tavares the following day.

As I worked, I thought about Bonita Golde and what she had said to me. Her declaration of love was startling. I had believed that she and Fat Vincent were together. He was quite fond of her, and I could see why. But he knew about her feelings toward me. As pleasing as Bonita's declaration was to hear, I did not know how to receive it. Did she want me to reciprocate? Would I see her again? Would I have to go back to Alicia? And what about Maisa? My emotions became clouded with these questions, and I had no answers to any of them.

I had not seen Maisa since Bonita's declaration. But I knew she had not taken it well. Maisa had declared her love for me in Santa Teresa, and it had remained constant for this entire expedition. I knew she was waiting for me to give my declaration of love to her. But I couldn't do it—not for her and not Bonita. I just didn't feel that it would be the right thing to do at this time. I planned to see this expedition through to the end and fulfill Oscar's prophecy. Being in love with someone right now would distract me away from doing that.

I believe you are the one who will unite this land as one, and the Great Forest will not be a barrier between us anymore.

That sentence from Aunt Maxina's letter came to mind as I pondered these things. I'd read her letter when I was leaving Charlesville to come to Santa Sophia. She was the first person to believe that I would be the one to fulfill Oscar's prophecy. I had to see this through, not only for myself but for Aunt Maxina.

I want you to know that I will be all right even if Xavier finds out that I helped you escape Charlesville.

I hoped that Aunt Maxina was doing well. If Uncle Xavier found out what she had done, he would treat her harshly. I couldn't help feeling that if that happened, this entire expedition would not have been a risk worth taking.

My thoughts were stormy and distracted while I tried to study. On top of all my personal issues, I still needed to find out what was the issue here in Issabella. How much did the konseho of Kammbi know about me? And how much did the people of this city believe and follow the Book of Kammbi to the letter? In Santa Teresa and Alicia, that had not been the case. People in both cities had created their own interpretations of the Book of Kammbi, and it had brought division of many kinds. I needed to find out if it was the same issue here in Issabella before my hearing with the konseho. They thought I was here for their approval, but I knew I was here to fulfill the prophecy. I had a higher purpose. I continued to pray every morning after I arrived in Issabella. Prayer had been an unexpected boost for me, and I liked the fact that I could communicate honestly. Kneeling on the floor next to my bed was still uncomfortable. Diakono Copperwith explained to me that that was the way he prayed every morning after awakening. He felt that position in prayer was the proper one in order to communicate with the Eternal Comforter. I was still not sure about that line of reasoning, and I wondered if his knees did not ache after praying in that position for so many years.

Despite my questions, I was starting to believe that I was communicating with the Eternal Comforter in prayer, and I knew I would need his guidance for the rest of my time here in Issabella.

#

"How many children did Oscar Ortega have?"

"Four," I answered. I sat across from Morrim Sperrie and Diakono Prescott in the morrim's office.

"Who was the oldest child?" Diakono Prescott asked.

"Niomi."

"When is the Festival of Sinquinta?" Morrim Sperrie asked.

"The twenty-first day in the fifth month of Aym."

"What does the festival signify?"

"The fifty days that Oscar Ortega traveled from his homeland, Guadharra, to the Ortega Hills."

I glanced over at Diakono Copperwith, who gave me a reassuring smile.

"Keep your eyes on us," Diakono Prescott snapped.

I nodded and returned to looking at them both. I started feeling that nervous energy churning in my stomach.

"When were those northwestern hills named the Ortega Hills?

"Year 39 A.O.A." Sudden uncertainty hit me. "A year after Oscar Ortega died?"

"Incorrect, Diondray," Morrim Sperrie said. "It was 43 A.O.A., five years after Oscar Ortega's death. Niomi became the first governor of Santa Sophia and named those northwestern hills after her father."

"I did not read that in the Book of Kammbi."

"It is not in the Book of Kammbi," Diakono Prescott added. "But if you are the one to fulfill Oscar's prophecy, then you must know the entire history of Oscar Ortega. The konseho of Kammbi will test you on it."

The nervous energy in my stomach began to make me lightheaded, and I knew I needed to stand up. I also needed to look away from Diakono Prescott. His glare unnerved me.

"Morrim Sperrie, I believe we should take a break," Diakono Copperwith said, rising.

Morrim Sperrie looked at me with concern. "I agree, Diakono Copperwith. A break is needed."

"We just started with the session. He will not be able to take a break during the hearing. We have to strengthen him to push through it," Diakono Prescott said as he also rose.

I got up and started pacing.

"Diakono Prescott, you still have not learned how to read people," Morrim Sperrie said. "Our guest was getting uncomfortable for the past several minutes. If that same scenario happens during the hearing, the konseho of Kammbi will give him a grace period. They will want him to be at his best for the hearing."

I smiled at Morrim Sperrie, thankful for her understanding. I knew from that moment she believed I was the one who would fulfill Oscar's prophecy. She would do everything in her power to make sure I was ready for the hearing in thirty-seven days.

"Thank you, Second Esperah Holloway," Morrim Sperrie said to the stout second esperah who entered the office with a glass of cherry juice.

Second Esperah Holloway handed me the glass as I returned to my seat. He bowed and exited the office.

"Are you ready to continue?" Diakono Copperwith said. I nodded, but I had a question for Morrim Sperrie before we continued. "What made you decide to become a morrim? You are the first woman morrim, and I believe you are an outsider like myself."

Morrim Sperrie gave me a surprised look at first and then smiled.

"I don't think that is an appropriate question," Diakono Prescott said, but Morrim Sperrie and I both ignored him.

"Diakono Copperwith has told me about your struggle with the Eternal Comforter since you arrived north of the Great Forest," Morrim Sperrie started. "I shared that same struggle. How could an unseen spirit guide you in every life-making decision? How could an unseen spirit communicate to you without you thinking that you were just talking to yourself? That was a hard concept to embrace. However, I decided to trust that unseen spirit placed inside of me by Kammbi. Because of that trust, I became the first woman morrim in the cities north of the Great Forest."

"So believing in the Eternal Comforter just comes down to trust?"

She smiled. "First, you have to declare your belief in Kammbi and follow him. You have to believe that his sacrifice, as acknowledged during the Festival of Sinquinta, was for all of humanity. Once you have done that, then you receive the gift of the Eternal Comforter. And then yes—you walk with him by trust."

I finished drinking my glass of cherry juice and placed it on the table. "Diakono Copperwith has explained that to me throughout this expedition. Both of you make it seem easy to just believe and follow Kammbi. But I have seen already in both Santa Teresa and Alicia that people have added their own interpretations to their belief and following Kammbi. Is it the Eternal Comforter guiding those people as well?"

Morrim Sperrie smiled. "Diakono Copperwith was right. You are perceptive, Diondray. I'm beginning to believe more each day that you are the one to fulfill Oscar's prophecy. People will always add their own ideas and thoughts to what has been shown them. There is a misconception amongst those who believe and follow Kammbi that everyone will follow the words of the book literally and understand them perfectly, without room for any other type of interpretation. That will never be true. Human beings are flawed and impure. And we continue to promote the mistaken idea that if we can become pure ourselves, then we can achieve what it truly means to become a believer and follower of Kammbi. Kammbi is the only pure one, because he alone carried the dual status of god and man in one being. We will never achieve that kind of status, no matter how strongly we believe in Kammbi and follow him."

"That is true. And so, because we are imperfect, there will always be room for individual interpretation from each city north of the Great Forest," Diakono Prescott added.

I glanced at Diakono Prescott after his comment. His intense look remained.

"Those basic beliefs have been handed down from Kammbi for us to believe and follow. People will always try to add to those basic beliefs in the name of sophistication and evolution. But it will always come back to those basic beliefs. And to answer your question, Teresa was a morrim even though she did not receive the title. So I had every right to become a morrim, and the guidance of the Eternal Comforter confirmed it," Morrim Sperrie added.

I turned all of this over in my mind. "So I have to embrace the basic beliefs before I can truly fulfill Oscar's prophecy?" I asked.

"You already have embraced the basics, Diondray Azur," Morrim Sperrie answered. "You would not be here in my office otherwise. But you are trying to grasp it with your own logic. I would tell you to let the logic of these basic beliefs connect with your heart. When you allow that connection, the Eternal Comforter will forever guide you."

#

"We would like to welcome back Diondray Azur of Charlesville," Andres announced.

The patrons applauded. I looked out from the stage at the audience to get a read on how ready they were for my themily. Positive energy washed over me from their applause, and I was ready to give the reading.

What is love?
Is love something that you feel?
Is love something that you already know deep inside of you?
Is love something that can grow over time?
Is love something that can elude you no matter how much you want it?

Love tends to come in a variety of ways,
But what happens when someone declares their love to you
And you do not reciprocate that declaration?
Should they keep continuing to pursue love?
Should they wait for your reciprocation?
Or should they just move on?

I would tell those who have made their declaration of love
That timing is the key,
Because heartfelt intentions at the wrong time
Can be taken by the recipient of the declaration
Like those who have never given a declaration of their love
And that person ends up thinking their love was unrequited.

The recipient of that declaration
Could have something else in their life
That they are preoccupied with
And that preoccupation could keep them from
Giving the love
that the beneficiary wants from that person.

It returns to the question,
What is love?
If you know the answer
Then you will know that love can exist
Even if your declaration has not been reciprocated
Because love has a way of revealing itself
When you least expect it.

I finished the themily and looked out at the patrons. They did not applaud right away, and I could tell they were still trying to absorb my themily. I saw astonished looks on their faces. Like I had read something to them that they did not expect.

I looked over at the table to where my group was sitting. Mr. Cortes was talking to the man with the thin-rimmed glasses whom I remembered from the fashion show. Felicia and Maisa smiled at me. They were pleased with my reading.

"Thank you, Diondray Azur," Andres announced as he returned to the stage. "Love is definitely mysterious, and your words of wisdom are something we should take into thoughtful consideration. Give him another round of applause."

The patrons rose from the seats and applauded as I turned to leave the stage.

I arrived at our table a few minutes later. Before I could sit down to have dinner, Maisa ran up and wrapped her arms around me.

"I knew you loved me," she said softly in my ear. "I was waiting to hear something from you about it. I understand. I will wait until the time is right."

I returned her embrace. For the first time, it felt like the right thing to do. She didn't know I had written that themily for Mara years ago because of her declaration of love for me. I'd never thought I would be reading the same themily for a second time to someone else. Hopefully it would keep Maisa at bay for a while longer. Also, that themily had been for Bonita as well. I hoped those words got back to her too. Love was a distraction that I did not need at this moment.

"Those were great words of wisdom," Mr. Cortes said as I finally sat down at our table. "I would like you to meet someone. This is Deputy Julian Santiago."

I greeted Mr. Santiago with a handshake and noticed how far those thin-rimmed glasses stood away from his face. I was surprised they did not fall off of his nose upon our greeting. Mr. Santiago carried himself like a man who knew his status in this city.

"He is a deputy at the konseho of Kammbi," Mr. Cortes continued.

"With words of wisdom like that, I'm looking forward to our upcoming hearing with you, Diondray Azur," Deputy Julian Santiago said after our handshake.

His words were encouraging—but intimidating too. For the time I realized the konseho of Kammbi had already heard about me and were making their preparations for the hearing as well.

Chapter 19

"The konseho of Kammbi is made up of two sections," Morrim Sperrie stated as we finished our latest study session. "There are padres (tenured members) and deputies (nontenured members). Julian Santiago has been a deputy for several years and is looking for his opportunity to become a padre.

"He is probably the most important deputy in the konseho of Kammbi." Diakono Prescott added sternly.

I glanced at Diakono Prescott after his comment. He had not taken a liking to me yet, at least as far as I could tell. There were twenty days to go before the hearing, and I sensed that he would test me the entire time to see if I was truly the one who would fulfill Oscar's prophecy.

"I'm not surprised he would be spending time with Mr. Cortes," Diakono Copperwith said. "Their ambitions would create an instant connection with each other."

"Plus, Deputy Santiago will use any angle to get leverage with Senior Padre Ashland," Diakono Prescott added.

The diakonos were in sync about Deputy Santiago. I wondered how much Mr. Cortes had told him about me.

"It tells me that the konseho of Kammbi are taking your claim seriously," Morrim Sperrie stated. "Deputy Santiago will make sure they know everything about you before the hearing."

"The konseho know that Morrim Sperrie and I are training you for the hearing," Diakono Prescott said. "They will test your entire knowledge of the Book of Kammbi, looking for any inconsistencies to refute your claim. We must make sure that you are totally prepared for it." "He will be prepared for it, Diakono Prescott," Morrim Sperrie answered.

"Deputy Santiago is the most knowledgeable about the Book of Kammbi and will listen carefully to how Diondray answers their questions. He will hone in on any incorrect answers and capitalize on it."

Diakono Prescott looked genuinely concerned. Deputy Santiago bothered him in some fashion.

"We will prepare Diondray to the best of our ability and leave the rest to the Eternal Comforter," Morrim Sperrie said. "If he is the one to fulfill Oscar's prophecy, then a deputy from the konseho of Kammbi will not be able to stop what is going to happen for this entire land."

She smiled at me. I was beginning to feel like she was a kindred spirit. Not only did she believe in me, but she reminded me of Aunt Maxina for some reason.

"Mr. Cortes has his own agenda for being with us," Diakono Copperwith interjected with a grimace. "My wife and I had our concerns about him. But we had to honor Diondray's decision to allow him to come with us on the second expedition."

"You made that decision?" Diakono Prescott asked me.

I faced him and replied, "Yes. I believed it was the right decision at the time, and I stand by it. Mr. Cortes may have his own agenda, but it has not come into conflict with the expedition."

"I appreciate the leadership you exhibit," Morrim Sperrie said. "As you know, Oscar Ortega allowed Diego Carranza to join him when he returned from Guadharra. Diego had to become a believer and follower in Kammbi in order to come with Oscar. He agreed, and Oscar allowed him to become the one businessman who is forever remembered in the Book of Kammbi."

"I took that section of the Book of Kammbi into account in making my decision. I believe the same result will happen again," I replied.

Diakono Copperwith shook his head. "Diondray, I have explained to you that Diego Carranza and Oscar Ortega had a well-established relationship prior to Oscar coming to the land for the first time. Oscar made sure he adhered to becoming a believer and follower in Kammbi. Diego agreed with that stipulation. Remember when you met Phyllis Carranza at Oscar's statue in the marperia at Santa Sophia. She is his great-granddaughter four generations later. Phyllis told me how Diego's faith in Kammbi was handed down from one generation to the next. Because of Diego's adherence to Oscar Ortega, the Carranza family will be forever remembered in the Book of Kammbi. You do not know if Mr. Cortes truly believes and follows Kammbi. You don't even know if he really believes in you."

"I can only take a man at his word. He said he is a believer and follower in Kammbi. Mr. Cortes knows the Book of Kammbi just as well as any of you. And what I've learned from reading in the Book of Kammbi is that the Eternal Comforter is the only one who can judge that," I replied.

Diakono Prescott nodded. "You have read the Book of Kammbi and taken our study sessions to heart."

That was the first concession he had given me so far. I would take it as a small step in the right direction.

"Diakono Copperwith, I hear your concerns, and I assume you expressed them to Diondray back in Santa Teresa. Let's not go too far with it. Diondray exhibited leadership and made a difficult decision. We know from the Book of Kammbi that the Eternal

Comforter will always protect those who have been chosen." Morrim Sperrie said and smiled at me again.

She was right. After she said it, I realized that the Eternal Comforter had protected me the entire time I had been in these cities north of the Great Forest.

#

It was fifteen days before the hearing, and this would be my first excursion into Issabella besides Tavares. I needed to spend some time in the city before the hearing, and I wanted to get out from the kahall.

Percival drove me away, and I stared out of the window at the marperia. It was triangular shaped and small compared to the other marperias I'd seen here in the north. I looked to see if there was a statue or some landmark signifying the city's history, but I did not see one. Disappointing.

Maisa was sitting next to me, and my thoughts turned to her. I had not seen Bonita Golde since that night at Tavares. She must have gone back to Alicia by now. Maisa had not mentioned her since that night. I knew that it was still creating separation between us. Maisa would never be totally comfortable with me until Bonita Golde was completely out of the picture.

"Issabella is a nice city," she said as she placed her hand on my shoulder. I was still looking out the window.

"I'm looking forward to finding that out," I replied while looking at the bubble-shaped cars that passed us by. "I've been hidden in the kahall so long it's starting to feel like Santa Teresa."

"Mr. Cortes has made sure your name is known throughout the city."

I turned from the window and faced Maisa. "I'm sure he has."

"Your themily readings at Tavares have been the talk of the city. Mr. Cortes and Felicia have made sure of that fact."

"I know that Percival continues to take both of them to the konseho each day."

"Yes. Mr. Cortes has gotten to know Deputy Santiago of the konseho of Kammbi. He has taken us around the city to allow Mr. Cortes to talk about your arrival in Issabella." She giggled. "He speaks about your themily readings while promoting his clothes."

"Of course," I said. "Did he apologize for his role with the mine?"

"No, he has not," Maisa said with a slight frown. "However, he assured me that the ownership transfer would go smoothly."

I scooted back in the seat. "I spoke with the Copperwiths about the position he took on the ownership transfer. Diakono Copperwith has expressed concerns about Mr. Cortes. He has never truly been on board with my decision to allow him and Felicia to join us."

"Annalisa has stressed those concerns to her husband," Maisa answered. "I believe his concerns come more from her than him."

"Actually, I believe both of them feel the same way about the businessman," I replied. "I defended my decision in our last study session with Morrim Sperrie and Diakono Prescott. They both respected my decision and believed I made the right choice."

Maisa smiled and patted my thigh. "Because they know you are the one to fulfill Oscar's prophecy. And any decision you make will be guided by the Eternal Comforter."

I leaned back in my seat, still unsatisfied. "Maybe so, but I've been getting the feeling Mr. Cortes's real reason for wanting to come on the second expedition has not been revealed yet."

"I agree with you, Diondray. But remember, the Eternal Comforter is guiding you, and any agenda the businessman has will not harm you. You have been chosen, just like Oscar Ortega. Trust in that more than anything else."

I nodded at Maisa and embraced her, giving in for the moment to my desire to hold her.

"I will wait for you, Diondray Azur," she said softly inside of our embrace.

I knew she would. And for the first time, I knew I would wait as well.

#

Our exploration of the city was fun but uneventful. When I returned to my room at at the kahall, I went back to work on the themily for the konseho of Kammbi. I stopped writing and picked up the Book of Kammbi from the desk. I wanted to reread the entire book to make sure I did not miss anything Deputy Santiago would bring to light at the hearing. Also, I would spend these last days in prayer each morning. If the Eternal Comforter was truly guiding me like Maisa had said, then he would answer my prayers on how to handle the hearing.

I finished reading Issabella's section in the Book of Kammbi and placed the book on the right side of the desk. I said a quick prayer and continued writing the themily. But this time, I started over, going in a different direction. My entire time in these cities north of the Great Forest was becoming clear to me. Issabella believed that the Eternal Comforter gave everyone a role to live out as a believer and follower of Kammbi. She did not understand her role, because she could not grasp the concept of a spirit living inside you. When the connection between her, Oscar, and the other disciples was revealed to her, she knew the Eternal Comforter had created that connection and understood her role.

I realized that being a believer and follower of Kammbi did not mean suspending your mind and logic to believe in the unseen. It was about trusting in something outside of you. Human beings have an inherited selfish nature and will always revert to their selfishness especially in times of trouble. The Eternal Comforter wanted all believers and followers of Kammbi to trust in the gift they had received.

The people in the other cities of this region did not fully trust in the Eternal Comforter. They trusted in themselves. That's why they had different interpretations from each city about the Book of Kammbi. Even though the people believed and followed Kammbi with their words and outward displays of devotion, ultimately, they did not really trust the gift from Kammbi within themselves.

Oscar Ortega had always trusted that gift. Even though he committed an act of passha with Mother Adrianna and attempted reconciliation with Charles, he still trusted. Oscar trusted the Eternal Comforter when he left Guadharra to come to this land, and so he knew his role despite his shortcomings. The people of this region had not trusted in the Eternal Comforter alone, and my themily at the hearing had to address that.

Chapter 20

It was the next-to-last day in Issabella. Morrim Sperrie explained they might extend the hearing beyond one day and wanted to start it today instead of our last day here in the city. I arrived at the hall of the konseho of Kammbi shortly after eating breakfast. Our entire group ate together in the kahall of Issabella's cafeteria. Morrim Sperrie and Diakono Prescott joined us as well. I received encouragement from everyone, and Morrim Sperrie said a prayer before we left for the hall.

The konseho of Kammbi met in an impressive building to behold. Mr. Cortes asked Percival to drive around the building so we could get a full view of it before entering. It was a long, rectangular building that took up several blocks just north of the city's marperia. The reddish-brown mud and wood common to this region were the materials making up the outside. The mud colored the entire building except the entrance doors, one on each side of the building, and appeared like it had just recently been painted. The white entrance doors gave a striking contrast to the rest of the building, and Percival pointed out the tastefully embossed letter "K" on each door. The façade had three pillars that rose towards the skyline and gave the building a regal appearance. The left and right pillars had a white letter "K" at the top, while the center pillar had a white letter "O," and each letter was positioned symmetrically to represent the name of the building. I must admit I wanted Percival to drive around again so I could get another look at this majestic place.

Percival parked, and we exited the autobus to be immediately greeted by guards. They were all young men who appeared to be close to my age of twenty-three. The guards wore brown shawls and had blank expressions on their faces as they led us up to the main entrance. Our group was quiet, as it seemed that everyone knew the time had arrived for the conclusion of this expedition. I was not sure of what to expect at the hearing, even though I felt prepared by Morrim Sperrie and Diakono Prescott. Would Oscar's prophecy be fulfilled? Or not? Somehow, I sensed that we had not reach the fulfillment of the prophecy.

The guards led us through the main hallway with white "K"shaped chandeliers hanging from the ceiling. There were paintings of men and women dressed in shawls engraved into the walls. I realized some of them were the disciples from the Ryianza as well as from the Baramesa.

Some of the guards veered right onto another hallway and took the rest of the group to a different area of the building. I watched them walk away and immediately missed their presence. I realized that I'd come to rely on their support. I could not have traveled to these cities north of the Great Forest without them. Despite our disagreements at times, they meant a lot to me.

A couple of guards led me through the main hallway to the back entrance. I adjusted the travel bag on my left shoulder as the guard on my right opened the door. The sunlight greeted me instantly as I exited the building.

"Diondray Azur." A deep, baritone voice called my name.

I placed my right hand on my eyes and looked to my left, seeing bleachers that rose as high as the building. There was a stairway between the bleachers with people sitting on both sides of it. The bleachers were made from the same reddish-brown mud as the building, and behind them was a river. The Issabella River.

"The konseho of Kammbi greets you," a wrinkle-faced man with disheveled white hair said from the lowest row of the bleachers. The guard brought me to the open area in front of the bleachers, and I felt all the eyes of the konseho of Kammbi staring at me. "I believe the claim has been made that you are the one who will fulfill Oscar's prophecy written in the last chapter of Oscar Ortega's writings in the Baramesa."

"That claim has been made," I answered.

I scanned the bleachers and saw elderly looking men on the left side of the stairway and younger looking people, men and women, around Mother's age on the right side of the stairway. I thought there had to be at least a hundred members. "I'm Senior Padre Arthur Ashland," the wrinkle-faced man announced. I looked over to the left side of the room, where I heard his voice. "There are fifty members of the konseho above me. They are all padre members of the konseho of Kammbi."

"You are the tenured members of the konseho of Kammbi," I replied.

Senior Padre Ashland smiled. "Yes, we are. Morrim Sperrie and Diakono Prescott of the kahall of Issabella prepared you quite well."

I noticed the entire konseho nod their approval at my response. To my own surprise, I didn't feel nervous, even with all of them looking down at me. I didn't even feel a need to pace the open area.

"There are fifty members to the left of me," Senior Padre Ashland continued. "They are the deputy members of the konseho of Kammbi. And you probably know they are the nontenured members. Even though their status is not of a permanent nature, the deputy members have quite a bit of influence here at the konseho. After I declare the opening of this hearing on the twenty-third day in the tenth month of Coter, as attended by all the konseho members, I will allow Deputy Julian Santiago to conduct it. Do all members of the konseho of Kammbi acknowledge this declaration?"

"We do," all the members said in unison.

"Then this hearing has been declared," Senior Padre Ashland stated. "Deputy Santiago, you may begin."

I recognized Deputy Santiago's face from Tavares restaurant. His rimmed glasses still looked like they were going to fall off his face. He sat on the right side of the bleachers at the bottom row in a similar position to Senior Padre Ashland. The deputy looked eager, but I could not tell if he was a friend or an enemy.

"We meet again, Diondray Azur. This time it is in my arena. I'm looking forward to finding out who you really are."

I nodded.

"Also, I want you to know that the rest of your group are watching this hearing from inside. We do not want a hearing influenced by someone's support system. However, we at the konseho of Kammbi know you have been well prepared by Morrim Sperrie and Diakono Prescott of the kahall of Issabella."

"I have."

"I understand that you have in your possession Oscar Ortega's copy of the Book of Kammbi, the very book he left as a gift to his out-of-wedlock son, Charles."

I winced at that last comment and replied, "I do. I found out about this copy of the Book of Kammbi when my Aunt Maxina took me to Ama's Faddar back in Charlesville and showed this book to me."

Deputy Santiago glared at me. "May we see it?"

I nodded and pulled the travel bag off of my shoulder. I unzipped the bag and pulled out the Book of Kammbi. It felt like the pages were going to crumble in my hands.

"Guards!" the deputy snapped.

A guard came immediately and seized the Book of Kammbi out of my hands. "Be careful!" I said.

The deputy smirked as the guard handed him the Book of Kammbi. "I can see you have grown fond of this Book of Kammbi, and I understand from the morrims in all the cities you have visited that you have read it as well."

I had gotten used to having that Book of Kammbi in my possession and felt like it belonged to me. "I have."

Deputy Santiago stared at the cover for a moment and then flipped the pages. I was trying to read his face, but he remained expressionless. "Guard, give this to Senior Padre Ashland."

The guard grabbed the book from the deputy and walked over to Senior Padre Ashland. The old man clutched the Book of Kammbi in his hands as the guard walked away. He placed the Book of Kammbi on the ledge in front of him and nodded at the deputy.

"Let's see how much you have read, Diondray Azur," Deputy Santiago remarked.

Finally. I was ready to start.

"How many books are in the Ryianza of the Book of Kammbi?" Deputy Santiago asked. "Seven."

"How many books are in the Baramesa?"

"Seven."

"Who were Kammbi's first disciples before Oscar Ortega?"

"Carlos, Gregory, and Jorge. Each of them has his writings in the Ryianza."

"What does *Ryianza* mean?"

"Covenant."

"What about *Baramesa*?"

"Promise."

"Who did Oscar Ortega meet with when he first arrived from Guadharra?"

"The elders of the Makala tribe."

"What was the woman's name who caused Oscar Ortega to commit an act of passha?"

"Mother Adrianna."

I heard a gasp from the entire konseho of Kammbi after my answer. I could tell they did not like it.

"Why do you call her 'Mother'?" the deputy asked. I straightened my shoulders. "Mother Adrianna gave birth to Charles Azur, the founder of my hometown, Charlesville. She traveled from the northwestern hills of this land after being rejected by her own tribe while pregnant. When she arrived amongst the Makala tribe and became a part of our ancestors, she gained her name."

"Do you know that by our tradition she is considered to be the other woman?"

"Yes, I do. I have learned in my travels throughout these cities north of the Great Forest that she has not been honored or sometimes even mentioned. Oscar Ortega was a great disciple of Kammbi, but he failed in this area of his life. However, I thought that the people of this region would be a forgiving people. Considering that one is allowed to pursue an act of aphemmia and be absolved of their acts of passha according to the Book of Kammbi, it would seem grace befits Kammbi's followers. Oscar Ortega pursued an act of aphemmia when coming south of the Great Forest and trying to establish a relationship with his son, Charles. And I believe that Mother Adrianna deserves to be forgiven too."

The entire room gasped again. I cut my eyes from one section of the bleachers to the other section and noticed the astonished looks of some of the konseho members.

"So you believe the other woman deserved aphemmia?" Deputy Santiago continued.

"Mother Adrianna," I shot back. "Every one of the disciples in the Book of Kammbi pursued aphemmia when they committed an act of passha. Why can't Mother Adrianna be shown aphemmia as well?"

Deputy Santiago smirked. He knew I was right about Mother Adrianna.

"Morrim Sperrie and Diakono Prescott have prepared you well, and you have read this Book of Kammbi that has been in your possession," Deputy Santiago continued. "You have brought an idea that no one in this region has ever considered. It's a fair point. The other woman was rejected by the Mayza tribe and made to leave her people. Even though she was willing get involved with a married man and our greatest disciple and so has guilt of her own, it was Oscar who brought this act of passha on himself, and he received aphemmia from Kammbi and the Eternal Comforter. Why could she not also be forgiven?"

"That other woman was not a believer and follower of Kammbi. And the Eternal Comforter did not reside inside of her," Senior Padre Ashland erupted.

I faced Senior Padre Ashland and replied, "She was not given a chance to return to her people. In Oscar's next-to-last chapter of his writings, he spoke about meeting with the Makala tribe. Those tribe members mentioned that Mother Adrianna spoke often about her people and how she missed them. But when you are rejected and cast out, how can you pursue aphemmia? What chance are you given? And if the teachings of the Book of Kammbi were not meant for those outside of this region, then I would not be here standing before you."

Senior Padre Ashland's expression dropped. He nodded slowly, and I knew I had just made some headway at this hearing. The looks of the other members of the konseho had changed from astonishment to concern. They had never expected Mother Adrianna to be spoken about in such fashion.

"You have challenged our traditions throughout your expedition," Deputy Santiago said. I looked away from Senior Padre Ashland and faced him. "We will continue this hearing tomorrow and hear from some people in each city who have been affected by those challenges. This hearing is adjourned."

I felt a tug on my shoulder and turned around to see it was the guards who had brought me here. They escorted me away from the area and led me back to the building. I was surprised at how abruptly the first day of the hearing had ended. I wanted to continue. I knew my response about Mother Adrianna had caught them by surprise, and Senior Padre Ashland had agreed with my comments. I'd thought I would be pacing restlessly upon being questioned, but I had felt calm the entire time. I knew that the Eternal Comforter had begun to answer my prayers.

#

I was back in that spot in front of the bleachers for the second day of the hearing. After yesterday's hearing, I did not have the Book of Kammbi in my possession for the first time since I came to this region. I felt a part of me was missing, and I hoped they would return it to me after today's hearing.

Before we got started, I turned to the right of the bleachers and stared at the Issabella River in the distance. I thought about the people of the River district in Alicia. Their reverence for the river god when he rose from the river flashed through my mind. Worshipping something for years and then finally seeing it was a powerful thing. Had they accepted the correct interpretation of the Book of Kammbi when the river god urged them to? Had the morrims and diakonos of that city brought those people into the fold? That scene at the river had been a life-changing event, and staring at this body of water brought it back to me like it had happened yesterday.

"I see that you like water," Deputy Santiago said, interrupting my thoughts as I looked out at the river.

I faced him as he sat in the same position from yesterday. "I spent a lot of time looking at the Bay of Charlesville back home. The river reminded of that time."

The deputy smiled. "I would like to visit Charlesville someday. Maybe your arrival will begin to facilitate that possibility."

"This is day two of the hearing," Senior Padre Ashland announced and interrupted my conversation with the deputy. "You gave us some thought-provoking responses yesterday and provided us with the Book of Kammbi you claim belonged to Oscar Ortega. We had an intense discussion after the hearing ended. The entire konseho of Kammbi wants to learn more about the person who is standing before us. Deputy Santiago will continue on with today's portion of the hearing."

"Diondray Azur, let's continue where you left off from yesterday," Deputy Santiago started. "You gave a passionate response about that other woman being able to receive aphemmia."

"Mother Adrianna," I interjected.

Deputy Santiago stopped his opening remarks and replied, "I can understand that you might take offense to her being called the other woman. Unfortunately, the people of this region have always viewed her that way, and I use the name she is known by. But I do want to be respectful of your position. I will begin to call her Mother Adrianna."

The konseho of Kammbi began to murmur. It seemed they did not like him making that concession.

"Quiet!" Senior Padre Ashland bellowed. "Deputy Santiago has started the hearing. Our chatter about his comments can wait until he has finished for today."

The room fell silent immediately. There was no question about who controlled the konseho.

"Thank you, Senior Padre Ashland," Deputy Santiago continued. "Mother Adrianna's position will be taken under consideration by the rest of the konseho of Kammbi after the hearing. Now, I will turn my attention to the effect your arrival north of the Great Forest has had on our people. You arrived in the city of Santa Sophia on the first day in the fourth month of Lir. One of the first people you met was Second Esperah Leo Carranza, from the kahall of Santa Sophia. Now, he will speak about his time with you."

I recognized that wide smile with the whitest teeth I had ever seen, as well as his stocky build as he was brought to an area a few feet away from me. After he smiled at me, he faced the konseho in the stance I had seen during my time in Santa Sophia. That stance revealed his sense of duty and servitude, which I had questioned in our time together. I had come to admire his servant's heart and was glad that I'd had my first connection in Santa Sophia with him.

"Welcome, Second Esperah Carranza. Can you describe your experience with Diondray Azur in Santa Sophia?"

"I first met Diondray Azur on the date you mentioned, Deputy Santiago," Second Esperah Carranza began. "He arrived in the newcomer's assistance area of the kahall and told me he was from Charlesville, a city South of the Great Forest. I'd heard for several days prior to his arrival that someone unexpected would be coming to our kahall."

"Where did you hear that from?" Deputy Santiago interjected.

Second Esperah Carranza stood like a statue and replied, "Diakono Copperwith had been saying it. I, along with the other second esperahs, did not know why Diakono Copperwith spoke with such conviction about a stranger arriving at the kahall. It was out of character for him. I asked around and learned that Diakono Copperwith had met with a woman from the same city prior to Diondray Azur's arrival."

"Who was this woman?"

"Maxina. Diondray's aunt."

Second Esperah Carranza had known about Aunt Maxina's arrival in Santa Sophia prior to me coming! Why had he not mentioned that to me? Was that the reason he was so receptive when I arrived?

"When I met Diondray, I made the connection immediately between him and his aunt. Diakono Copperwith told me they were related," Second Esperah Carranza continued.

"What has been the effect of his arrival in Santa Sophia?"

"I remember a conversation I had with Diondray. He questioned why I believed in Kammbi so strongly. I told him it was about trust. As you know from the Book of Kammbi, Kammbi wants us to trust him in every area of our lives. I could tell Diondray struggled with trust in his life. He asked why I served as a second esperah, and why it seemed like I had conformed to Kammbi instead of being myself."

"Would that not give you pause to believe that he was not the one to fulfill Oscar's prophecy?"

Now I was really starting to squirm. All the calmness I'd felt at the start of this hearing was gone.

But Second Esperah Carranza surprised me. "Actually, I believe the opposite. I knew that Diondray was questioning me from an honest place inside of him and not out of rebelliousness like most men of his age. He was trying to come to grips with the issue of trust, and that made me believe he could be the one who would fulfill Oscar's prophecy."

I saw surprised looks from many of the konseho members at the second esperah's comment.

"How so?" Deputy Santiago asked.

"Oscar Ortega wrote in his prophecy that someone from his bloodline would fulfill his prophecy. He stated that person would not be what we expected or even wanted. However, he would have to learn to trust in order to fulfill the prophecy. Oscar Ortega himself had to trust Kammbi when he left Guadharra and came to the northwestern hills of the land. It took fifty days by foot, and if he did not trust Kammbi and the Eternal Comforter, he would never have become our greatest disciple. With Diondray's questioning of me, I knew he had started the process of becoming the one to follow in Oscar's footsteps."

"I appreciate your answers, Second Esperah Carranza, and thank you for your service to the kahall of Santa Sophia," Deputy Santiago said.

The guards surrounded Second Esperah Carranza and led him away. I wanted to walk over to where he was and embrace him. It meant a lot to me that he believed in me. But I had to stay where I was.

I looked up at the members of the konseho of Kammbi. They were talking amongst themselves about Second Esperah Carranza's comments, and I knew he had made an impression on them.

"Now, it is time to hear from someone from Santa Teresa," Deputy Santiago continued. "This is the second city that you visited on your expedition."

The guards returned a few moments later with Resa Dorrado. She stood in the same position as Second Esperah Carranza and did not face me. Annika was dressed in a sky-blue shawl as the resa she had become. She looked happy and peaceful. I could have stared at her for the rest of the hearing. I knew my decision to help her had been the right one. I hoped I would get a chance to speak with her before she returned to Santa Teresa.

"Resa Dorrado, can you describe your experience with Diondray Azur in Santa Teresa?" Deputy Santiago asked her.

"I met Diondray Azur on the twenty-fourth day in the fifth

month of Aym at the kahall of Santa Teresa. I had never met anyone from south of the Great Forest, and his skin color was darker than I had seen on another human being. It was his words written on paper that first drew me to him."

"A themily?"

"Correct, Deputy Santiago," she continued. "Diondray read a themily to me when I first met him, and immediately I had a sense that we would be forever connected."

I smiled at her. I realized how special Resa Dorrado had become at that moment. The Copperwiths spoke about her significance in Santa Teresa, and when she became resa at Kahall Angelica it made sense that we would be forever connected, like Oscar and Teresa.

"Did you immediately believe he was the one who would fulfill Oscar's prophecy?"

"Not immediately," she answered. "I started to believe that he was the one when he came to our home for dinner and brought Oscar's copy of the Book of Kammbi with him. After Diondray explained that it had been in his hometown of Charlesville for all those years, I knew he was the one."

"I see," Deputy Santiago remarked. "You are now a resa due to him helping you break a tradition in Santa Teresa that all women marry at age twenty-one. I understand that Diondray caused your wedding to Turner Perez to be stopped."

Resa Dorrado remained expressionless during her questioning. I knew answering this particular line of questioning would be difficult. I wanted to stand beside her and strengthen her, but once again I had to stay where I was. "That was the most difficult day of my life. I was being forced to go through with something I never wanted. My father insisted that I get married and that no unbeliever from south of the Great Forest was going to stop that wedding. I must admit I hated my father for the first time on that day. I prayed to the Eternal

Comforter the entire day to find a way to stop the wedding. I knew that Diondray planned to help me, but I didn't know how he could. My emotions were all over the place on that day. But when I saw him come up to the stage at the Kahall Angelica, I knew I would not be getting married. He and Madre Harriet changed my life."

I started to pace, reliving that day in my mind and remembering the anguish on her face as well as Turner Perez's. They should have never gotten so far with the wedding and been placed in a position like that.

"Remain in place, Diondray Azur," Deputy Santiago commanded.

I stopped pacing and returned to my spot. I did not want to draw attention to myself any more than I just had.

Deputy Santiago continued, "I understand that you and your father are not on good terms. Do you think what happened was worth the breaking up of your family?"

Resa Dorrado remained expressionless. I sensed that she had to come peace with the ramifications of her decisions. "Deputy Santiago, I love my father. I was a daddy's girl, as the adage goes. However, I do believe my decision not to get married at twenty-one was the right one and bigger than me. It took a stranger, who I will admit that I'm forever connected to, pointing out the unfairness of that tradition. The people of Santa Teresa allowed this tradition, which contradicts Teresa's words in the Book of Kammbi, to continue for over two hundred and sixty years. Something is wrong with that. No one from the other cities in this region or even the members here in the konseho of Kammbi wanted to correct this wrong-headed tradition. Now, because of Diondray Azur, it has all changed. The women in Santa Teresa have a choice, and I believe from the guidance of the Eternal Comforter it was the right thing to do, even though I do not have the same relationship with my father I once had. Moreover, it all confirms that Diondray Azur is the one who will fulfill Oscar's prophecy. Oscar's words from his section in the Book of Kammbi said that person would be someone you would least expect. He was correct about that."

The konseho of Kammbi erupted in chatter. Resa Dorrado was challenging their authority, and it probably bothered them.

"Silence, members of the konseho of Kammbi," Senior Padre Ashland announced over their chatter.

The konseho obeyed his command and became silent. "Thank you for your answers, Resa Dorrado. We will take your words under consideration," Deputy Santiago remarked.

The guards reached Resa Dorrado and led her away, and I already missed her presence. I knew I would see her again. I felt grateful for her responses.

"Diondray Azur, we have one more person to hear from. You were recently in the city of Alicia, and we want to know about the effect of your time in that city."

The guards came moments later with Bonita Golde. She had the same expressionless stare at the konseho as had Second Esperah Carranza and Resa Dorrado. I whispered a quick prayer to the Eternal Comforter about remaining calm. I would need it for her portion of this hearing.

"Bonita Golde, can you describe your experience with Diondray Azur in Alicia?" Deputy Santiago asked her.

"I met Diondray Azur briefly on his first day in Alicia, the thirteenth day of the seventh month of Yul," Bonita Golde answered. "However, my real impression of him came when I invited him to Fat Vincent's house to play Blacks."

"Do you know that playing Blacks is gambling and considered an act of passha?" Deputy Santiago said sternly.

"Yes I do, Deputy Santiago. But I learn a lot about people when they are playing a game where something is at stake."

Deputy Santiago smiled warmly at her answer as the rest of the konseho of Kammbi murmured behind him. I knew from his expression that he had played Blacks and was not bothered by me doing so, even though it was an act of passha.

"On what date did you invite Diondray Azur to play Blacks?

I turned away from Deputy Santiago and looked over at Bonita. She wore a fitted red jumpsuit with a yellow plaid pattern that captured my attention. Bonita dressed like she was at a fashion show, in stark contrast to Second Esperah Carranza and Resa Dorrado. I wondered how the konseho felt about it. "It was the twenty-second day of the seventh month of Yul," she answered. "He was nervous that night. It was refreshing to see a man not overconfident about his surroundings and wanting to fit in with the people at the house. It showed me immediately that he cared about people and did not feel like he was above them."

I looked down and soaked in what she had said about me. I had always considered myself the outsider. I never fit in with my family or the people on the east side no matter how hard I tried. And now I'd just heard this woman say she noticed how much I wanted fit in with my surroundings. I felt included for the first time in my life.

"Did that impression make you believe he was the one who would fulfill Oscar's prophecy?

"It was not that impression that convinced me, but something else," she answered. "Diondray played Blacks with us several times during his time in Alicia. I noticed how Fat Vincent and the others at the house became comfortable with him after each game. I knew the people of our district would be open to his claim."

"In what way? Have not the people of the River district rejected belief in Kammbi and the Eternal Comforter in order to believe in the river god?"

"That is true, Deputy Santiago. But we rejected belief in Kammbi and the Eternal Comforter because most of the people in Alicia refused to acknowledge the role of the river god at all. Diondray listened to us about our beliefs and did not dismiss them outright. He explained about his own spiritual beliefs and how they had been misinterpreted in his hometown. The people of my district identified with that misinterpretation and felt they had a kindred spirit with Diondray."

I had never felt more included in my life as I listened to Bonita's answers. I did not know if I would ever come back to Alicia again but hoped that our paths would cross again.

"His ability to relate to the people of the River district was the reason that convinced everyone to return to believing and following Kammbi?"

"Like Oscar Ortega did. He came to meet Alicia and Dexter. Oscar Ortega treated our forefathers with respect as he taught them the teachings of Kammbi. The morrims and diakonos of our city have forgotten that. Oscar Ortega embraced the river god instead of rejecting it. And the people of our district could see the same thing in Diondray Azur. And the river god himself came to the festival and acknowledged Diondray, as you must have heard."

The members of the konseho of Kammbi murmured again. Deputy Santiago raised his hand to silence them.

"How did the river god's acknowledgment of Diondray affect the people of the River district?" he asked.

"When the river god acknowledged Diondray Azur as the one who would fulfill Oscar's prophecy, we all knew that if we believed in the river god, then we would have to embrace the river god's wishes. The river god himself told us to worship the high One, Kammbi. After the festival, the people in our district all began reading the Book of Kammbi again and attending kahall services on the first day of each week."

I looked away from Bonita to Deputy Santiago. He was smiling. I sensed that he was pleased with her admission that people of the River district had become believers and followers of Kammbi.

"Bonita Golde, the konseho of Kammbi appreciates your response to our questions. You have given us more insight into the effect that Diondray Azur has had in this region of the land. However, I believe you have one more thing to say before you are dismissed from the hearing."

I took a deep breath and murmured to myself. I knew what she was going to say.

"Deputy Santiago, I came to Issabella weeks ago before this hearing and participated in a fashion show put together by the Santa Teresa businessman Mr. Frederic Cortes. I knew that Diondray would be in attendance that night at Tavares restaurant."

I looked at Deputy Santiago and saw the eagerness on his face. "Go on," he said.

"I revealed to him that I love him, Deputy Santiago," she continued. "I loved him from the first moment I saw him at Hotel Dexter. It was something about him that brought out a love I did not expect. I took him to Fat Vincent's house and brought him into our environment to see how he would react. And when he played so well and seemed comfortable among the people of our district, I loved him even more. Fat Vincent played along like he was my man . . . but that was a ruse to see how Diondray would react. "

I began to pace as Bonita revealed her love for me to the entire council. Fat Vincent had known all along how much she loved me. I wanted to leave the area and head toward the river.

The konseho erupted after her admission. I knew I had lost some credibility with them.

"Please return to your position, Diondray," Deputy Santiago instructed. "Quiet to the members of the konseho."

The members obeyed as I returned to my position. I looked over at Bonita Golde and saw the tears flowing down her face as she was led away by the guards. Her love for me was genuine as well.

"I want to thank Bonita Golde for her candor and honesty. Her words will be taken into careful consideration upon conclusion of this hearing," Deputy Santiago continued. "However, there is one other matter that needs to be discussed. Guards, please bring Maisa Merez, Mr. Cortes, and Felicia Hargrove here."

My heart was beating fast, and my entire body shivered. I knew that Bonita's admission would be a strike against me somehow. I wished I had known of her love for me in Alicia and could have addressed it before I left that city.

The guards brought Maisa, Mr. Cortes, and Felicia to the area where Bonita Golde had stood. I saw the pain on Maisa's face, as I knew she'd heard Bonita's admission from where they had been inside the building. But Mr. Cortes and Felicia had smirks on their faces, and I sensed something else was getting ready to be shared.

Deputy Santiago once again did the talking. "We have found out that Maisa Merez is an heir to Silver Mine 12 in Alicia, the mine that was owned by Marco Phillip Merez. Maisa Merez has applied for transfer of ownership with the help of Mr. Cortes and Felicia Hargrove. The konseho of Kammbi has reviewed and decided we can grant the transfer of ownership on one condition."

Maisa's pained look turned into a frown. "What's the condition?" she asked curtly.

"In order for you to get transfer of ownership of Silver Mine 12, you must remain in Alicia. You cannot continue with Diondray Azur, as he will have to continue to prove whether he is the one to fulfill Oscar's prophecy," Deputy Santiago answered.

"What do you mean?" Maisa asked, clearly upset. "I want that ownership transfer, but not at the expense of being with Diondray!

He's the reason why I came on this expedition. I cannot lose him."

I felt my heart sinking into my stomach. I understood what was happening and who had put us into this situation.

"Is there a reason why you cannot lose him, Maisa Merez?" Deputy Santiago asked.

Tears erupted over Maisa's face as she moved away from the businessman and his assistant. "I love him too. Before Bonita Golde!" she said. "I have revealed my love to him as well. I was determined to wait until he proved himself as the one who will fulfill Oscar's prophecy. I have known we were meant to be together since we met in Santa Sophia."

The konseho murmured again. Deputy Santiago waved his arms, and the members became quiet. "Yes, I knew about your love for Diondray. Mr. Cortes shared that with us. Members of the konseho, you have just heard two women declare their love for Diondray Azur. Those declarations will be taken into consideration as well."

I faced Mr. Cortes with anger running through my body. I knew what was coming next.

Deputy Santiago continued to instruct Maisa: "You can continue with Diondray Azur, as he will have to travel south of the Great Forest and share what he has learned with his people to see if they can become believers and followers of Kammbi. If he can do that, it will prove he is the one to fulfill Oscar's prophecy, and he will have done something that Oscar Ortega could not do. Also, if you go with him, the ownership of the mine will go to Mr. Cortes."

"You bastard!" Maisa erupted and charged toward Mr. Cortes. "I should have known that was your goal all along!"

The guards grabbed her before she could reach the businessman. I felt sick inside and realized that I had made a mistake in allowing Cortes to come on the expedition with us.

"Before you take her away," Deputy Santiago continued, "what is your decision, Maisa Merez?"

"Let me go," she snapped. I looked at Deputy Santiago, and he nodded to the guards. They released her from their grasp.

Maisa wiped the tears from her face and began walking toward me. I gathered myself and collected my thoughts. I heard chatter from the konseho as she approached.

"Diondray," she started and grasped my hands. "I have revealed my love to you and declared that I would wait for you to fulfill Oscar's prophecy. However, I have found something that will make my family proud and allow our name to be forever remembered. I cannot give that up. I will accept the condition of ownership transfer and inherit the mine."

I nodded and embraced Maisa. I saw the smirk on the businessman's face and a look of disdain on Felicia's.

The guards came and released Maisa from my embrace. She kissed me on the lips before she was pulled away. I watched her leave the area, and I had never felt so much pain in my life. I loved her as well.

"Maisa Merez has made her decision, and she will be the new owner of Silver Mine 12." Deputy Santiago announced. "This hearing is adjourned. Now, Diondray Azur, you will get the chance to prove if you are the one who fulfills Oscar's prophecy."

I watched the guards take the businessman and his assistant away as I heard a growl coming from the river. I knew immediately what was coming toward me.

"Reuel the Leopard!" Deputy Santiago blurted.

The leopard nuzzled my right leg, and I reached to caress his head. I knew the cat's arrival would have to be factored into the konseho's conclusion about who I was becoming.

Thanks for reading Diondray's Journey, the second book of The Diondray Chronicles and joining him on his adventure in Kammbia.

If you enjoyed it? Diondray's adventures began in:
Diondray's Discovery, Book 1 of The Diondray Chronicles

And will concludes in:
Diondray's Roundabout, Book 3 and the final book of The Diondray Chronicles

Ciscoe's Dance is a new novel set in Kammbia that takes place after the events of The Diondray Chronicles. Coming in the fall of 2020.

Also, I have released Marion's 25, the first non-fiction title of my favorite 25 books. Avid readers should be able to find some new book recommendations to add to your ever-growing TBR List!

If you want to keep up with all things Kammbia, then go to Marion's webpage: https://marion-hill.com/entry-into-kammbia/

Or you can connect with Marion here:

Blog: https://marion-hill.com/

Email: marion@marion-hill.com

Instagram: https://www.instagram.com/?hl=en

Goodreads:
https://www.goodreads.com/author/show/8202665.Marion_Hill

Bookbub: https://www.bookbub.com/profile/marion-hill-e4d3343b-634b-45e9-bcdf-294c03430436

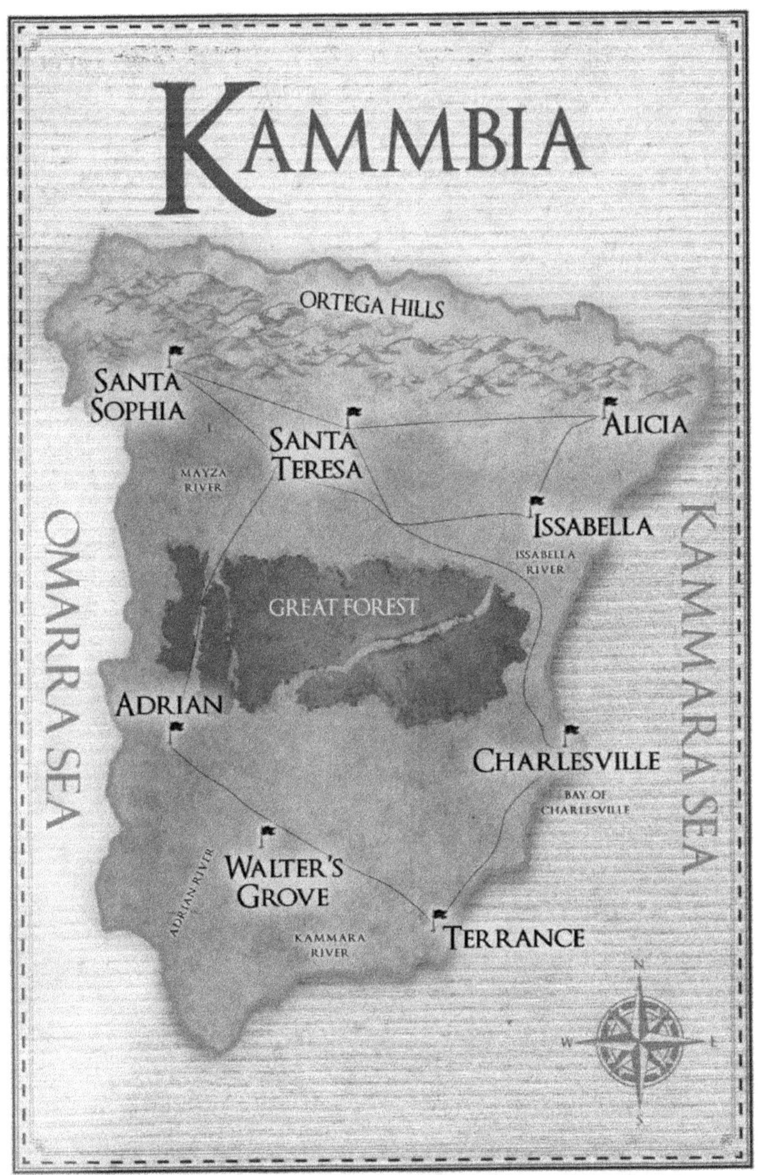

KAMMBIA
ORTEGA HILLS
SANTA SOPHIA
SANTA TERESA
ALICIA
MAYZA RIVER
ISSABELLA
ISSABELLA RIVER
GREAT FOREST
OMARRA SEA
KAMMARA SEA
ADRIAN
CHARLESVILLE
BAY OF CHARLESVILLE
ADRIAN RIVER
WALTER'S GROVE
KAMMARA RIVER
TERRANCE
N
W
E
S